PERESTROIKA IN PARIS

PERESTROIKA IN PARIS

JANE SMILEY

THORNDIKE PRESS

A part of Gale, a Cengage Company

LIBRARY OF CONGRESS CIP DATA ON FILE.
CATALOGUING IN PUBLICATION FOR THIS BOOK
IS AVAILABLE FROM THE LIBRARY OF CONGRESS.

ISBN-13: 978-1-4328-8720-9 (hardcover alk. paper)

Published in 2021 by arrangement with Alfred A. Knopf, an imprint of The Knopf Doubleday Publishing Group, a division of Penguin Random House LLC.

Printed in Mexico
Print Number: 01   Print Year: 2021

PERESTROIKA IN PARIS

PART ONE

ONE

Paras had won her race. She had jumped all the jumps with a great deal of pleasure, and, she thought, in excellent form. The number-two horse, a chestnut gelding from down south somewhere, had been so far behind her that she hadn't been able to hear his hoofbeats on the turf (and of course the crowd was yelling, too). She had, she thought, almost danced across the finish line. Everyone was happy — the jockey did a backflip off her, the groom gave her a kiss, and Delphine, her trainer, gave her a hug and three lumps of brown sugar, not to mention an excellent feed of carrots when she was all cool and calm after the race.

Since it was the last race of the day, and, indeed, the year — it was early November — the van, which already had its four horses, had left before her race began, so as to come back and get her, but now the van was late, the stable was empty, and Rania, her groom, had, she said, gone to the bathroom, and why not in the stall, thought Paras, but she could never get an answer to this question.

Twilight was descending over the vast green expanse of Auteuil Racecourse. The jumps had dimmed into dark shapes against the still vivid green grass. Admiring this, Paras did something that she often did — she pressed against the door of the stall, and this time something happened that had never happened before — it swung open. After a moment, Paras stepped carefully out onto the fine, crunchy gravel and snorted. Everything remained quiet. She could see now that every stall was empty and dark — in fact, the green of the racecourse was the brightest color around, so bright that, for a moment, she didn't dare head out there. But Paras was a very curious filly.

At her feet were several items that Rania had left behind — the grooming box, full of brushes, Paras's blue blanket, and something that Paras knew was called a "purse." This was the only thing that interested Paras — she had seen lots of purses, and heard even more about them — she had, in fact, just won a purse, and so, she thought, this would certainly be it. She dropped her nose, snuffled a bit, and found the handle. She picked it up, and trotted out of the stable yard onto the racecourse. Really, she thought, for a horse who had just run a long race, and with fourteen jumps, she felt quite full of beans. She kicked up her heels and gave a squeal.

To begin with, Paras had no idea of making a getaway. Not only did she like racing, and Delphine, and Rania, and her "owner," Madeleine, and several of the other horses, as well as her nice clean stall up there in Maisons-Laffitte, she really didn't know much else — none of the horses did. All had been born on pleasant farms in the country, and all had come to Maisons-Laffitte when they were hardly more than babies, and all had been galloping and eating and riding in the van and racing and galloping and eating and racing for quite a while, as long as Paras could clearly remember, actually. It was an active life, and in Maisons-Laffitte there was plenty to see of a morning, especially if you raced over jumps. But the horses did talk among themselves about what else might be out there. Some worldly ones who had traveled from down south, or from across the sea, had seen different courses. They lorded it over the others a bit. There were also those who talked about escaping this life, but they never talked about what else they might do. Paras did not think that any of them were as curious as she was.

And here was the grass — turf, they called it, but grass, really, as thick and green and appetizing as it could possibly be, and a racehorse never got to eat a strand of it, never even thought of doing such a thing. A racecourse was for racing. Paras took a few bites.

It has to be said that the grass was delicious — sweet, fragrant, flavorsome, and a little fruity-tasting. A mouthful was excellent chewing — not too light, but not at all tough, like hay. And it was nice to bite off the living stalks. She walked along, nibbling, occasionally trotted, occasionally kicked up her heels, and even reared twice, just for the fun of it. She was careful to keep track of her purse, though, and always circled back to retrieve it before she got too far away. Pretty soon it was completely dark, but Paras didn't mind. She could see quite well in the dark.

She romped and grazed, and minded her purse, sniffed a jump here and there, and recalled her race. She inspected interesting herbs and bushes, got into the woods, and then there she was, at the side of what she knew was a road. Roads were for vans —

she had traveled many a road.

Across the road were several interesting sights: More trees, more paths. Some tall buildings. Another road that ran between them. Cars — she was quite familiar with cars — parked and quiet beside the buildings. Here and there, the buildings were lit up. There was grass, and it was that, in the end, that lured her across the road. Her shoes rang on the pavement with a pleasing resonance. She lifted her tail and arched her neck and blew out her nostrils a few times. Soon she had left the park far behind.

No one knew that Frida lived in the Place du Trocadéro, but she did. Frida was an elegant German shorthaired pointer, ticked all over, but with a brown head and two brown patches on her back. She sat proudly here and there about the Place, making believe that she belonged to this human or that one and was simply waiting to be taken home after a nice walk. There were so many crowds around the Place du Trocadéro that no one noticed her, and so much food thrown out that maintaining her figure was as easy as could be. She was also careful to groom herself from top to bottom every day. Frida was intimately familiar with the Place, because her former owner, Jacques, spent a lot of time there — seven roads entered a nice roundabout that encircled a small green space with plenty of trees and bushes, which meant that the cars had to slow down, which meant that Jacques was more likely to receive a contribution. Up the hill was a crowded cemetery where Jacques liked to sleep when the weather was warm; Frida went up there in the evenings. Two large buildings separated by a slippery exposed area that Frida didn't like (Jacques called it the Palais de Chaillot) overlooked a large park full of paths and trees that swept down to the river. This meant that there was always a place to run around, and plenty of humans strolling here and there — also good for contributions. Frida bathed regularly in the pool below "the Palais." You could not be a dog in Paris and be dirty or smelly — if you were, the gendarmerie would take you in for sure.

Frida had never been taken in by the gendarmerie. Jacques had impressed on her that such a fate was unspeakable — every time he even saw a police car or a policeman in the distance, he got up off the pavement, picked up his dish, his mat, and his guitar, and led Frida into some alley or other. Jacques knew every alley, every courtyard, and every cemetery, especially

14

on the west side of the river, and he and Frida had slept in many of them. And then, one morning, in a courtyard a little ways down the river, he didn't wake up, and here came the gendarmerie, and Frida slipped away. She watched from a distance as they picked him up, put him in a van, and drove him off, and she never understood that. They left his guitar behind. Frida visited it twice and sniffed it for evidence of what had happened, but she could not figure it out. It was hot and bright and the leaves were all over the trees when they took him away, and now it was getting cold and the leaves had fallen, and Frida had to admit that, in spite of the occasional pats she got from passersby, she was a lonely dog, and not quite sure what to do. Jacques had been her only friend, and Jacques had had no friends. How to make a friend, either dog or human, was a mystery to her. It was not only that Jacques had been solitary and protective, it was also that dogs in Paris, on leashes, neatly garbed, kept to themselves. If Frida approached one, it barked instantly, loudly, reporting her misbehavior.

Which is not to say that when she saw Paras by the light of dawn, cropping grass inside the fence of the Place du Trocadéro, Frida knew that they were going to be

15

friends. She knew nothing at all except that she had never seen such a thing before. Here was a horse, not attached to a carriage, a light, graceful-looking horse, wolfing down the grass. Frida plopped down on her haunches as if Jacques had ordered, "Frida! *Assieds.*" Frida stared. Frida barked two barks. The horse's ears twitched, but it didn't lift its head.

A dog had to be careful around horses. They had big feet and big teeth, and they could be quick or they could be clumsy. Jacques had sometimes liked to give the white carriage-horses a bit of apple when the drivers weren't looking, but he had never allowed Frida to sniff or explore them. Even so, Frida finally stood up and hopped over the little fence and approached the horse, not so much to sniff the horse itself, but to investigate that item near to it, an item that looked very much like a leather purse. As far as Frida was concerned, there was nothing quite as fascinating as a leather purse. Humans carried them all the time — big and small, fragrant and not so fragrant, always clutched tight. Out of leather purses came all sorts of things, but most especially coins. When Frida and Jacques positioned themselves carefully on the street, Jacques picking tunes on his guitar and Frida looking alert and friendly, the coins had rained into their dish. Frida had come to understand that they were good things, mostly by watching Jacques smile as he counted them every evening.

Frida slid in her quietest and most bird-stalking manner toward the purse, nose out, head down, ears pricked. The horse continued to munch the grass.

Maybe if the purse had had a zipper Frida would never have been able to open it, and this story would have happened differently — Delphine would have found Paras and taken her home to Maisons-Laffitte, and Frida would have had to think of some other way to gain a friend. But in fact the purse had a magnetic snap, and opened quite easily. Once the flap was open, Frida pushed the purse a little bit with her nose, so that the contents were revealed, and what she saw in there was money. Yes, there was also a lip gloss and a hairbrush, but mostly there was money, made of paper, in all shades (a dog sees red as brown and blue as blue, green as pale yellow). She knew which ones Jacques found exciting — Frida did not have much experience with the palest ones, but once, outside Saint-Michel Station, when Jacques had been playing and singing, a tall man in pointed-toed boots

17

and a big hat had walked by, stopped to listen to the entire song, and said, "Thanks, brother," then dropped one of those pale notes into the bowl. Jacques had to snatch it up before it blew away. Now Frida nudged the flap closed and stepped back.

She bumped smack into the horse's front legs. The horse was standing over her, staring down at her. That was how interesting the money was — she hadn't even heard the horse approach. Frida froze, and the horse sniffed her, snorting a little bit (which was frightening), but not showing her teeth. Frida cleared her throat and sat — with dignity, she thought. The horse touched noses with Frida, then put her nose on the purse. Frida knew this meant, "The purse is mine." Frida sneezed. She often did this when she was nervous. Finally, she managed to say, "Are you lost?"

The horse said, "I don't know."

Frida said, "Are you from around here?"

The horse said, "I don't know."

Frida had never been to the racecourse, even though it was only a few kilometers away.

Frida said, "What's your name?"

The horse said, "They call me Paras, but my real name is Perestroika, by Moscow Ballet out of Mapleton, by Big Spruce. I am

18

a descendant of Northern Dancer and Herbager, and I go all the way back to Saint Simon on my dam's side."

"What does that mean?" said Frida.

"Those are my ancestors. Some were very good racehorses —"

"Did one come from Moscow?"

"Where is Moscow?"

"It's in Russia. You can hear people speaking Russian right here in Paris." Frida had heard her human, Jacques, and another busker talking about this from time to time. They said that Russians loved Paris. She said, "You must know that 'Perestroika' is a Russian word."

"I didn't know that," said Paras. She'd thought it was a nonsense word, like "giddyup" or "Wowsiedowsie." It had a sharp rhythm, too, like the rhythm of a good trot.

Frida began to think that maybe the horse didn't know what she had in her purse, either.

Paras said, "I am a filly, three years old, soon to be a mare."

Frida said, "Filly? Mare?"

"Female."

Frida thought, "You think I don't know that just by your scent?," but she didn't say anything.

The sun was now completely up, but

19

nothing was going on in the Place du Trocadéro, which never came alive until lunchtime, anyway. Frida picked up the handle of
the purse in her teeth and walked away, to
the part of the grassy area where not so
many humans might see them. Paras followed her. Frida dropped the purse in the
grass. For now. Frida sat and regarded the
horse. She said, "What do you eat?"

The horse glanced around and said,
"What do *you* eat?"

"Oh, it depends. Sometimes a little onion
soup. A bit of steak, if I'm lucky. Lots of
bread. Cheese. Old croque-monsieur. The
occasional leg of chicken or lamb. Bones.
It's a varied diet around here. Heavy on the
cheese."

"Oats? Maize? Hay? Apples? Carrots?"

"Well, the Pâtisserie Carette has some nice
apple tarts, and they serve grated carrots in
some of the salads. But it's expensive."

"What does that mean?"

Frida regarded the horse some more. She
was so big and yet so dumb. Well, "in-
nocent" was a better word. Obviously, she
had been taken care of her entire life and
had no idea how the world worked. Frida
offered, "Nice purse."

"Is it? How do you know?"

"Have you looked inside?"

20

"Is there something inside?"

Frida didn't say anything, and Paras returned to cropping the grass.

After a moment, Frida went over and lay down right beside the mound of dirt where the flowers had been in the summer and the spring. She didn't curl up tight, the way she did to go to sleep. She assumed her thinking position, her head up, her forelegs out in front, and her hind legs tucked under her, a position in which she could keep her eye on things, but also relax a little. It was certainly true that a dog did not live all her life on the streets of Paris without learning how to recognize a sucker when she saw one. The horse seemed to like the purse, and Frida did not have to steal the purse in order to steal all or most of the money. She could nose it out of the purse and scoop it into her mouth and take it to her spot in the cemetery and secrete it there. She had a big mouth, and she was adept with it. If, for example, you grabbed a pigeon for your morning meal, you had to do something about the feathers, and Frida had done that sort of thing a few times. How to take the money was not the point.

Could a dog with lots of bills leave Paris altogether and go back where she came from — back to the place Frida did remember, but not well, where there were plenty of trees and huge fields to run in, where there were pheasants and geese and partridge and deer, animals that were beautiful and inspiring and difficult to stalk? She hadn't stalked any of them, because she was only a puppy, but her mother, and then the other dogs she knew as she got older, had talked all the time about ways to approach, how to go undetected, avoiding anything that would make a noise, like a fallen leaf or a twig. And then Jacques had taken her away (had he bought her or stolen her? She never knew) and brought her to Paris. With lots of bills, could she pay her way on the train and get back to a place like that, as Jacques had? A year ago, she and Jacques had taken the train to a city called Lyon, where Jacques had left her in a room alone almost all day and had also put his guitar away. Yes, they had had a bed to sleep in, but in the end, sleeping in a bed didn't make up for those tight four walls that made both of them nervous. They had taken the train back, and even though the leaves were off the trees and the puddles were hard and cold, they had been quite happy when they returned. And they had made a lot of money, too — Jacques had had her sit in front of the dish without her wool coat on, and the shivering had upset the ladies passing by in their fur coats, and soon they'd have a pile of coins in the dish. It might be nice to go to a place where she didn't have to pretend all day and all night that she had a right to be there when most of the humans she saw all around her did not think that she did have that right. But she had to admit to herself that she didn't know how she would do that, even with lots of money.

Paras understood perfectly well that Frida was a dog. Dogs had their uses. Delphine had a dog in the stable yard — a small, bright, spotted dog named Assassin, a Jack Russell terrier, who spent all night and most of the day hunting rats, although she was willing to chase a ball and give the rats a rest around suppertime. Assassin and Paras had discussed the rats from time to time. Paras didn't mind rats, and neither did most of the other horses. You always knew when a rat was around — they made a lot of noise and had a distinct odor, and if they ate a few morsels of grain or bits of hay, well, it wasn't much, in the end. Assassin did not personally hate rats, either. But, as she explained to Paras, there was something about the way they moved — low and quick along the floor and then into a hole! — that just drew her like a magnet. She was good at rat killing, and the pleasure of the game had only increased of late, because, as she killed off more and more rats, the ones she hadn't killed got to be the smart, fast ones. Whereas she had formerly gotten a rat every couple of days, now she was down to a rat a week, and more avid than ever. Assassin had a busier life than Paras did around the barn, and sometimes Paras envied her: she was not bored, ever. Paras gazed at the dog for a moment, then said, "Do you kill rats?"

"I hate rats."

"Why?" Must be a dog thing, Paras thought.

"They taste very bitter." In fact, she had only eaten one — already dead, in the street — just to try it.

"Why would you eat one?"

"Why else would you kill one?"

"Our dog at Maisons-Laffitte kills them all the time. She snaps their necks and drops them and walks away."

Frida sniffed, then said, "Do they give her dog food, then?"

For some reason, Paras was embarrassed to say that they did. She said, "She doesn't like it much."

"Some dogs will eat anything," said Frida.

After a moment, Paras said, "So — is that

24

what dogs talk about all the time? Food?"

Frida put her nose to the ground, smelled a few fading plants and the damp soil, then said, "Yes. What do horses talk about?"

"Who won the last race. Who's going to win the next race. A few spend all their time making excuses, but I don't like to talk about that. Everybody talks about their relatives. Some horses won't talk to you if you aren't related to Northern Dancer, but other families aren't as snobbish." She thought for a moment, then said, "To tell the truth, the last day has been rather nice, no blah-blah-blah about Dad's family and Mom's family and brothers and sisters." She thought for a moment. "We talk about the jockeys, too."

"What are those?"

"When we run in races, the jockeys go along. Some stay with you better than others."

"They run, too?"

"No, they ride us."

The dog looked startled, then said, "That must slow you down."

"It does, but, between you and me, not every horse knows the way, so they have their uses. A lot of horses won't admit it, though. There's a lot of complaining."

"What are you chasing?"

25

Paras pondered this question, then said, "I don't know."

That seemed to end the conversation.

Paras went back to cropping the grass, but the morning was passing, and Frida knew that eventually the cafés would open and humans would show up, stalking their lunches. And they would certainly notice a horse and a dog by themselves in the Place du Trocadéro. How to solve this problem for Paras, Frida had no idea. It was one thing for a dog to position herself in an alert and friendly way here and there about the cafés and shops, but a horse was considerably bigger than a dog and expected to be attached to a carriage. At the same time, humans stalking their lunches in Paris sometimes didn't notice what was going on around them. And there were a lot of statues all over the city — for example, way up there on a pedestal above them was a black horse that never moved, with a tail that appeared to be waving even when the wind wasn't blowing. Frida had never seen anyone look at that.

The purse would catch the eyes of certain humans, though, and Frida did not want any human looking into the purse, so she went over to Paras and sat down in front of her, waited patiently for Paras to sniff a few more bits of grass and take another bite, then said, "You can stay here, if you're quiet, but you" — she didn't say "we" — "should hide the purse. It has . . . money in it." Then she said, "Humans love money, and someone might take your money."

"Does it taste good?"

"No." Frida had actually tasted money from time to time, just out of curiosity. Then she said, "But if you are going to live in Paris, you need plenty of it."

"What do you do with it?"

"You give some, a little, to humans and they give things back to you."

"Like what?"

"Like . . . carrots and apples."

Paras looked at her and pricked her ears. Then she said, "What is 'Paris'?"

"It's where we are. This city. Don't you know anything?"

Paras said, "I told you. I'm only a filly. I won't be a mare until January first. Then I'll know lots more things. How old are you?"

Frida didn't answer. She didn't know.

For a moment, Frida thought that, in spite of the money and the purse, the horse wasn't her concern. She could go back to her little cubbyhole up in the cemetery and pretend that she hadn't seen Paras and that

27

her life was the same as always. But then she thought that, if her life was the same as always, she didn't quite know what she was going to do. Just talking to Paras had been a change for her — even the dogs who didn't bark at her, when they looked at her face, then looked for her collar and leash, and saw that she had neither, simply looked away. Frida sighed. Sometimes the thing that you wanted to do did make you sigh, just because it was a hard thing to do.

It was not a pleasant day now. It had started out sunny, but the clouds were scudding in and the wind was picking up. Frida did not smell rain in the wind, but the leaves that hadn't been cleaned from the streets were lifting around them. Paras noticed, too. Frida said, "Are you tired?"

"I am," said Paras. "I had a hard race yesterday, and I was exploring most of the night."

"Do you lie down when you are tired?"

"Of course I do," said Paras.

"Well, I think you should take a nap. I'll show you a spot." And she led Paras around the little grassy park to the spot where there was a hedge and some other bushes. She said, "Maybe if you curl up next to the hedge and make yourself as small as you can, no one will see you."

28

"What will happen if they see me?"

"They will take you to jail." Jacques had always told her that if she wandered away from him, looking like a dirty stray, she would be put in dog jail, and it would be even more confining than that room in Lyon.

Paras could tell from the way Frida scowled and shivered when she talked about it that jail was a bad place, so she followed her over to where some bushes were cut into strange shapes and she nestled down as tightly as she could in a more or less hidden spot. She tucked her back legs underneath her and folded her front legs, and curled her neck around and tucked her nose in beside her hooves. She was a limber, slender horse, and a nimble bucker, so this was the way she liked to sleep. Frida brought along the purse, and pushed it under the hedge with her nose. She made sure that the magnetic lock was closed and the purse itself was well hidden. She said, "After lunch, I will come up with a plan."

"Lunch?"

"It's when humans come here to eat. But the cafés are all shut up today, so they are going to eat inside. That's good for us."

Paras was sleepy, indeed. She blew the air out of her nostrils and let her eyelids drift closed. Pretty soon, she was making a ruffling noise with her lips. Frida sat nearby and watched her, as she had so often watched Jacques before he disappeared.

TWO

It may be that the humans around the Place du Trocadéro did not notice Paras — maybe they were busy, or cold and looking down at their feet as they trotted from building to building. It may be that the leaves were blowing around and the clouds came and went, and the sun and shadows flickering together blinded the humans to the sight of a bay filly, nicely grown, sleeping by the hedge below the statue of the other horse that stood in front of the giant building. But there was someone who was watching, who had seen the whole thing from the beginning, who knew perfectly well that Frida lived in the neighborhood and that she was a free dog, and this someone was Raoul. Raoul was a raven, and he had a nest in a tree just down the Rue Benjamin-Franklin. He lived there alone most of the time. He was different from the other ravens he knew in that he liked Paris. The others, especially the females and the chicks, preferred the woodland to the west, which the humans called the "Bois de Boulogne," or the countryside. Raoul had seen plenty of that, but for a bird his age, which was old old old, there was more to do and more to see in the city, and not so many arguments. Ravens were an argumentative lot, and Raoul had had his fill of it. Perhaps the other ravens didn't know that he had a mate, Imelda, who was almost as old as he was. The two of them had plenty of offspring, so many that they had parted amicably when she had indicated to him that she was tired of reproducing, and also of listening to what she called his never-ending observations.

He watched Paras sleep for a while, then watched Frida get up and walk over to the only café where the tables sat in the open, and nose out a piece of bread that had slipped under a chair and been missed by the cleaners. After she did that, she sat near a medium-sized child and stared into the child's face, and, sure enough, the child handed her something else, maybe a piece of cheese. Then the child's parent scowled and shook her finger, and Frida walked away. A few times, Raoul had tried to persuade humans to give him things he wanted, but they had just laughed at him. However, it didn't matter. Raoul would eat anything — he especially liked ants, which were tiny but crisp and salty — and he was, he would admit, a little fat.

Raoul flew back to his nest and curled up in there. It was in a good spot — protected on one side, but with a view of the neighborhood. The neighborhood was full of birds, ones that Raoul considered frivolous, like sparrows, buntings, warblers, swallows, and tits. Not to mention woodpeckers in the trees, and thrushes on the ground, and pigeons, pigeons everywhere. Paris was a city of birds, and if the starlings were kings, then the ravens were knights. The avian city was a raucous place — most of the time Raoul couldn't even hear what the non-bird population was saying, the Aves were so loud.

For the rest of the day, Raoul thought of Paras as simply an oddity — something that would pass as all oddities did, and Paris was full of oddities, always had been. Out in the country, the days were monotonous, the sun came up, the rain fell or it didn't, the wind blew first from one direction and then another, the grass grew, the females and the chicks squabbled about every little thing.

Paras slept for a long time, and woke up nervous. She was not in her stall, either at Maisons-Laffitte or at the racecourse, and she did not recognize the bizarre cubical plant that ran along her back and made it itch. She was lying in dirt. She snorted and nearly jumped up, but then she saw Frida, sitting with her front feet neatly together and her haunches square. Frida said, "You slept for a long time. It's dusk."

And certainly it was; the sky was darkening more rapidly than the earth. The buildings all around, though, retained a pale glow, and that was what told Paras that she had made a terrible mistake when she pressed open the door of her stall at the racecourse and gamboled out into the world.

Frida said, "Of course, the days are pretty short now." She shivered. Paras shivered, too. Paras extended her foreleg and lifted herself, then shook. Leaves fell off her back. She grunted. Frida stuck her nose under the cubical, inedible plant (Paras had tried a bite), and pulled out the purse. Paras had forgotten about the purse. Right then, a raven flew in front of Paras's nose and landed on the grass between her and Frida. Paras was wondering how to get back to the racecourse — really, she had been very confused, but getting back to the racecourse was the best idea — and Frida was wondering if her new friend, and, okay, her new source of funds, was going to disappear. It was because she was wondering this, and therefore distracted, that Frida didn't go for the raven at once. She had never killed a raven, but a bird was a bird was a bird, and she was a bird dog. However, the raven cocked his head and looked her right in the eye, and she dropped that idea. Paras, the curious filly, leaned forward and stretched out her nose and sniffed the bird. He allowed this. He said, "I speak seven languages."

Neither of the other two said anything, so Raoul preened himself a bit, then said, "French, English, German, Spanish, Romany, Basque, and Chinese. You may not know this, but all birds speak Chinese; however, there are so many dialects that sometimes we have a hard time understanding each other." He cleared his throat and marched around in a little circle, slowly lifting his wings and lowering them, then spreading his tail. He said, "Tell me your names, please."

Paras said, "Perestroika, by Moscow Ballet, out of M-M-M—"

"Thank you, that is sufficient. And you?" He lifted his wing at Frida. She said, "Frida."

"That's all?"

Frida nodded.

"I am Sir Raoul Corvus Corax, the twenty-third of that name. My establishment is just over there, on the Rue Benjamin-Franklin, but the family estate is out in Châteaufort — that's straight to Versailles, then right." The horse and the dog looked at Raoul blankly, as horses and dogs so often did. He cleared his throat again. "Let me say that, from my aerie in that tree" — he lifted his right wing this time — "I noted that you two damsels seemed to be in distress."

"I'm hungry," said Paras.

"Ah," said Raoul. "Please correct me if I am wrong, but as an *Equus caballus,* you dine on rough grasses, small plants, grains, seeds, root vegetables, and apples when you can get them."

Paras nodded.

"A nutritious diet high in fiber, but let me say, as an Avis, low in variety and piquancy. No doubt when you come to, say, a fly or a cricket in your hay, you spit it out?"

36

"I do."

"And yet," said Raoul, "the entire insect kingdom is both flavorful and nutritious in the extreme — concentrated doses of trace minerals, and many naturally occurring remedies for whatever ails you. Ahem." He looked at Frida, who said, "I've tried those things."

"I'm very hungry," said Paras.

"I believe that I can come to your assistance, and enable you to realize your destiny here in the wonderful city of Paris. I am told by my far-flung correspondents, mostly albatrosses, that this is the finest spot in the world, and I know it well. And let me say this, you are fortunate in one or two respects, even in addition to your serendipitous encounter with myself. It may look from here as though verdant and well-watered fields are absent from our vicinity. But an aerial view, could you somehow attain such a thing, would persuade you differently." The dusk had now advanced. They waited until there were no cars anywhere. Paras hoisted herself to her feet, and then Raoul said, "Follow me."

And so they did, Frida suspiciously, Paras hungrily. Raoul flew ahead of them, swaying lightly in the breeze, maybe half a meter above Frida's head and two meters in front of her. Frida carried the purse. Paras seemed to accept that the purse had become the dog's responsibility. Raoul brought them to the road, to a low fence, less than a meter high. The approach was terrible, Paras thought. She was just attempting to gauge the footing when Frida pushed it open with her nose and went through. Paras followed her.

The path ran downward beside a high curving wall and was, in one place, quite narrow. But Paras caught some bites of grass, and took a drink from a small pond. The grass was short and not very tasty, so she tried a few leaves here and there. When the path widened, however, they came upon a rolling green prospect. Paras snorted. Raoul lifted his wings, stuck out his toes, and landed on a tree branch. He said, "I think I may say that this is the pride of my *domaine*. The humans have named it the 'Palais de Chaillot.' "

"You own this?" Frida set down the purse.

"What is ownership these days?" said Raoul. "I oversee it. That is my only claim." Then he said, "You said you were hungry?" He lifted his wing and gestured in a large semicircle, taking in the entire park. "The insect kingdom is yours for the asking, and, of course, small children and older adult

38

humans are always dropping things as they wander in their aimless way around the greenery and the paths."

Paras began grazing, but she was still careful to step around benches and bushes. Frida did not want to look hungry, but she was, so she checked under a few of the same benches and bushes without taking her eye off the purse, and she even got up on her hind legs and peered into a trash bag. Her reward was a half-eaten shish kebab wrapped in a pita. A human had taken a bite or two and tossed the rest, still in its paper, into the garbage bin, which was full, so the sandwich was right on top. She found it a nice change from cheese. Raoul hopped along the paths, snapping up this and that. When he got near the purse, he touched it with his beak. Frida was certain he would not be able to lift it, but even so, she said, "That's the horse's purse."

Raoul pecked at it.

Frida walked over, picked it up, and carried it a few steps away, where she set it down and sat over it.

Raoul said, "Is this a precious object?"

"In a way."

They stared at each other. Finally, Raoul said, "Ask yourself, do not Aves live free and clear of such things as possessions?

What is a nest but a temporary assemblage of bits and pieces — of trash, if you will — collected and molded into a comfortable, but always ephemeral, dwelling? Most Aves live to see the world, not to claim it. Even territorial Aves, such as myself, make their claims as a gesture, merely to start an argument with other territorial birds. We live to fly. We live to argue. What is in the purse?"

"Money," said Frida. "Lots of money."

"Aves use money all the time."

"They do?" said Frida. In all her life in Paris, she had never seen a bird pay for anything.

"I have a ten-euro note right in my nest. You get it nice and wet and press it for a bit, and it makes a superior bed. Sturdy, soft, smooth."

"You found a ten-euro note lying around?"

"Yes. On a desk. Through an open window. In and out in a matter of moments."

Raoul went back to pecking the border of the path, and soon enough came up with a caterpillar. He pecked it, tossed it, opened his beak, gobbled it down. Paras continued to graze. She was now just a dim figure in the darkness, but Frida could hear her. Time, she thought, to take the purse and slink back to the Place du Trocadéro; this raven, this Raoul, could show Paras the way

40

to the racecourse, the best place for her. But she had to think about it, so she lay down, and then she stretched out, and then she rolled, and then she rolled back the other direction, and between one thing and another, she was a little surprised to hear a loud clipping and clopping from the other end of the park. Raoul said, "Where is she going?"

Frida said, "You can fly — you tell me." And Raoul soared into the dark.

Paras was, indeed, a curious filly. The fact was that the grass in the park that swept down the hill to the river in front of the Palais de Chaillot was good enough to satisfy her appetite temporarily, but not delicious. And so she wandered along, taking a bite here and there, trying a few leaves, wondering, as she had so often in the past, what was ahead, where the bright lights were. She quickened her step and then crossed a narrow street.

All her life, Paras had heard the humans talking about her — she's nervous, she's sensitive, she's spooky, be careful, she can get out from under you in a second. The way Paras saw it was that she was interested in lots of things, and there were lots of things that she had never seen before. Unbeknownst to the humans, she was farsighted. There had been many times, out on the racecourse, on the training track, and even in the barn, where she had looked up and said, "What's that?" or, "Do you see that?" and the horse beside her had said, "What are you talking about?" If there was something to look at, a smart and curious filly was obliged to look at it, and she did. Delphine had learned over the months just to let her look. Quite often, when they were out training, Delphine let her stand there on her own, her reins loose, while she stared at the trees or the other horses or the wind blowing over and through the jumps, and then, when Paras figured out what she was looking at, she went along, doing her job. Now, at the end of the park, which was dim and green, she saw something she had never seen before — a group of small horses in proud, alert postures, standing absolutely still, not even grazing or nosing each other. She stepped carefully toward them.

She would have thought they'd snort or turn their heads, or at least flick their ears, but they did nothing of the sort. They only stood there, their necks arched and their nostrils flared. She got closer, step by step, then stood very quietly, and finally stretched out her neck and sniffed one of them. He was cold and hard, and smelled something like a truck. She snorted and backed up.

Frida, glad she had found Paras, said, "Haven't you ever seen a carousel before?" She leapt up onto the platform that the horses were standing on and sat down. Raoul swooped over Paras's head and landed on the haunch of the nearest horse, where he fluffed his wings and then assumed a knowing posture. He said, "Perhaps you ladies do not understand the demands of offspring. They require entertainment, none more so than humans, who seem to take years before they start foraging for their own sustenance, and so what is there for them to do? We Aves often discuss this mystery, the idleness that is endemic among humans, and yet they thrive —"

Paras touched the curving mane of the horse again with her nose and said, "A useless beast." She was disappointed and turned away.

It was now that the curious filly made her choice, and she made it just for that reason — she was curious. She could have turned left, gone back up the grassy hill. She could have stared at the fountains and the brilliant façades of the golden buildings that stretched grandly to either side. But, instead, she followed the scent of the river, and the sound of her own hooves ringing on the pavement. She crossed the bridge at a trot, tossing her head. She said to herself, "Why not? Let's see what's over there."

Delphine and Rania had looked for Paras for eighteen long hours. The night she escaped, taking the purse and Rania's phone, Rania had had to wait, impatiently, for Delphine to return with the trailer. It was almost midnight, but they had unhitched the trailer, driven around Auteuil, peering into the dark as best they could, then gone back to Maisons-Laffitte. In the morning, they got up, fed the other horses, came back into town, drove around the Bois de Boulogne and Longchamp, everywhere they could think of. A very long day, and now Delphine was alone and extremely tired, but unable to give up. She and Rania had passed Paras twice the night before without seeing her — once when Paras was curled up, sleeping in the Place du Trocadéro, and once when she was following Frida down the garden path. The reason they didn't see her then was that they were not looking for her — they assumed that she was lost in the Bois de Boulogne, which was a very large park, many kilometers around and many kilometers across. The reason Delphine didn't see her this time, when Paras was standing just beneath the Tour Eiffel, was that she was looking in the other direction, toward the river. Delphine did get a funny feeling, though, and so, just beyond the Avenue de la Bourdonnais, at the Avenue Bosquet, she decided to turn around. She drove south again. But by the time she was passing the Tour, Paras had noticed the pond that was outside of the tower lights and had walked into the darkness. Delphine got to the Pont de Bir-Hakeim, decided not to think crazy thoughts, and went across the bridge, back to the Bois for one last look.

THREE

The pond beside the great four-legged brilliant thing that Paras could not see to the top of was inside a low fence, but this time, the footing of the approach was fine. Paras backed off five strides or so and popped over it. The grass inside the fence was rich and deep, and the water in the pond was good enough. In Paras's experience, everywhere you went, the taste of water was different. Here it was rich and dirty, but with a sweetness, too. She was thirsty, and drank her fill. Frida soon appeared, and she, too, jumped the fence. Her form was good, Paras thought, in spite of the weight of the purse between her jaws — knees tucked, a little kick of the hind legs to clear the top metal bits. Frida took a drink. And then the screaming began. Paras was startled, and snorted and reared, but Raoul, who floated in, wings stretched, and landed on a low branch overhanging the pond, cawed dismissively and said, "Mallards. Common. *Anas platyrhynchos.*"

Sure enough, the screecher was a shining green duck, plump and well preened. He waddled toward them, stopped, and screamed again. Behind him was a duller bird. Raoul said, "She would be the wife." He sniffed. The wife quacked several times: "I don't think you should do that, honey. I think we should mind our own business. Lower your voice! Look at her, she eats grass! What's the harm?"

Paras walked along the edge of the pond. It was entirely fenced in, but the fence was low, and there was plenty of vegetation. She could see that dawn was approaching, and this seemed a favorable place to take another rest. Frida yawned. Paras yawned. Paras went to a spot in the lee of a wall, lay down, and curled up. Frida hid the purse, and then lay down beside her. As she drifted off, Paras realized that her decision had been made.

The mallards were named Sid and Nancy. Sid allowed Paras and Frida to sleep — he had other matters to attend to, particularly preening, which was time-consuming, but if you wanted to swim, it had to be done. When the horse and the dog woke up, though, he felt that he had to make explicit

47

his view that they had invaded his territory: he screamed himself hoarse, in spite of Nancy's incessant advice to calm down. Finally, he flew away. Nancy sighed, shook her head, and flew after him. Late in the night, they came back. The horse and the dog were still there, and so was the raven. Ravens, in Sid's experience, lived off the efforts of others and considered themselves very smart. He pondered screaming at the raven, too, but he suspected that the raven would ignore him, or perhaps get some other ravens and mob him. That would not be a pleasant experience. Sid decided to keep his trap shut. Nancy, he could see, was relieved.

It didn't take Paras long to adjust to her new surroundings — daylight hours inside the fence, in the shadow of the bushes, nighttime roaming the Champ de Mars. Adjustment to new events was something she was used to, and, anyway, the grass in the Champ de Mars was flavorful, quite comparable to the grass at the stud farm where she had spent her youth, thick and juicy, and there were other small plants and tufts of delicious weeds here and there, enough to hold her interest. In some ways, the Champ de Mars reminded Paras of places she had always known — it was green and enormous, like a big pasture, though flatter. Houses encircled it, cars ran through it, but not across the grass. There were trees and ponds and places to lie down for a good roll. Beneath the giant tower, she could smell the river and see the hill rising on the far side. At the other end, there was yet another grand building, but not many people went in and out of it, at least at night, when Paras was out and about.

Frida was not so sure about the Champ de Mars — it was too exposed for her taste, and there were so many humans around that Frida worried about the purse. Jacques had brought her here only once, in an attempt to play his music for humans standing in line at the base of the giant tower, but he and Frida had been sent off by an abrasive fellow in a uniform. Paras evidently liked it, though, and so Frida decided to stay. After a few days, she found a soft spot among the bushes beside the pond and dug a deep hole. She was good at digging — she had sharp toenails and strong paws. The effort was satisfying in its way — once the hole was big enough, she could not only hide the purse in it, she could curl up on top of the purse and take a rest. She enjoyed the hole. She felt good in the hole, maybe

49

the best she'd felt since Jacques had been carried off.

The real question for Frida was what to eat. Though she was a hunting dog, she was not much accustomed to game, given all the scraps of human food she had eaten over the years. She caught a vole, but the flavor was pretty rank. She did not feel comfortable stalking and killing Sid and Nancy as she came to know them. There were other birds. Sid often said to her when he saw her staring at one, "Go ahead! Kill it! I know you want to!" But in fact she didn't know how to, except by chance. She had yet to see a rabbit. Squirrels weren't worth the trouble. And there was plenty of money. The scent of a nearby meat market was very strong — depending on the breeze, it wafted over the entire grassy park, saying to Frida, "Beef, lamb, pork, chicken." It drew her, and so, one morning, perhaps the third morning after she and Paras settled next to the pond, she trotted toward it, right down the allée, under the trees, and then up the first street and the second, as if she were following her master home from her walk. When she found it, it reminded her of Jacques, who had quite often gone into such places and come out with some bones for her, or a piece of chicken. She lingered outside the door, but she knew that she could not appear hungry or desperate, or the shop owner would call the gendarmerie. She went back to the pond, stopping at a trash bin to snare a rind of cheese and half of an egg sandwich.

She returned the next day and the next, but remained undecided about her strategy. She was sitting quietly beside the vegetable market, enjoying the scents from the meat market. It was a sunny day for so late in the year, and the doors of both shops were open. Ladies with bags and baskets had been going into and out of the vegetable market, but now the traffic had slowed. The proprietor stepped into the street, his arms crossed over his chest, and regarded her. Frida straightened up, as if she'd been ordered to "stay" by her owner, and tried not to look at this man. He was tall, with a big nose and big feet. He wore a long white apron. He stepped closer, and his eyebrows lowered, as if he were wondering about her. He looked one way up the street, and then the other, and the street was empty. Just for the moment, there was no one to pretend that she belonged to. He came toward her, leaned down, stretching his hand out as if to grab her.

Frida knew that there were some dogs

51

who would have snarled and maybe bitten the man's hand, but she was not that sort of dog. What she did was offer him her paw and look him in the eye, then look away. The man laughed, shook her paw, and said, "Bonjour, mademoiselle." After a moment, Frida politely removed her paw. The man stood up, smiling, and went back into the shop. He returned and tossed her a small roll, which, of course, she caught neatly and gobbled down. Then she rose and trotted away, very dignified, back to the Champ de Mars, where Paras was curled up for her afternoon nap and the mallards were floating in the water the way they always did, Sid in the lead and Nancy just behind him. Raoul was nowhere to be seen.

Frida took a drink from the pond, which stank terribly of duck.

It was the sight of a plastic bag filling up with a puff of air and lifting itself out of a garbage bin that reminded Frida of what Jacques had taught her about money. When it drifted to the ground and skidded off, she ran after it, secured it with her paw, and took it between her teeth. Here she had spent the entire summer scuttling about, pretending to be owned by someone, and losing lots of weight, when what she really had to do was perform a few tricks. Humans were pushovers for tricks. They always laughed and gave you a treat. How many times on the street with Jacques had she rolled over, or covered her eye with her paw, or put the toy in the guitar case, or balanced the piece of bread on her nose and then tossed it and caught it? Jacques, of course, did tricks, too — playing songs and sometimes singing. Tricks got you money, and then you took the money and exchanged it for what you wanted. The thing she must do was put some of the money into the plastic bag, then carry the bag to the meat market.

It could not be said that the bag was easy to manage in the breeze rising off the river, but she did uncover the purse, nose it open, and take a bill in her mouth. She then scratched at the bag with her paws, and, when the edges came apart, pushed the bill between them. She picked the whole unwieldy object up in her mouth, then kicked the loose dirt back over the purse. She looked around. The only humans she could see were running ones, rushing away through the trees. Running humans never looked at a thing, Frida thought. Perhaps they could not do two things at once, which was why she had never seen even the fastest ones catch a pigeon.

But the meat market was not open. The succulent offerings in the windows were dark; the lights were off. Even the fragrance had dimmed, though it was quite rich and varied just at the base of the door. Frida felt her haunches sag in disappointment. And then she saw that the proprietor of the vegetable shop was standing in his doorway, his hands underneath his apron. He smiled and said, "Mademoiselle!"

There was a table just inside the door. Frida trotted over to the proprietor (she felt that the trot was a dog's most self-possessed and dignified gait), stood up on her hind legs, put her paws on the table, and spit the bag onto its surface. The man looked at her, then picked it up and saw the note inside. He laughed. There would be no chicken, Frida thought, but there would be a roll, and maybe cheese. She went farther into the shop. She stood on her hind legs and looked into every bin. The man, Frida thought, was actually rather intelligent. If she paused at the bin, he put something from that bin into the bag. As a dog of the streets, she had eaten plenty of vegetables, and though it was true that she had no use for a raw potato (fried potatoes were quite a different matter), she didn't mind green beans or carrots or even a leaf or two of

romaine. And her bill didn't go very far —
a bread roll, beans, carrots, romaine, another bread roll. The man took her bill
politely, smoothed the handles of the bag
into a circle, and held them out. Frida
opened her mouth, and he gave her the bag.
Then she left the shop, heading briskly
down the street as if her master were waiting for her. She could hear the man laughing as she ran.

Paras was still lying down when Frida
returned, but she was awake. Raoul was
perched on her rump. He had just finished
telling her what he knew about the word
"perestroika," which wasn't much, something about either always making plans or
letting things turn out as they would and
making the best of that. ("If that wasn't
horseracing," Paras thought, "then what
was?") Now he was telling her about an
argument he was having with another raven,
who claimed the head of Benjamin Franklin, which was immediately below Raoul's
nest. "Everyone knows that a raven's territory is spherical," said Raoul. "It is widest
around the nest, and then diminishes outward. I have almost no claim to the hillside
below my nest, but the head of the statue is
well within my territory, and I could make a
case for the lap, too —"

Frida dropped the bag in front of Paras, and it fell open. Paras nosed out a carrot, bit it in two, and munched it down. She said, "How delicious! I'd almost given up hope. You'd think they'd plant a few of these in such a large park, but I haven't found them."

"I bought it," said Frida.

"Ah, commerce! A concept, I must say, that we Aves have given the world." Raoul flapped his wings, but it was only a flourish of self-congratulation. He didn't fly away; rather, he sidestepped over to the bag and helped himself to a green bean. This drew the attention of Sid and Nancy, who walked out of the pond and stared. Paras took another carrot and bit it in two. Frida ate the second half, then one of the small rolls. It was fresh and delicious. "No apples?" said Paras.

"I don't quite know what an apple is," said Frida.

Malus domestica," cawed Raoul. "A waxwing will eat an apple." He coughed as if this was an unusual affectation. "I have tasted apples."

Sid and Nancy waddled closer, then sat down. No screaming or quacking. Frida took the second-to-last piece of bread out of the bag, carried it over to them, and

56

dropped it. Jacques had never minded sharing his food with others. Sid ate part of the bread; then Nancy ate the rest. Sid said, "We've eaten apples. A child tossed us some bits just a few days ago. They're all right."

"I love them," said Paras.

Frida knew this was a hint.

The next day, Frida supplied herself with another bill and went to the market earlier in the day, just when every shop on the street was opening. She of course went to the meat market first — she could hardly help herself, the fragrance was so enchanting — but the woman who kept the shop was sweeping the step. She waved her broom at Frida and said, "Ahh, shoo, shoo! Get!"

Frida backed away and sat down, still staring at some pale, fat, featherless carcasses in the window.

She felt a pat on the head; the man said, "Ah, dear girl, you have returned again! The chicken is indeed very lovely."

Frida had found with Jacques that if she was still and steady and opened her eyes very wide, he was more likely to do as she wished, and, indeed, the man held out his hand, took her bag, and removed the bill from it. Then he went into the meat market. She stepped carefully up to the window and touched it with her nose beside a pile of meaty bones, and he put two of these in the bag, paid for them, and came out. He did not give her the bag, though. Instead, he carried it to his own shop. Frida followed him. When she was across the threshold, he took two coins from the register and said, "Mademoiselle, I owe you two euros from your previous visit." Frida indicated that she would take something from each of the bins closest to the street. When she had spent all of her money, the bag was heavy in her jaws, and she knew she would have to set it down more than once on her way back to the Champ de Mars. But the bones motivated her.

The bag broke as soon as she set off.

The man clucked, clapped his hands, and said, "Oh dear!" And then he gave her another bag, this one sturdy.

Between them, Raoul, Paras, and Nancy identified the fruits — orange, apple, pear, another apple, lemon, banana. Paras took the two apples; Raoul had seen lemons but never tried one; and Nancy took the orange. No one knew what to do with the banana, so they left it beside the pond. Frida carried the bones to her hollowed-out retreat and gnawed them happily.

There was a human who knew that a horse lurked about the Champ de Mars. He had seen her the first morning, inside the fence around the North Pond, when she stretched and snorted and hoisted herself to her feet, then made her way to a bit of grass half hidden by some bushes. His name was Pierre, and he was the head gardener of the Champ de Mars. Pierre loved the Champ de Mars, thought it was the oddest spot in Paris — out west, right along the Seine, flat enough to have begun as a hundred-hectare training ground for the students in the École Militaire, then large enough to host horse racing (before that moved to Longchamp), then to host what was now called a world's fair, not to mention the Tour. It was full of grass and trees and gardens and cars and ponds and trash (Pierre did the best he could with that), over a kilometer long and half a kilometer wide, peaceful sometimes, busy other times, especially in the summer, but not so much now, in the late fall.

That first morning, he'd watched the horse for a while, and his immediate instinct had been to have her caught and vanned away. But she was a beautiful horse — a rich bay with a long tail, a thick mane, and large, expressive eyes — and the more he looked at her, the more he thought that, at least for now, she gave the Champ a certain style: every landscape needs a figure in it, perhaps especially a figure that is only intermittently visible, that is mysterious and alert. He caught sight of her often, and watched her when he could. He saw from her footprints and her manure that she was jumping out of the fenced area to graze in the evenings. Perhaps the tourists didn't notice her, or, if they did, thought that because she was inside a fence during the day she was provided by the authorities as a picturesque gesture. Perhaps his employees did notice her, but it was not for them to say anything if he didn't. So everyone wordlessly shoveled up what she left, as they cleaned up after dogs and cats and birds and foxes and once an ocelot that had escaped from its owner on the Avenue de Suffren, a much more troublesome beast than a horse. Pierre knew he should wonder where the horse came from, and report her, but, for now, he reassured himself that he was not in Animal Control, and if they wanted her, they could come and look for her themselves.

FOUR

Although Frida didn't like the mallards because of the smell, and Raoul continued to disdain them as common common common (you saw them everywhere — did Paras realize they would mate with any Anatidae?), Paras considered Nancy good company, and extremely patient. Sid, Nancy said, did not live here all year round. He appeared every autumn about this time, decked out in green. He stayed with her for a while, and then flew south. He was sensitive to the cold. Winter migration was statistically the norm, but if you lived in Paris, well — Nancy cocked her head, then went on — it was an issue between them, but she was a homebody. She liked her territory. The pond had frozen over completely only one time. Down south (she had gone with him once), you had to put up with chaos. The worst of it around here, according to Nancy, was that, in addition to her own six or eight or ten eggs (one year she laid twelve), if she didn't hide her nest well, other eggs could turn up, and there you were, you had hatched some completely alien little thing before you knew what was what. Her last bunch had just flown off a month before. Nancy pushed them out as soon as they could go — she realized that she was a bit impatient about it, but they were well cared for and strong, and she felt that she needed at least some time on her own, didn't Paras agree? Paras of course agreed, since she liked to have a lot of time on her own.

In half a year, late in the spring, there would be another migration — only the drakes that time of year. And good to see the back of them. A drake plus ten nestlings was too much. "What were the nestlings' names?" asked Paras idly.

Nancy shook her wings and cocked her head. She said, "I have no idea. It's your mate who names you, not your mother."

"For horses," said Paras, "it's humans. Our dams just call us 'sonny' or 'honey.' But humans don't seem to know the difference between two horses unless they name them, so we allow it." She confided in Nancy that, even if a horse didn't have showy white markings, he or she always had distinctive cowlicks and dapplings and ways of moving. It was a mystery to all the racehorses that they had to wear not only jockeys but brightly colored cloths so that the humans could tell them apart. In even the most crowded race, every horse knew who was who. Some horses found the politics of it all quite nerve-racking, but, as a front-runner, Paras didn't pay much attention to that.

Sid was a bossy one, but Nancy quacked that she could not complain, and she had never closed herself off to him, as some ducks did, not only to interlopers, but to their own mates. He was a good provider, and a duck had to be fat, because the ducklings would slim her down to nothing if she didn't take care of herself ahead of laying time. And anyway (Nancy lifted her wings and tossed her head), Sid knew how to shake a tail feather. Quack-quack-quack. Paras found it soothing to walk around the grass, taking bites of this and that and listening to Nancy. Where, she asked, did the drakes go? Nancy had no idea. Of course, they said that they roamed far and wide — to the mountains, to the oceans, etc. But a duck had no way of knowing. Except for that one sojourn to the south, Nancy had lived in the Champ de Mars for years. It was an excellent spot, no matter what certain mallards said about other neighborhoods. There was plenty of cover, plenty of water, plenty of food. The noise didn't bother her — she hardly heard it anymore.

"It is noisy around here," said Paras.

Much of the noise was made by Sid, whose high-pitched mode of expression made Paras's ears flick. Sid was in charge of the nest, and he had decided that this year, since Paras and her friends were always present, they needed to build it in a safer spot. So he marched about the pond and the neighboring groves, trying to make up his mind. "There, you see," he said, "the outer edge is too far into the open. Very dangerous, but if we make the nest smaller, that has its dangers, too. We haven't lost a duckling in three years. It's a point of pride for us, and I speak for Nancy as well as myself, because we each have our duties and responsibilities, and my responsibility is the nest." Sid stepped carefully, looked here, looked there, kept going. "Can't be too far from the water," said Sid. "Very vulnerable if they have to walk far. Owls at twilight, hawks during the day, foxes anytime, dogs for that matter, cats. You ask anyone, mallards are fair game." He coughed and glanced over his shoulder and shuddered. "Rats."

"I don't mind rats," said Paras. "They clean the place up."

"They are ruthless. There has never been a rat who let an egg be!" screamed Sid. He walked up the face of a large rock, and plopped down in the sun. Sunny days were few and far between lately, but Paras didn't much mind the rain. It was easier to live outside in all weathers than it was to be confined to a dark stall, unable to see much, but hearing every little thing, day and night. All the horses complained about being cooped up, even the least curious ones. And then, when the humans took you out, they got spooky when you were startled by something. The better riders just sat there, and said, "Ah-ah," but a sensitive filly like Paras could feel in her very bones that their hearts were pounding. If you lived out, there wasn't much that surprised you. Paras could see things all over the Champ de Mars — humans large and small, dogs large and small, birds of all kinds soaring and swooping. If you lived out, every noise had a reason, every sight a before and an after. No surprises. Pretty soon, Nancy joined Sid on the rock, and both of them seemed to go to sleep.

Paras stretched, shuddered all over, and stepped out into the open space. In the last few days of rain, there hadn't been many humans around; the sunshine would bring them out, so Paras thought she should go for a little trot before they showed up. She jumped the fence and headed down the allée, head up, ears up, pace brisk. It felt good. She flicked her tail and rose into a canter. The footing was firm, wet but not at all slippery. She enjoyed the sound of her own hoofbeats. She had been bred to race thirty-two hundred meters; a good gallop gave her the opportunity to blow out her lungs and get some exercise. At the big building at the far end of the Champ, she came down to an easy walk, turned around, and trotted back, pausing here and there to take some bites of grass. The few humans running not far from her either didn't notice her, or pretended not to notice her, but their dogs kept barking: "Who are you! What are you doing here! I never saw you before! You don't belong here!" Paras ignored them, and if a human looked her way, she lifted her head and trotted all the more proudly. Frida said that there was a way to conduct yourself "as if" you had your own human about. You were calm and proud and never threatening, because you didn't want to scare anyone. You kept your distance — humans did not like strange animals to come too close to them — and you did not ever look at them unless they were looking at you. In that case, you could give them a friendly glance — I would like to know you if I had the time, but I am busy at the moment. The other important thing was to be as clean as you could be, and so Paras tried to roll in wet grass as often as she could, and to stay out of the mud. Paras was a well-bred horse, so she liked to be clean, anyway.

When she got back to the pond, Frida had returned from the market. There were, of course, fragrant apples and pears, arugula, a few carrots, and an artichoke. Paras ate the artichoke first. It was a bit like taking medicine, but she enjoyed them — you couldn't eat sweets all the time. Of course, Frida had also brought Nancy's, and especially Sid's, favorite item — blackberries.

It was Paras who noticed the boy.

There were occasionally boys in the Champ de Mars, and there were occasionally girls, but boys and girls were always attached to regular-sized humans. If she had ever in her life seen a solitary boy, Paras could not remember it. But now here was a boy. He was, in addition, staring at the five animals eating their treats, his feet wide apart, his hat pushed back on his head, and his hands in his pockets. As Paras watched, he took two steps toward them and stopped again.

Raoul finished his arugula and noticed the boy. He cawed several times, flew upward, and landed on Paras's haunches. Frida said, "What are you talking about?," because the wind was blowing in the wrong direction for her to scent him; then she saw the boy. Raoul said, "Chase him off."

"Oh dear," said Frida.

"What? What?" screamed Sid.

Paras knew that Sid was upset because the boy was not far from the building site of the new nest. Nancy kept her opinions to herself.

Frida said, "I saw this boy down the street from the market. I didn't realize that he was behind me."

"He followed you and you didn't even notice?" cawed Raoul.

"The bag was very fragrant. I couldn't smell anything else."

"Chase him off," cawed Raoul.

The boy held out his hand.

Now Raoul started walking around in small circles, cawing like mad. Twice he flapped his wings, but the boy didn't under-stand the hint. He just stood there. Paras could see that Nancy and Sid were torn between eating the remaining blackberries and taking off. They kept watch on the boy and snatched a few. Frida sat. The boy took another step toward them. He was looking at Frida, but then he glanced at Paras. Frida suddenly stood up, and said to Paras, "Let's go." She took off, running away from the boy, toward the other side of the Tour, a less protected part of the Champ de Mars. Paras cantered after her. In a green area beyond the other pond, they stopped and looked back. Raoul had flown away; Nancy and Sid were nowhere to be seen. The boy was standing, staring down at their treats. He squatted and touched something, then stood up and walked away. In the grand panorama of the Champ de Mars, he looked very small.

Paras had a dream. Perhaps it was the apples that gave her the dream, but she didn't dream of apples — she dreamed of oats. She was standing in a summery green field with other horses, nibbling shoots of grass that grew among the yellow flowers. A gate opened, and a fellow came through, wearing a hat and carrying four buckets. He hooked the buckets to the fence, and Paras and the other horses went over and thrust

69

their noses into the buckets and started munching on the oats. They were sweet and crunchy. When she woke up from the dream, it was early — not even the barest shimmers of light at the far end of the Champ de Mars. Frida was stretched out beside her. Paras rolled up onto her chest and then levered herself to her feet. Frida didn't wake up.

If a curious filly wanted to walk down a street, her hooves clanging on the pavement, to look into windows without being seen by humans, then this was the time to do it, the only time when all was quiet. She crossed the field, glanced down one street, then turned down the next one. There may have been humans who awakened in their warm beds, looked at the dim windows, and said to themselves, "What is that noise?" They may have pulled the covers over their heads and decided they were dreaming, or they may have gotten up, looked out the window, and seen nothing. Possibly, it was that time of day when the security guards stationed here and there and a couple of members of the gendarmerie had the greatest difficulty staying awake, and so they didn't watch the street as carefully as they might have. At any rate, Paras loitered and stared as she strolled along. Doors were closed, awnings were rolled up, windows were dark, the smell was mostly the damp pavement itself. She touched her nose to the cool metal of the automobiles, and the cool surface of the glass, and the stone buildings. She sniffed iron fencing, and nipped off tiny fugitive plants that grew through cracks in the pavement. She looked ahead, she looked back, she even looked up. A single dog was out and about, but he circled around her, his head low, his tail low, his ears low. He looked like a sad dog, not at all the proud beast that Frida was. There were cats here and there, squatting in corners, their paws tucked under their chests, their eyes slitted. They saw her — she knew this, because their heads turned as she passed. One, a black one, gave off a low meow as she walked by. Paras nickered in response. She might have seen a fox, too, slipping around a building, waving its orange brush, but foxes were elusive.

Then she saw a light in a window. She stopped and snorted. A figure within the light was busy staring at something, touching it, shaping it. Paras watched. The door was slightly open, and a strip of light fell onto the pavement. And a scent billowed out. Paras was drawn to the scent. She stepped closer.

71

Anaïs sensed that she was being watched. She glanced up and saw nothing but the darkness of the big windows that looked out onto the Avenue de Suffren. She had set her baking pans on the tables in the shop, and would carry them into the *cuisine* when they were ready. She shook off the feeling and went back to forming her rolls, her favorite part of baking. She had already baked the baguettes and the larger loaves. The croissants and *petits pains au chocolat* were in the ovens. Henri would arrive soon for the *tartes* and the *galettes.* But Anaïs was trying something — a roll with a hint of sweetness, cut into diamond shapes and dotted with fennel seed, then baked until the fennel seed turned crisp and golden. She heard a noise and looked up again. A horse's head shone in the window, nostrils flared, ears pricked. Anaïs nearly jumped out of her skin. The two pans rattled as she bumped them. She exhaled, "Ahh!" The horse's head turned to one side and then turned back, still staring. Anaïs coughed. Then she pulled herself together, wiped her hands on her apron, and went over to the coffeemaker. She picked up two lumps of sugar and went to the door, which she opened carefully.

The horse stood still for a moment, then

approached her. It took one lump of sugar carefully off Anaïs's palm, then the other one. The horse's lips were velvet. Anaïs put her hand on the horse's neck and stepped out into the street. The horse eased backward. Anaïs looked toward the École Militaire, and then she looked toward the Quai Branly. No one in sight. The horse's neck was soft and warm, and Anaïs could not help stroking it under the heavy black mane, down and down. The horse dropped her head as if enjoying it. The air was cold. Anaïs shivered, stepped closer to the horse.

Anaïs didn't have much experience with horses — she had ridden in a carriage twice and watched races on the television. About horses she knew only that they ate sugar and that they liked oats. Except that now she knew a third thing, that they had warm, fine coats. She stopped petting the horse and stepped back into the comfort of the bakery. In the corner, in a bin, Marie, who managed the café side, kept a supply of oats. Anaïs found a bowl and scooped some into it. When she went back outside, the horse had continued down the avenue. It was staring into a lighted shopwindow at bins of vegetables. Anaïs called out "Hello!" and made a kissing sound with her lips. When the horse turned its head, she rattled the

73

oats in the bowl.

Paras did not know the concept of dreams coming true — in fact, she did not quite know that a dream was different from being awake. She did know that after her dream of the oats she still felt hungry, as if she hadn't actually eaten any oats, but she was too young, as yet, to be philosophical about it. Nor did it strike her as an unusual coincidence that, having dreamed of oats, she would now be offered some. But she did feel that Anaïs was a remarkably sympathetic human — similar to Delphine in her demeanor, but requiring nothing, and not likely to pull a halter from behind her back and put Paras in a stall. Paras did not want to return to a stall. She finished the oats and licked the bowl. Anaïs laughed. Then she petted the horse two more times along the warm spot under her mane. She stepped back and said, "I hope you return." Paras tossed her head, then continued down the avenue until she saw the grass of the Champ de Mars reappear. Anaïs went back to her workstation, but not before washing her hands and arms scrupulously and changing her apron. She knew so little about horses that at first it didn't occur to her to report the animal. If a horse lived in Paris, and could stroll down the street gazing into shopwindows, Anaïs thought, then that was the horse's business. Later, though, thinking back on her experience, she thought: if, indeed, it was an actual horse.

FIVE

One morning, after a cold rain the night before, Frida was making her way to the shop. Frida avoided cars automatically — cars sometimes moved in unexpected ways — but she was an alert sort of dog, and no car had ever come near her. On this day, she could see that the cars were slipping, jerking, acting awkward and dangerous. She pressed herself a little closer to the shops. And then it happened: two cars screeched and bumped. An old old woman had stepped into the street, stumbled, fallen to her knees, and there was the boy she had seen in the Champ. He took both of the old woman's hands, and she struggled to her feet. One of the cars had rammed the trolley she was pushing. The boy looked frightened, but the old old woman seemed unaffected. The boy pulled her back onto the sidewalk, grabbed the trolley. Cars began to honk. Frida trotted over to the boy as he stood beside the old old lady, and Frida did something she had seen a Great Dane do once: she stood against the old lady, leaned into her. In a moment, the old lady regained her balance. She was a polite old lady — she reached down and petted Frida on the head. Frida accompanied the old lady and the boy to the vegetable shop, and sat quietly next to the dented trolley outside.

Although his shop was in a prosperous neighborhood, Jérôme was familiar with troubled lives. The village he had grown up in, north of Toulouse, was not a wealthy one, and, of course, here was Madame de Mornay, a regular but infrequent customer, who lived right down from the shop, on the Rue Marinoni. Madame was a hundred years old, Jérôme suspected, and she had in her care a boy of eight or so, who must have been her great-grandchild. The dog was sitting calmly outside. Jérôme had gotten into the habit of selling vegetables to her every other day, and of including a marrow bone or two in the bag. Usually, the dog brought a ten-euro note, but sometimes she brought a twenty. Once she brought a hundred-euro note, and though Jérôme was surprised at this, he carefully made change (how could a dog carry a hundred euros' worth of vegetables?), rolled the bills up, and tucked them in among the leaves of the head of romaine she bought (and why would a dog eat romaine?). Jérôme had grown convinced that some housebound owner was sending her out, and now he thought that this must be her.

Madame was blind but alert. She made her way deeper into the shop. Each thing she asked for, Jérôme gave to the boy, who placed it in Madame's hand. Madame felt it over carefully. Jérôme held a basket, and the boy put each item into the basket. Then the boy paid, Jérôme handed them the bag of vegetables, and they left. Outside, the boy put the bag into the trolley and went into the meat market, then the bakery. The boy never spoke, nor was he spoken to, but he seemed to know exactly how to serve Madame. She kept him dressed in nice clothes, and she made sure, somehow, that he did as he was told. Madame was invariably polite and always paid in cash. She, too, was nicely dressed, and never without a hat. But Jérôme suspected that their life on the Rue Marinoni was a sparse affair. That the boy should, one day, appear with the dog did not surprise Jérôme. She was a beautiful dog — large for the streets of Paris, but elegant. However, Jérôme was saying nothing — the dog paid her bills.

Jérôme watched the dog follow the boy and the woman. They rounded the corner and disappeared.

The woman, Frida knew, did not realize she was following them, but the boy did. He turned and looked at her several times, even whistled so that she would approach him, but Frida kept her distance. They came to the end of the row of buildings, to a door in a high fence that was covered with ivy and other plants so thick that even Frida could not see through them. The boy took a key from his pocket and opened the gate, helped the woman in, then pulled in the battered trolley. Frida heard him open what must have been the door to the house; then he came back to the gate and stood there, staring at Frida. She approached him, licked his hand, but did not enter. Gates would always close. Jacques had made sure that she was suspicious of that. Frida trotted away.

Madame Éveline de Mornay was not yet a hundred, but if she lived for three more years (and one month), she would be. Her grandfather had come from Domme, a lovely hill town on the banks of the Dordogne, a place Madame had loved to visit. He had come on one of the first rail lines, built during the Second Empire. He had made a great deal of money in soap and creamy lotions scented with lavender and verbena, then bought this house abutting the Champ de Mars, not far from the École Militaire. Éveline's father had been killed in the First World War — she was three years old at the time and didn't remember him. Her husband and her brother had been killed in the Second World War. Her son had died in Algeria, and her grandson and his wife had died in an automobile crash on the Périphérique. She now had this one child left — his name was Étienne. He was eight years old, almost exactly the same age as this twenty-first century, a century that Madame had never expected to see. With each death, Éveline had closed a room or two in the large house she lived in, and now she and Étienne made use only of the *cuisine,* the dining room, her father's old study, which she used as a bedroom, and the small library, which now belonged to Étienne. There was a telephone, but it hadn't rung in years — maybe Étienne didn't even know what that sound was. Étienne had taught himself to read — there were books not only in his room, but all over Great-Grandmama's house — and after that, he had taught himself to count, to add, to subtract, to multiply, and to divide. Others might have said he was dangerously isolated, but he was used to it, was leery of other children. What his great-grandmama told him of the outside world didn't make him want to go out there, and he thought that if he could learn to do these things on his own, there was no reason to make himself known to the other children or at the school.

But sometimes he did feel lonely. For a while, he'd enjoyed the company of a neighborhood cat, but the cat had vanished. After that, he'd left crumbs for a pair of pigeons on the sill of his window, but the pigeons remained shy. He'd been watching Frida now for two weeks, and he knew for certain that she lived beside the pond to the north of the Tour, and that a horse lived there, too.

Raoul witnessed Frida's adventure from his perch on a second-floor railing down the street from the vegetable shop — he also observed with some amusement the human fracas that ensued when the two automobiles hit each other in the street, and their drivers jumped out and began cawing loudly about who was at fault and who should have been paying attention. One of them shouted at the old old lady, but she marched on, oblivious, her hand on the boy's shoulder, Frida at her side. Nor did the boy turn to look. Now Raoul sailed along above them, riding the lightest of breezes, simultaneously keeping an eye on Frida and watching for stray *frites* on the sidewalk — sometimes he could swoop down and scare off a pigeon; it was good sport, he thought. The lady kept her hand on the boy's shoulder and seemed to react to nothing. When they stopped at an intersection, she looked nowhere, and as they crossed the street, she paid no attention to the cars nearby. At last, when the boy and the old old lady came to their house, Raoul swept into the nearest hazelnut tree. After Frida left at a run, he floated about the place, glancing in through this window and that. All was silent and dark. The court was overgrown with grasses and weeds, but he was pleased to note some late blackberries, thick and brambly in one corner. He perched on the old, heavy branches and picked here and there among the half-fermented berries. When the boy appeared at one of the lower windows, then opened it, Raoul flew off.

But he stayed away from Paras and Frida for the time being. They might be oblivious to the brouhaha about the mallard nest, but he could not be. Any bird knew that a nest was a nest, and subject to the whims of fate. In the fork of a tree, on the ground, under the eaves of a building, in the corner of a chimney, in an attic, in a thicket of bushes — anywhere you built a nest, something could happen to it. Who was it, Raoul tried to remember, some dove he had known years ago, so proud of himself for building the nest in a warm, quiet, hidden spot that turned out to be the engine of an automobile. When the owner of the vehicle returned from his vacation, the nest had gone up in smoke. Sid had none of the sense of larger perspective that every bird should get with age. He would not accept that each spot had its advantages and disadvantages, and that fate would take its course no matter what. He asserted that he had been here and there with his band of drakes, to the ocean, to the ice, to the sandy shore, but Raoul Corvis Corax, the twenty-third of that name, had his doubts. It would come as no surprise to Raoul if it turned out that Sid and his band had made it no farther than Lac du Der-Chantecoq, where they strutted around, bragging about Paris all summer, and swimming in the calm of that domesticated body of water.

All the same, his own nest seemed empty and dull to him. He was so bored with his nest that he had let his rival, Maurice, enact his claim upon Benjamin Franklin's lap, which Maurice had promptly ratified by defecating in every possible spot. Raoul thought he was spending too much time flying back and forth to the pond, urging Sid to come to his senses and build the nest. Winter, real winter, was at hand. Paras was as furry as a kitten.

That evening, Raoul arrowed back to the Rue Marinoni. He perched on the stone sill of the single lighted window. Inside the room, the boy sat in his bed with his back against the headboard. His covers were drawn well up, but he held a book in his hands. Raoul watched him for a bit. Through the next window over, he saw the old old lady, still and maybe dead (though that was impossible to know without pecking her corpus here and there). Her nest was spare and neat. There were three surfaces, and on each surface there was a single object precisely in the center.

Raoul jumped to the next sill. This room was so grand that Raoul could not see to the end of it. It was dark, quiet, and cold — he could feel the cold through the glass. There were many objects in the room, as in all the rooms of every human dwelling that he had ever spied into, but all of the objects were swathed, even the objects hanging on the walls near the window. The room seemed to have been waiting a long time for the coming of someone. Raoul flew back to the lighted window, landed on the sill, pecked lightly on the pane. The boy looked up.

Étienne was reading *Vingt mille lieues sous les mers*. There were two copies of it on his shelves, a very old copy that was hard to hold, and a newer copy. He had read it once before, but he understood it better this time. He was up to the part about Atlantis. When he imagined the sea, he thought of the Seine, but there would be no other side, and the boats traversing it would be bigger than houses. Étienne didn't mind not understanding things. There were many things that his great-grandmama did not understand, but she was patient about it; whatever it was, she sought to touch it or to hold it or to smell it, and after she had been with it for a while, she would nod and smile. She could make very nice food in her little *cuisine* even though she was unable to hear anything and, Étienne thought, did not see much anymore, either. Each morning, he stood in front of her while she sat in her usual chair, and she touched his hair to discover if it was tangled, his shirt to make sure it was buttoned properly, his shoes and the cuffs of his pants to know that he was neat, straight, and ready for the day. She herself wore the same clothes almost every day.

A raven was perched on the windowsill, and once again, it pecked the glass — Étienne saw him (was it a him?) do it. The raven then cocked his head and looked at Étienne, as if he was asking him to open the window. It was very late — the clock said almost midnight. It was cold outside, and Étienne's pajamas were thin, but he slipped out of bed and opened the window. He could have sworn that the raven nodded his shiny black head before hopping into the room. Étienne was a little surprised, but not terribly surprised. Animals in books did all sorts of things, and that was mostly what Étienne knew about animals, or about anything, for that matter. Since the weather was cold, he closed the window after the raven entered. Étienne went back to his bed, and got under the covers.

Now the raven hopped to the table, then onto a stack of books, then onto the back of Étienne's desk chair, then onto the rim of the lamp shade. He looked here and there, every so often pecking something. He stood over the core of an apple on the corner of the desk, pecked it, dropped it. Finally, he hopped to the footboard of Étienne's bed and looked at him, cawing mildly, not making much noise or, Étienne thought, arguing about anything. At last the bird fell silent, and the two of them stared at one another. It occurred to Étienne to reach out and pet the bird, but he decided against it and kept his hands warm under the covers. A moment later, the bird hopped to the book, which was lying open on the counterpane. He turned his head back and forth, looking at the white, shiny pages, then tapped the book gently with his beak. Perhaps he decided that there was nothing in it for him, because he suddenly lost interest and walked across the bed, then flitted to the windowsill and pecked at the glass again. Étienne got up and opened the window. The raven flew into the very dark night (clouds, no stars). Étienne closed the window. No book he had ever read spoke about such a thing, but Étienne was not surprised. If every new thing were to come as a surprise, he knew he would be surprised every hour of his life.

SIX

Now that she had explored the Champ de Mars, eaten oats out of Anaïs's bowl a few times, and in general made the best of her surroundings, Paras could not quite remember, or even imagine, her former, regimented life. To stand in a stall all night and most of the day? To hear the other horses banging their buckets, kicking their walls, making grunts and whinnies, pawing the straw, knocking their chests into the door? To go out always at the same time every morning? To eat what they put in front of you day after day? Yes, she had banged her stall door when she heard the food coming, but it was not exactly because she was hungry, it was because she had nothing else to do. Paras knew that she had left because she was curious and didn't know any better, not because she was dissatisfied, but, well, this freedom, these friends she had made, and this strange field were all more intriguing than anything else she had ever seen. When the grass was spare or the ground was frozen and the wind howled, it occurred to her to go back, but she was well aware now of what she would be giving up. Horses did what they were told — every yearling learned to be led here and there, learned to spend most of his or her time in a stall, learned to be groomed and tacked up, learned to step forward and step back, learned that humans had their foibles and their faults, but it was better to go along and get along. Every two-year-old you met had already been mounted, ridden, galloped, and, sometimes, raced. Horses who got injured came back and reported that they had stood around day after day, week after week, with nothing to do and no one to relate to — a good reason not to get injured.

Delphine and Rania had treated her kindly, and she had had no complaints about them. The other woman she saw sometimes, her "owner," was also kind and gave her plenty of cookies and carrots. Not all of the other horses she spoke to out on the course could say the same, and some of them, even the nice ones, quite resented how they were handled — the whipping and the spurring especially. Or their trainers hardly knew their names, much less their preferences. And she had enjoyed racing — the hot, stretching efforts of the galloping, the coiling spring over the fences, the exhilarating sense of competition. Here on the Champ de Mars, there were no winners or losers, just humans and animals and birds going about. A canter was a canter, a trot felt good (especially when it was cold, and it was getting colder by the day). But the thrill of racing seemed a part of the past, something worth giving up in order to be able to satisfy her curiosity and do things as she pleased. She enjoyed Frida and Raoul and Nancy and even Sid. There was an owl who dropped by in the night, when Raoul had gone to his nest, and the owl had a few things to say. There were foxes who appeared, even though Frida told them repeatedly to stay away, barking with that deep, resonant bark she had that was so startling when you first heard it. Possibly, there was a human, too, because from time to time a carrot or an apple or a lump of sugar would appear on the concrete abutment beside the pond, and certainly these treats were meant for her, since they were horsey sorts of treats. But that human, whoever it was (and Paras did not think it was the boy), was making himself or herself scarce.

Sid made up his mind about the nest. He put it exactly where it had been for the last three years, among the weeds under the thickest branches of the trees to the north of the pond, not far from where Paras curled up each day — she could just see it from her spot. Once it was built, Nancy made a home of it — she wallowed about in it, stamped on it, worked it into a comfortable shape, then settled in and stayed there for long periods of time. After completing his work, Sid took off, with complaints, for the south. "Screech-screech-screech, you should come with me, I won't be gone long, I will linger around Évry in case you change your mind." Nancy put her head under her wing. After Sid was gone, Paras asked, "Where is Évry?"

"A day's flight. He says that every year, even though I never go."

For many days, the weather was tolerable and the grass was thick enough in spots; but it got dark earlier, and the number of humans in the Champ de Mars diminished day by day. Paras was hungry, and she visited Anaïs more often. Anaïs was not like Delphine or Rania — she was shy with Paras, and, Paras thought, a little afraid of her. She rarely came too close, and she put her hand out to touch Paras as if it were at the end of a pole. But her touch was gentle and smooth. She would lay her palm under Paras's very abundant mane and stroke her from the cheek to the shoulder slowly, her hand flat, like a smooth cloth. Paras had always been ticklish with the curry comb and the brush, but she had enjoyed the rag they used to shine her up so that the sunlight gleamed off her coat. When Anaïs gave her the oats, she held the bowl away from herself, as if Paras might step on her (she would never do that), and Paras was careful to eat slowly, neatly, not spilling any oats onto the pavement. She offered Paras a few other delicious things, too — bran, wheat bits mixed with molasses (something Delphine had fed her as a treat). She mixed shredded carrots in with the oats, and once she had fed her an apple tart. Each time Paras visited her, she lingered as long as she could, but if the sky was beginning to lighten, or the dogs were waking up, or an automobile could be seen passing on the Quai Branly, Paras made sure to walk away, always in a different direction, so that Anaïs would not see her heading back to the pond. She had never seen Anaïs in the Champ de Mars. Anaïs, like all humans, had given her a name; it was "Chouchou." Since Anaïs was at the shop every time Paras went there,

Paras assumed that the shop was where she lived.

Paras's coat was thicker this year than it had ever been — if she were still at the racetrack, Rania would have clipped her by now, and she would be wearing blankets, light during the day, heavy at night, and even a wool square over her haunches during training. Her coat kept her plenty warm, though — as long as she stayed fairly dry, it fluffed up nicely whenever she moved around. Trotting about, really moving, was the most warming thing, but she was, as always, careful in her choice of when and where to get this exercise. Her fluffy coat was the reason, when she left Anaïs this time (honey, shredded beets in the oats!), that she got back to the pond without realizing what Frida pointed out after she jumped over the fence. Frida said, "You do understand that you're covered with snow, don't you?" Frida was lying with her forelegs and her hind legs curled underneath herself. Now that she thought about it, Paras could just feel a little cold weight along her spine. She put her head down and shook herself. Snow lifted off and fluttered around her. Where it landed, she touched it with her nose. It was light and intriguing.

Frida said, "Look where you came from."

Paras turned around. She hadn't thought she was trotting through snow. She knew snow — quite often it crunched under your hooves. Once, when she was a yearling, she and her three companions had been let out in new snow. They had frolicked and floundered, the thin, frozen surface giving way so that they dropped through it and then leapt out of it again. Now she saw that the whiteness receded into the distance, and there, in a long line, leading to the spot where she had jumped the fence, were her hoofprints, round and dark in the smooth, blank field. Frida said, "You'd better hope that those fill in by morning."

Paras looked upward. The air was thick with sparkling flakes; a light breeze whirled them around, but they fell and fell, into her face, into her eyes. She glanced at the pond — it was white, too, around the edge. Paras crunched through the ice until it was in fragments around her cannon bones, cold and sharp. The water in the middle was covered with a film of ice that was not yet white, but almost. She tapped it with her nose; it broke; she took a long, freezing drink.

Frida sighed.

Paras suspected that she was thinking sad thoughts — she had come to understand

94

that many of Frida's thoughts were sad, that there had been that human who had mysteriously disappeared, that without a human a dog was a little ill-at-ease in a way that a horse was not. Dogs, evidently, saw humans as friends, whereas horses saw them as co-workers. "Well," said Paras, with her new-found sense that everything would work out, "at the moment, I'm tired and full, so I'll sleep, and then we'll see."

"What are you full of?" said Frida.

Paras pretended not to hear. For now, she wanted to keep Anaïs to herself; anyway, she didn't think Frida would care for oats.

After Paras curled up and went to sleep, Frida lay still for a long time, trying to keep her feet warm and her nose curled under her knee, but more than once, she could not resist looking at those hoofprints. Finally, she rose to her feet and slinked away, looking back once to see if Paras had awakened, but no — not even her ears flicked. Frida knew from her recent experience that a horse didn't sleep as much as a dog did, but she was asleep now. Frida took off at a run.

Frida could follow the hoofprints perfectly well — not only by sight, but also by smell, and the fact of the matter was that even a human would notice that Paras had defecated on the dirt road to the north of the pond. What surprised her was that the hoof-prints went to the other side of the Champ de Mars, away, from Jérôme's shop, toward the Avenue de Suffren, a street Frida had explored several times and had never found of the least interest. She might have enjoyed exploring the soccer field, but the fence was too high, and she might have visited one of the dogs she heard barking in the area, but all of them seemed to be safely locked in upstairs rooms. She had visited one vegetable shop, but the man there stayed inside, unlike Jérôme, and none of the customers had noticed her. Nevertheless, the hoof-prints stopped at this shop. As far as Frida could tell, everything all up and down this block was closed up tight. She sniffed all the doorsills, growled at a couple of cats but asked no questions, and looked at the hoofprints again. Next to the vegetable shop was a bakery. Frida paused, put her forefeet on the windowsill. The light was dim, and she could see nothing. The glass was cold, with frost creeping upward in tendrils; she could smell nothing. In frustration, she gave a little whine. The door opened, and some-one wrapped in white exclaimed, "Out! Out! Get away, bad dog!" Frida backed up into the dark street, and ran off. It was snowing harder now — Paras's hoofprints had nearly disappeared. When she got back to the abutment, Paras hadn't moved, and Nancy was so soundly asleep that she didn't even flinch when Frida touched her with her nose. Nancy, she thought, was a fool — a dog was a dog, and a mallard was a mallard. Frida might exert all of her willpower but still be overcome by instinct, especially if Nancy were to move, but Nancy remained as still as a rock — her feathers, fluffed, were chilled, too. And so instinct did not kick in. Frida lay down in her spot and thought happily about carrying her bag to her usual shops early in the morning, when Jérôme was just taking in supplies and organizing them. He might give her something ugly — something that humans would not like, but that was fine with a dog. He'd done that before. She fell asleep and dreamed of a nice knucklebone.

Paras woke up first, and she did not understand where she was. Something was hanging over her. Something else was all around her. The only warm spot was right beneath her chest. She shook her head and blew out her nostrils, and the air that came out was a white fog. Then she shook herself, and with that, the whiteness encompassing her splintered and fell in little pillows to the ground. She realized that it was snow, that the branches that normally arced above her as she slept had been weighted down with it. They now trembled and lifted, and she could see the world. Not that there was much to see — the earth was white, the trees were white, the pond was white, the sky was white, and the air, too, was still white with flakes drifting downward in the stillness. She turned her head. Snow was mounded against her side almost to her withers. She made her skin shiver; the snow shivered, too, and slipped off.

It was only then that she began to feel cold, and to feel cold meant, as always for a horse, that she had to move. She stretched her foreleg and started to stand up, but Frida was there instantly, saying, "Be careful! Be careful!" She dropped two carrots in front of Paras's nose. How disappointing they were tasteless, floppy carrots — but she ate them. Frida pressed closer. She said, "The snow is higher than my chest. I had to bound over to the market. It took me forever and was exhausting. I could hardly bring anything back. The streets are not much better than the Champ. No cars anywhere."

Thanks to Anaïs, Paras had had that full feed — oats, honey, beets, but also bran —

almost more than she could eat, though she had eaten every morsel. She was not hungry — but she did expect to be hungry. For the first time in many days, she began to feel a little nervous.

She hoisted herself to her feet.

Thoroughbreds are nervous horses — you heard that all the time, and it was a compliment. It meant that they were quick and smart and attentive. There were non-Thoroughbreds up where she had trained and mostly lived, in Maisons-Laffitte, and all the Thoroughbreds congratulated themselves on not being as dull as those others, with that odd hair around their fetlocks, and those heavy heads and thick coats. You might not be a winner (and every Thoroughbred was well aware of who won, who placed, and who showed), but at least you were a Thoroughbred, and that counted for something. But to be nervous meant to run here and there, and it was pretty clear, even if Frida had said nothing about it, that running about was not a good choice right now.

Up in Maisons-Laffitte, Delphine was also looking at the snow, and there was more of it than there was down in the city. She had just finished shoveling the walk that led from her small house to the road. Soon she

99

would get on the little tractor she kept for barn work and push the snow away from the horses' stall doors, out into the middle of the yard. And at some point, the men who took care of the entire training facility would plow the roads. The horses would keep their blankets on today, and she and Rania would take them out into the yard and walk them for an hour around the pile of snow. She had ten horses; all this would take most of her day.

She didn't have to worry about them for the moment — the night before, she had given them each an extra hay net to get them through the morning as well as the night.

None of her stalls were empty; she still wondered and worried about Perestroika, but another horse had come to take her place, to be trained for the spring season. There was a stall nearby that she used for storage — if Paras turned up, she could put her there. But she had lost hope. No one said it, but everyone thought it — Paras was surely dead. Perhaps she had wandered from Auteuil to the Bois de Boulogne and died there, and her carcass, stripped by vultures and foxes, was hidden in a ravine somewhere. Perhaps she had been kidnapped. A stolen horse might be doing something somewhere. Paras's markings were not unusual — a plain white star, two little cowlicks in typical spots, otherwise, a red bay, no white stockings. Delphine would recognize her, but to the average person she would look like a multitude of other horses. Delphine had scrutinized horses at all the racetracks she'd been to — in Deauville, down south, in Chantilly — for that telltale luxuriant forelock, those intelligent eyes, those wide nostrils, but she had seen no horse that looked like Paras. She had contacted the racing authorities at France Galop, she had put up signs, she had advertised in newspapers and on Internet forums, she had told all of her friends more than once, she had called all the stud farms in France, England, and Ireland, just in case a mystery mare might show up to be bred, though how a thief might pull that off, she had no idea. But someone else might — a fellow trainer named Louis Paul (and everyone knew that wasn't his real name) was said to have stolen horses in the past. And he didn't like women trainers, said they were ignoramuses and deserved no support. Once in a while, he went out of his way to mock her if she didn't do well in a race. There were plenty of stories about ringers in the racing world — horses disguised to look like other horses so that they could run in a race they might win. She had notified Animal Control. Of course, a stolen horse could be sent to the slaughterhouse, but for what? A handful of euros? And surely any slaughterhouse would recognize that Paras was sound, well fed, young. Delphine had contacts at a few slaughterhouses, too. It was a mystery, as if the horse had vaporized into space.

She, Madeleine, and Rania had taken it very hard — Rania hadn't wanted Delphine to agree to train the new horse, a gelding named Jesse James, but Delphine could not do without the income, and it had seemed too sad to do as Madeleine wished — as Madeleine offered to pay for — to hold the stall, empty, bedded, waiting for the filly's return. The race Paras had won was not prestigious — it was not as though, at least at this point, she was worth hundreds of thousands of euros — but, unlike many owners, Madeleine didn't care about that. What all three of them cared about was the filly, soon to be a mare, Paras herself. As a trainer, Delphine thought she might have been harder-hearted than Rania or Madeleine. Training racehorses was a business; you had to accept that anything could happen and still you had to get on with it. And she had gotten on with it, but she couldn't give up the conundrum. Paras was Delphine's very own cold case.

Of course, the other mystery was what had happened to Rania's handbag, which might have disappeared at the same time — when Rania came back to the stall from the bathroom and found the door open, found the grooming box tipped over, found Paras gone, she had forgotten about everything but her phone, even though her handbag was full of money — she had put her whole week's salary down on the race and won her bets. Paras had been something of a long shot — 12–1 — but the horses that ran second and third had been even bigger long shots — 30–1 and 50–1 — and since she had bet on all three of them, she had won a number of euros that Delphine shuddered to calculate. But Rania had been much more upset about losing the horse than about losing her winnings, and Delphine had not punished her for being careless — when you have to pee, you have to pee, everyone knew that. What everyone did not know was, what in the world had happened? The handbag had never turned up — Rania's keys and credit card and phone had never turned up. Only her little mirror lay there on the gravel outside the stall, glinting in the deepening dusk — a clue, but a clue that no one could understand.

Without telling Madeleine, Delphine had spent a hundred euros of her own to call an animal psychic. They had spoken on the phone; the woman, who was in the west of Ireland, had taken her credit-card information before "casting about." Delphine had given the woman — Áine was her name — all of Paras's particulars, including color, date of birth, cowlicks, racing history, breeding — and at her end of the line, Áine had cast about so long that Delphine had thought the line was dead and said, "You there? You there?" Finally, Áine said that Paras was walking down the street, looking into shopwindows, but since she herself had never been to Paris and didn't know French, she could not say what was written over the shops — all she knew was that the windows were dark, but that Paras seemed healthy and active. These remarks were so ridiculous that Delphine simply put them out of her mind and swore that she would never be fooled again. Walking down the street, looking into shopwindows, indeed! What was she looking at? Designer platform heels? A hundred euros down the drain! But even so, she found a single grain of comfort in the fact that a voice — a rather deep, warm, and lilting Irish voice — had not said that the horse was dead. She pulled her hat more tightly down over her head, and marched, shovel in hand, across the road to the stables. She still had to shovel the snow away from the door to the storage barn where she kept the little tractor.

The horses saw her coming. None of them talked about Paras much — only six of them had known her, and she had not been one of those fillies who are friendly and agreeable to everyone. When she disappeared, the horses from England (there were two of these) assumed that she had been sold away. The horses from France said, if she had been sold, why were the humans so upset? Jesse James, the single, solitary horse from America, asked if she'd been running in a "claiming race," like they had back where he had come from, where, if you ran, another owner could pay some money and take you straight to his barn, but his accent was very strange, and no one answered him. According to the other horses, he was related to Paras — he had Northern Dancer everywhere in his pedigree — but because his grandsire was Nijinsky, he was big and brawny, a chestnut. Today, though, no one was worrying about Paras — it was cold, their blankets were dirty from lying down in the muck, the hay was a little dry. When all was said and done, they were Thoroughbreds — a day inside, a day walking, was not a good day.

SEVEN

Raoul was surprised at the snow, too — in his long life, he had never seen this much snow around Paris. Benjamin Franklin's lap was a dome of snow, and upon his bald head was a little white hat. An icicle hung from the tip of his nose, and even the back of his chair had a white railing. Raoul had huddled in his nest all night long, and he was hungry, but snow wasn't bad for your diet. Seeds dropped with the cold and were very nicely visible against the white. The trick was to wait until the sun had come out and melted the top surface. Later in the day, the top surface would freeze again, and an agile raven could hop gently around upon it, extracting chilly nutrients here and there. Also, anything that a human tossed landed visibly on the snow and was easy to see from above. This time of year, humans were rather careless, because they were rushing here and there, buying an abundance of things for what they called *vacances de Noël.* Some of these things fell out of their pockets and their bags. This time of year, Raoul allowed himself the occasional *palmier,* some pieces of meringue, even a stray nougat. Young humans, especially, tended to cry for something, eat a bit of it, toss it away, and cry for something more. A discreet *Corvus corax* could follow a small human down a street, picking up whatever he or she tossed, and be full in a short time. But he had to be discreet — if too many other Aves saw him, they would all be after the goods, and then the humans would chase them off.

The animals didn't know it, but Étienne did know it: this was the Feast of the Immaculate Conception. His great-grandmama had been up since before the sun, preparing herself for her long walk to the Mass. She had put on two pairs of socks, and some sturdy boots, gloves as well as mittens, leggings, a long wool dress, two sweaters, and her coat. Now she wrapped her head in a scarf she had knitted twenty years ago (four-ply cashmere — she could afford that then). A piece of lace, which she would wear during the service, was in her pocket. Étienne stood quietly as she patted him over to make sure that he, too, was suitably clothed. He was. It was a long walk at any time of the year, many times longer than the walk to the shops, but as far as Madame de Mornay was concerned, that only meant that you left plenty of time to get there. They opened the door and went outside. Étienne had cleared the step and the walk to the gate. Now he took along his little shovel, and as his great-grandmama moved down the walk, which had been not perfectly cleared by the city, he scraped bits of snow and ice to either side, widening her path. He was a good boy. The very few people who were out glanced at him and smiled.

It was to be a long Mass, and Étienne and Madame de Mornay got there in good time. Étienne left his small shovel outside, escorted his great-grandmama to her usual spot, about halfway down the center aisle. She did not kneel, but after she took off her coat, gloves, and scarf, set them aside, and put on her piece of lace, she sat quietly, with her hands in her lap, and closed her eyes to say her prayers. Madame de Mornay knew all the prayers there were in the book — she said them aloud even though she could not hear herself. She had once been a faithful churchgoer, in spite of her griefs, but now she could only manage it three times in the year — the Feast of the Immaculate Conception, Christmas Day, and the Pentecost.

Étienne took a seat behind her. When the church was almost full, and it seemed as though the Mass was about to begin, Étienne eased himself out of the pew, and out the back door. He estimated that he had two hours at least, and he ran for the Champ de Mars as fast as he could go, only stopping at his great-grandmama's house to pick up a bag of things that he'd been saving for a long time.

The surface of the snow was like a map of which animals had walked where in the course of the morning. Under the trees, along the allées that ran the length of the Champ, the snow was flattened by the footsteps of humans and their dogs, but deeper into the expanse of the Champ, there were the paw prints of cats and foxes, of geese that had landed, walked along, taken off again. Of a hare that had crossed the width of the Champ, and a rabbit that had scurried from one den to another. Squirrels had descended from their homes in trees, scurried across the snow, leaving a few nutshells, and returned to their trees. Ravens and other birds had landed, hopped about, taken off again. And Frida had raced toward the shops — she was cold, and cold made a dog hungry. Her track was straight — away from the abutment, back to the

110

abutment. There were no hoofprints. Étienne ran in loops around the places where he had glimpsed Paras over the last several weeks, but he could not see her. He got tired from running, set down his bag.

Paras could see Étienne, though. From her spot deep under the trees, where she was still curled up (so curled up that she could hear her own stomach rumbling), she could see him rise on his toes with his hands on his hips, and turn in a slow circle, looking everywhere in the Champ. Paras didn't need Frida to tell her that he was looking for her — she could sense it. And in the cold, dry air, she could just faintly smell a sweetness that would be coming from the bag. She could see that it was a big bag, and she could tell that it was a heavy bag. She had seen many bags in her day — not handbags, but feedbags. She flicked her ears and felt herself getting curious. Without thinking, she gave a little nicker. Nancy, who was huddling in her nest, all fluffed up against the cold, quacked, "Watch out!" But Nancy always quacked that. The boy had his hat pulled down so that only his nose and his mouth were showing. At any rate, Paras didn't think he had heard her — he didn't turn in her direction. She lay quietly, but she felt her curiosity getting bigger and bigger. Her nostrils stretched toward the boy. Her neck extended itself. Her eyes opened wider, and her ears went as far forward as they could go. Her tail stiffened, as if she were about to stand up, but she knew that she should not stand up. Or, rather, she knew that Frida had said that she should not stand up. Moment by moment, though, she was coming to think that nothing would be lost by standing up, by walking over to the boy, by nuzzling the bag, by sniffing the boy's cheek to see what kind of boy he was.

Now the boy jumped up and down, clamping his arms around himself, and then he made a noise like a horse does, blowing air out of his nostrils. He turned around again, looked in her direction for a long moment, then turned away. "He saw you!" quacked Nancy. "But he didn't see me! You quadrupeds don't know how to be still, do you?"

Paras didn't respond.

The boy opened the bag and looked into it. After a moment, he extracted something. Paras could see that it was a large carrot. He dropped it onto the surface of the snow. Although it smelled like a carrot, it didn't quite look like a carrot; it looked dark against the blinding whiteness. He picked up the bag and walked away, every so often stopping to take out something else and lay it on the snow. Paras couldn't sniff out what the other things were from this distance.

"He's tricking you!" quacked Nancy. "Don't fall for it. You know, they have these ducks that swim in the water. They look fine from above — handsome, you might say — and there they are, floating peacefully in a lake, as you are passing over, and always there is an argument about whether to stop and have a snack or whether to fly on, and the ones who stop — bam, they are dead. And those ducks that were there to begin with, they just keep floating around as if nothing has happened. Humans are horribly treacherous."

"That isn't my experience," said Paras. She could see a squirrel approaching the carrot. She knew the boy had left it for her. The squirrel looked this way and that. Another squirrel was nearby, too.

One thing Paras had learned in the Champ de Mars was that, if squirrels were walking around, then humans were nowhere to be found. She extended a foreleg, hoisted herself to her feet, felt the scratch of the branches as she left the trees and bushes that were her nest. She walked past Nancy's spot with her head down, and snorted at the squirrel as he reached his front paws toward the carrot, which smelled even sweeter and more delicious up close. The squirrel did not run away immediately, as Paras expected him to. He said, "Might doesn't always make right."

Paras had never spoken to a squirrel before. He said, "I'm hungry." She looked at him, then said, "It doesn't look as though you are hungry. You still have something in your cheeks."

The squirrel tossed his head and ran away. Paras took a bite of the carrot, then ate it piece by piece. She looked down the Champ. There was something else that the boy had dropped. She walked toward it.

She had been hoping for another carrot, but it was a head of romaine, a little wilted, more bitter than sweet, though parts of it were crunchy. She ate every morsel, including the fibrous stem end. The next item, not sitting high on the snow but sunk into it, looked like another carrot, but when she bit into it, it had a different flavor, and at first she stuck her nose in the air and wrinkled her lip, but she was hungry, so she ate it anyway. It was large, and by the time she was finished, she quite liked it.

The boy was standing over the next thing, dark and round. He did not retreat when she approached it. He stood still, then picked up the apple (any horse could recognize an apple from far away) and held it out to her, his gloved hand flat. The apple looked and smelled good. She could have bitten it in half right away, but since she was a curious filly, even though she was hungry, she stuck her nostrils against the boy's head and sniffed. He stood very still, but she didn't sense that he was afraid — humans could get quite a bad smell when they were afraid. She sniffed the top of his head. Then she waited a polite moment and bit the apple neatly in half, leaving the other half in his palm. She chewed on the apple. Like the romaine, it was chilled, but sweet and crisp.

The bag was sitting at the boy's feet. Paras did something that she knew was rude, that Delphine would have said "Ah-ah!" to: she put her head down and opened the bag with her nose. The contents of the bag smelled good — certainly more apples, romaine, and some carrots, some other things, possibly a beet. She lifted her head and stood quietly. A long moment went by. The boy took off his glove and stroked her on her cheek, very lightly. Paras nickered.

Off to her right, almost but not quite behind her, something ran across the snow. She swiveled her right eye and saw it was

115

Frida. She did not turn her head. She didn't want Frida to know that she had noticed her. The boy reached his hand into the bag, and now he had that very thing that no horse could get on her own, a lump of sugar. Paras lifted it neatly off his palm with her lips and took it in. She held it on her tongue and felt it begin to melt in there, the sweetest possible thing. She crunched it down and licked her lips.

Then she saw that Frida wasn't alone — Raoul was flying along just above her, and they were having quite an argument. Paras nudged the boy lightly on the shoulder, and he did what she wanted him to do — he picked up the bag and started walking away. She followed him, the snow a little watery, a little soft. She could feel it balling in her front hooves, not a pleasant sensation. Frida and Raoul got pretty close, about to where the not-quite-a-carrot had been; Frida came to a sliding halt and sat down. Raoul raised his wings and landed just in front of her. The boy stopped, stared at them, then reached into his bag. He rummaged around for a moment, held out his hand. Paras sniffed what was in it — it smelled sharp and salty, a little like the mineral block Delphine had always kept in Paras's feeder. Raoul cocked his head one way, then the other, then hopped over toward them. Finally, he flew up and landed on Paras's haunches, where he took a few steps in both directions (Paras didn't mind him walking on her — it felt like being scratched). He stretched downward, and the boy held whatever it was toward the raven in his gloved hand. Raoul took it.

"Excellent!" he said. "First quality! Provenance, the Costa Brava, or even North Africa. Very firm, and yet chewy, almost pulpy."

"What are you eating?" said Paras.

"Tenebrio molitor!" said Raoul, his mouth full. "Mealworms!"

"I ate one of those, once," said Paras. "It was in the oats." She wrinkled her nose in the air again.

Raoul hopped over onto the boy's wrist. The boy's arm dipped, but he managed to lift it, and Raoul perched there, picking the mealworms out of his hand one by one, then gulping them down. They did look rather large. When he was finished, he dipped his head in thanks, and hopped back onto Paras's haunches. The boy turned, picked up his bag, and continued across the Champ de Mars. Paras followed him. Behind her, Frida started barking her deep, startling bark. Raoul said, "Ignore her. As I said to

117

her, her life with that fellow, no matter how well intentioned he was, and, yes, I admit it, affectionate for a human, and he did not abandon her — I had to explain to her what death is —"

"What is death?" said Paras.

Raoul said, "I keep forgetting how young you mammals are. But, to finish my thought, he had his own issues, and if indeed he preferred to live out in the open rather than to take shelter, especially in the winter, well, look where that ended up, and, yes, I know he — as we Aves say — 'flew upward' in the summer, but damage accumulates in every species —"

"What's the problem?" said Paras. Frida was still barking.

"She thinks you are being captured and put in jail."

Paras stopped walking. She said, "She has mentioned that. But what is jail?"

"Oh, goodness, you know, a small enclosed space where you can't get in and out of your own accord, but must always bow and scrape and do tricks in order to achieve some sort of self-realization."

"A stall," said Paras. She turned her head to look at Raoul.

"Something like that," said Raoul.

"On a day like today, there's much to be

said for a stall."

"Have you ever been inside a house?"

"Where humans live?"

"Yes."

Paras, now walking along behind the boy, who was carrying his bag and moving at a decent clip for such a small human, said, "I knew a human who lived in our barn. Her horse lived in one stall, she lived in one stall, and her dog lived in the stall between them. Delphine made her move, though." She thought again. "Sometimes humans live above us. We can hear them walking around."

"You have enjoyed a very circumscribed life," said Raoul. "In my view — and, I would guess, the view of most Aves, especially *Corvus* — there is nothing quite as amusing as observing humans in their own habitats. They sleep on their backs with their mouths wide open, you know, and there is not much of this walking about that you see out of doors, looking lordly and in charge. It's all lolling and lazing and stoking themselves with food and drink. Gatherings are different. Quite often they flock together in large, bright rooms, and then they plume themselves and establish rankings. I would like to see a healthy flock of Aves fly into the room and perch on their heads. But, by themselves, they are something of a mess."

All of this time, Paras had been following about two paces behind the boy, and he'd been glancing at her. They'd crossed the Champ de Mars at an angle, taking the same route Frida always did when she headed for the shops. Frida had stopped barking, and was slouching along in the rear. Every so often, she uttered a sad whine, as if she had given up on them and was talking to herself. The boy now paused. Paras stepped up to him, and he offered her another item from the bag, a piece of bread. She could taste oats in it. It was delicious. Raoul landed in front of the boy and lifted and lowered his head. The boy seemed to understand. He opened the bag and held it for Raoul to look into.

"I thought I smelled *cacahuètes*," said Raoul.

"What are *cacahuètes*?" said Paras.

"Your diet is sadly limited," said Raoul. But he did not explain what *cacahuètes* were.

They had come to a building, much taller than a stable. A fence covered with impenetrable wintry vines surrounded it. Paras reached out and tasted the dead leaves. Plenty of snow, and the merest hint of a bitter, summer flavor. She spat the fragments out. Frida barked one time, but then sat and stared at them, her ears flat against her head. The boy opened the gate all the way, as wide as it would go. Paras stepped around it, and peered into the yard.

There was not much to see. The snow was not flat — it had mounded against the walls of the building and piled on the windowsills. The sun shone on the snow and the walls and made Paras blink, it was so bright. She snorted and tossed her head. The yard wasn't as tight as it looked from the outside — spacious enough to walk about in, though not to trot, private in spite of the brilliant sunshine — no branches to scratch her back as she got in and out. Open to clouds and rain and mist and breezes. But right now — not very appealing. Paras made no move through the gate.

Now the boy did something to the black door across from the gate, and then he opened that, too. It was much narrower than the gate, and a horse, or a dog, or a boy, had to climb a step to approach it. He opened it wide. Paras could not see inside — the sunlight on the snow had blinded her a bit — but she could feel warmth billowing out of the doorway like a fragrance, and so, even though Frida barked two sharp barks, and because she was a curious filly, Paras

121

went up the step and through the door (without banging either of her hip bones on the door frame), and Raoul flew in after her. The boy closed the door behind her, and also the gate, and it was a good thing he did, because there was a gendarme on the sidewalk, across the Avenue de la Bourdonnais, who could not believe his eyes. He thought he saw a horse go into a house that he passed every day, a house that he knew was very respectable and had been in the same family for at least a hundred years, but by the time he got there, the gate was closed and locked again. There were no hoofprints visible in the packed snow on the street or the sidewalk, and so he decided that he had, indeed, had too much wine the evening before, on the occasion of his daughter's engagement party, and that he had better avoid all alcoholic drinks for a few weeks at least. He did see Frida — he stepped toward her in what he considered a friendly manner (she was a beautiful dog; surely, she belonged to someone) and what she considered a threatening manner — he was wearing a uniform, after all. As his hand reached toward her, she backed away (without growling — a good dog never growled at a gendarme), then headed into the Champ de Mars, but away from, not toward,

Nancy's nest and her own den. She made believe she could hear Jacques calling her. The gendarme watched her for a moment, then turned around and went back to his rounds. He proceeded down the Avenue de la Bourdonnais toward the Avenue Rapp, and so he did not see Étienne emerge from the house, lock the gate behind himself, and run as fast as he could, back toward the church.

EIGHT

Every time she went to Mass, Madame de Mornay refused out of hand any sort of automobile ride home. She had her cane, and she had her boy. She allowed the curé to take her elbow and help her down the five stairs out of the church — that was a courteous thing to do, and even when she was a young woman, long long ago, she had allowed her husband to do the same. But then she waved her hand in a gesture meant to indicate that she had no need of him any longer, and she would see him another time, and even though he was worried about the snow (true, the streets were clear by now), he stood silently, with his hands folded, watching her and the boy, who was carrying a small shovel, make their way step by step by step. His predecessor, long retired, had considered her old in his day, and the curé himself was no longer a young man. Every time he saw her, he wondered if there were things he should do to help her and, perhaps, the boy. But he never did anything — he only saw them every so often, and had too much else to think about. He also knew that she would resent whatever he might attempt.

It took Madame and Étienne quite a while to get home, but Madame did not regret the trek. The Mass had been quite refreshing — a lovely performance by the choir (the baritones were especially good this year, their voices rich and expressive — though in fact she could not hear them, and was remembering another choir, from many years ago). She had taken Communion — last in line — and had thought her prayers (in Latin) if she had not said them aloud. She wasn't quite aware that Étienne had vanished during the service, because he was there with her when the Mass ended and everyone else had left. Perhaps she felt that his hand was cold and his cheek was cold, but that could be an illusion.

They trudged and trudged, and even though Étienne was eager to see what the horse and the raven were doing inside the house, he was, as always, patient with his great-grandmama.

Raoul had not meant to be left inside, with all the windows closed. He perched on each

125

of the windowsills in turn and looked out. When he was finished with the lower story, he flew up the grand staircase and into the rooms that were open (only two of these), and looked through those windows. He pecked at what looked like a grape or two hanging from the ceiling, but the grapes were plaster, and dusty at that. And so, when he saw from the second story that Étienne and the old lady were making their way along the Rue Marinoni, he flew down the stairs, and when the front door opened, he was gone before the old lady had even crossed the threshold.

Paras, too, had made use of one of the windows — she had stretched out in a square of sunshine on a nice thick carpet (though she didn't really understand what a carpet was), given a groan because she was so enjoying the warmth, and gone fast asleep. Horses don't sleep very long as a rule, but Paras was tired, and this time she did sleep, giving out quiet little snores that ruffled her nostrils and rose into the silent air of the old house.

All of her life, Frida had been a dog with a cool head. According to the relatives she could recall from when she was a puppy, a hunting dog had to be — you could not sight a quail or a pheasant, lose your mind, and go running toward them barking. Her relatives, as she remembered anyway, had been proud of their skills. A "good dog" took her time, moved away or moved toward, and only at the right moment did she race at the game, and then always silently, always intently, always moving as little of the surrounding air as possible — those were the rules. With Jacques on the street, she had been cool — standing still, sitting erect, resting herself as poised as a statue so that passersby would pat her head and then, the most important thing, drop coins into the dish. Little dogs might bark, but it was inappropriate for a big dog to respond in kind.

Now, however, she did not know what to do, and so she did an, admittedly, hunting-dog thing — she ran in circles about the Champ, as if she were scouting for game, but she wasn't, really — it was just that she had no idea what to do. She *was* looking for something, but it was not a bird — rather, an idea. On a sunny, snowy, still, and chilly day on the Champ de Mars, ideas seemed to be few and far between. Frida ran until she had worn herself out, at which point she realized that she was on the Avenue de Suffren. A few humans were out along the avenue, bundled up in thick coats with their faces wrapped, wearing gloves, and scurrying along. No one, as far as Frida could tell, even glanced in her direction. And running around had made her hungry. She turned off the Avenue de Suffren down the Rue Desaix, a street she did not know well. But there was a meat market there, she could smell it, and even if she knew no one in the place, it was something of a comfort just to lie down on the pavement outside, lean her back against the cold building, and pant for a while. She closed her eyes.

Frida had a perfectly good memory, and the picture of Paras and Raoul entering the gate and the door, and the door being closed behind them, was right there. Perhaps because she was so preoccupied, or perhaps because the air around the meat market was suffused with wonderful odors, when she opened her eyes, she was surprised to see that there was a woman squatting in front of her, neatly dressed in a coat made of a sheepskin (though with the fur turned inward), holding out her fist to Frida. Her fist was loosely clenched, and without really thinking, Frida did what she was supposed to do, she stretched her nose and sniffed the fist. She wagged her tail. It was a short tail, but the woman saw it, and smiled. She petted Frida on the head two times. It felt good. Frida hadn't allowed anyone to pet her — not even Jérôme, who sold the vegetables — since Jacques died. She had forgotten how pleasant it felt. The woman said, "You pretty thing! You have a coat like silk!" She petted her again. Frida stopped panting and let out a little huff.

The woman stood up and looked up the street and down the street. It happened to be empty. She looked in each direction again. No one. For the first time since the death of Jacques in the spring, Frida was found out. The woman said, "Dear girl! You don't seem to have an owner. Are you truly all alone?"

No human, Frida thought, but I have friends. Then she remembered the door closing on Paras and Raoul, and Nancy pre-occupied with her eggs, and she rested her head on her leg. The woman bent down and petted her again. She said, "You aren't terribly thin. You look as though *someone* looks after you." She squatted down again, and said, "You are a beautiful dog. I wish you belonged to me!" She opened her bag and pulled out a package, then unwrapped it, and offered Frida, very politely, a nice sausage, one of Frida's favorite items of food, one she hadn't had for a long time. The woman set the sausage in front of Frida's nose. Frida did not gobble it down. She sat up, looked the woman in the eye, and held out her paw. The woman took her paw, and said, "My pleasure." It wasn't until the woman walked away, back down the Rue Desaix toward the Avenue de Suffren, that Frida ate the sausage. The sausage did not solve her problem, but it calmed her down and warmed her up. It was a very nice sausage, not too sharp, but with plenty of flavor and density. It was a delicious change from cheese and bones.

Frida stood up and shook herself. As she walked back toward the Champ de Mars, she scented the woman — probably it was her sheepskin coat. She scented that she had turned left on the Avenue de Suffren; she scented that she had walked one block and crossed the street; she scented that she had walked another block and gone into a shop, then come out again. She scented that the woman had walked another half-block, then entered a door (Frida sniffed the bottom of the door) and closed the door behind her. Frida stepped back, looked upward. Perhaps she saw the woman looking out the window, but the light was against her — she couldn't really tell.

In the meantime, Étienne was escorting Madame de Mornay through the entryway of their house and into her room. He helped her remove her coat, and he hung it in her closet. He helped her remove her scarf and one of her sweaters, then her boots. He helped her into her slippers, put away her things. She was evidently very tired from her long day, and her lips were moving — he suspected that she was singing a few of the melodies or saying a few of the prayers she remembered so well. He'd seen Paras stretched out on the floor of the grand salon, her nostrils fluttering slightly and one of her hind hooves twitching. He very much wanted to visit her, but he knew that he had to fix his great-grandmama a cup of tea first, and bring her something to eat — they'd eaten nothing since the night before, because she believed in fasting before Mass. There were sandwiches she'd made for her return, a little ham, a little watercress, a little mustard. His great-grandmama yawned, but of course she covered her mouth very politely and patted his cheek. He ran to the *cuisine*, just happening to close the door to her room as if he had done so inadvertently. He ran past the grand salon again. Paras was still stretched out.

But Paras was not sleeping soundly. She

was lying still, not quite ready to get up. Getting up from lying down is a project for any horse, one that a horse must prepare for mentally. Legs are long, bodies are heavy; balance is attainable, but not without effort. Paras had often admired the ease with which Frida moved from lying down to rolling over to sitting up, and Frida was nothing compared with a cat. One of the cats at Delphine's barn had enjoyed sprawling on windowsills, watching mice and rats from above. Sylvie, her name was. More than once, she had leapt from the windowsill right onto an unsuspecting mouse. Delphine called it "an airborne attack." Sylvie called it nothing — she disdained making a big deal of anything. The boy ran past. Then he ran past again, at a slower pace, carrying some item, and disappeared. Paras rolled onto her breastbone, paused, shook her head.

Madame de Mornay felt invigorated by the sandwiches and the tea. She patted the bed beside her, expecting Étienne to sit down, as he always did, take a sandwich, and listen to her tell a little story. After a moment, he did; she felt the mattress dip. She gave him the plate, and said, "My dear, I keep thinking of something that happened to me when I was your age." And then she

132

told him how her own maman, after her father had died, had become quite fond of a man who lived in Normandy, who had a great estate not far from Deauville. She and her maman had gone to the estate twice, and now she could so easily remember those fields, those young horses running in the green grass, so playful. She said, "My life would have been so different if things had gone another way." She patted his head again, and then said, "I am so exhausted. Old memories are the ones that wear you out."

She lay down, rested her head on the pillow, and Étienne covered her with the old silk pelisse she preferred for naps. She fell to snoring almost immediately.

In the grand salon, Paras was at last awake and looking about. There was space, she had to admit. Even with all of the items that looked like shrouded haystacks pushed against the walls, a horse could wander around in this place. It was evident, though, both by the smell and by the look, that it had been a long time since any sort of equine had been here. There was no manure, for one thing, which was perhaps unfortunate, since Paras could discover a lot by investigating piles, or even single deposits that had been left by other horses.

She was not the sort of horse to snuffle for bits of hay and oats, as some horses did, but every pile of manure deserved a look. Nor did she see hay bins or grain buckets or a drinking dish. That she saw none of these was perhaps not a good sign, but at the moment, she was warm and curious, and so she levered herself to her feet and went to the corner, where she deposited her own little pile of droppings, out of the way, where she wouldn't step in it (she was a neat and tidy horse — Delphine had always praised her for this). It was a small pile, but it gave off a pleasant odor that made the grand salon seem just a little more welcoming and familiar. After that, she walked along the walls of the room, sniffing, and occasionally licking. It could not be said that she discovered much — only dust, and plenty of that. She sneezed.

And here was the boy. He stood at the end of the grand salon, staring at her. He held nothing in his hand, no apple or carrot, but she walked over to him anyway, and smelled his shirt.

Étienne hadn't really thought beyond the moment when the horse might come into the house. He hadn't thought that the horse *would* come into the house, and so he had made no plans for what he would do with the horse. He had never known a horse — only read about them, and in nothing that he had read did any author say that a particular horse had entered a house and gone to sleep beneath the window. He was a little frightened, but Étienne, a small but determined boy, had been frightened before; he did what he always did, he smiled, looked the horse in the eye. After a moment, he felt comfortable petting her. First he petted her cheek and the side of her nose; then, when she lowered her head, he put his hand under her bushy forelock and tickled her white star. Pretty soon, he was running his hand down her neck.

Paras had a thick coat, smooth and fluffy, not like the wool of the sofa or of a sweater. Étienne let his hand stroke her shoulder. She seemed to enjoy it. She dropped her head and closed her eyes.

But as she was standing there, she smelled that through a nearby doorway there was food and water. She hadn't eaten a real meal since her last visit to the bakery and café on the Avenue de Suffren. And she was thirsty, too, though she had licked and eaten plenty of snow earlier in the day. She walked toward the *cuisine*. Étienne saw where she was going, and went ahead of her.

In fact, there was quite a bit of food in the

cuisine. Madame de Mornay had a horror of running out of provisions, because she had, indeed, run out of provisions several times in the course of her long life, and she remembered those occasions in some ways better than she remembered the years of plenty. The question, for Étienne, was not whether there was food, but what does a horse eat?

The answer, as far as Paras was concerned, was "Let's try it and see." She went through the doorway, which was old and wide, and she clip-clopped first to the sink, where she licked the porcelain in a way that invited Étienne to put in the plug and run some water. He did so, and Paras took a long drink. When she was well and truly finished, Étienne pulled the plug. The next thing she did was to smell the remainder of a baguette that Étienne and his great-grandmama had purchased the day before. Étienne tore it into pieces; they were not especially hard, and Paras chewed them up and swallowed them down. They were not delicious, however, unlike the kale that Étienne pulled out of the refrigerator, which tasted to Paras of sunshine and summertime. There was a lot of it, and she enjoyed it very much, which was fine with Étienne, since he didn't like kale at all, and his great-grandmama made him eat it because she said it was very nutritious.

They moved on to carrots, parsnips, turnips, sweet potatoes, all of which Étienne was glad to see disappear from the larder (which was deep and wide, half a story dug into the ground, cool enough for extended storage; Etienne went up and down the steps several times, each time bringing up a surprise). Finally, he got to the potatoes. Paras sniffed them, and in other circumstances she might have eaten one, but now she left them alone and looked out the window. The window gave onto the courtyard. She could tell by the light that the day was coming to an end. Without really intending to, Paras continued through the *cuisine,* which, like the other rooms in the house, was a large space. At the far end was what had once been the door to which purveyors of food and wine had come, bringing everything Madame de Mornay or any other Mornay might need for suppers and parties. It was a large door, the same color as the wall, but Paras could smell that it led to the outside. She stood in front of it for a moment or two, investigating it, and then, by mistake, really, she bumped it with her knee and her hoof. After she did this, Étienne stepped in front of her and opened the door. This courtyard was different from the other one, not quite so large, and because of where it was situated, it contained hardly any snow, though it was somewhat gloomier and more overgrown than the courtyard outside the front door. Paras went outside and got rid of the water she had drunk from the sink. But it was still cold, so, after walking about for a few moments, she presented herself at the door again, and Étienne, who really quite liked her, stepped back and invited her in. He also gave her a lump of sugar.

And that was how the two of them agreed upon what the house was for and what the house was not for. That she had made a small mistake in the grand salon was fine with Étienne. He found himself a bucket, threw the manure out the window into the berry patch, and did a little mopping.

The manure was not unnoticed, except by Madame de Mornay, who was still sleeping soundly. If Paras had looked closely, she would have seen, in the corner of the grand salon where she'd made her deposit, a small hole in the wall where the floor molding had chipped and broken away. That hole was the entrance to a rather large estate belonging to Conrad and Kurt, father and son, two black rats who were part of a family of rats who had been living in the walls since long before the Mornays had ever been heard of. The rat family had once been quite extensive, with connections all over Paris, but some years before, a prolific tribe of cats had moved into the Champ de Mars, and reproduced to such a degree that most of the local rats, especially the smaller black ones, had either been wiped out or moved on to the Place des Invalides. Conrad and Kurt sometimes went for days without seeing, or, more important, hearing another rat in the neighborhood. The two main entrances to the rat estate were in the very storeroom where Étienne had gotten the kale and the carrots — one opening was not far from the flour bin (this one was larger, and normally used to carry provisions into the estate), and the other opening was down the wall a ways, behind the lentil bin. Kurt and Conrad and their predecessors had long since given up trying to chew their way into the various bins, barrels, crates, and even bags, because Étienne was not much good at cleaning up spilled provisions, and going down the short staircase had been too much for Madame de Mornay for years now. Kurt and Conrad were fat and lazy, though still much more stylish than brown rats. Many times every day, they went out the exit and in the entrance, picking up whatever Étienne left behind. This was largely the reason why Étienne didn't realize that the place was such a mess — Kurt and Conrad worked as his cleanup crew.

The estate was an enormous maze that ran all through the walls of the house and had several exterior openings as well. Conrad had sometimes gone out into the world in hopes of finding a rat or two, preferably black, preferably female, to join them in the estate. But the cat tribe was as avid and skilled as they had always been — they were everywhere, Conrad could sense them, he did not want to run into a lean and hungry feline when he was just trying to find a friend. Kurt was thus rather pleased to see, out the second-story window (his own aperture was a hole in the wall just below the sill), a certain canine pacing back and forth in front of the house. She had come at dusk, and now she walked for a moment, paused, lifted her head, sniffed, gave a single, urgent bark, then walked some more. Kurt knew which dogs were ratters and which dogs considered rats beneath them. This dog was just the sort who wouldn't look at a rat — all about birds, these dogs were. Even though Kurt had never heard of its happening, he could imagine taking such a dog on as a protector. Conrad said that this was a ridiculous idea, but Kurt thought that it was merely "imaginative." And Conrad agreed that, once you had a horse in the house, just about anything was possible. Conrad was old; Kurt was young. He knew that there were young female rats out there, and he thought of female rats more and more as he matured. He did not intend to give up on finding one of his own until he had at least tried something.

Instead of taking a little nap, which he sometimes did around dusk, Kurt gazed out the aperture until the canine moped away. Then he went through the wall into one of the uninhabited chambers and chewed meditatively on some linen drapes. He knew that Conrad was down in the storeroom, waiting to see what Étienne would leave for them. And it didn't matter to either of them that the horse might get some of what was rightfully theirs. There were plenty of provisions to go around, and always had been.

Madame de Mornay had expected her outing to take a lot out of her, and it did. When she woke from her nap, she was still exhausted. She rang her little bell, the one that called Étienne to her. He came at once, because it was very important to him that his great-grandmama stay in her room, at least until some idea of where to put the horse came to him — the grand salon and the *cuisine* were both places where Madame de Mornay spent a good deal of time. The library was a possibility, but it had hard, slippery floors, and windows onto the Champ de Mars. And whether Paras could or would be able to negotiate stairs was a question he had to answer. But the Feast of the Immaculate Conception had done Madame de Mornay in. She sat up in bed, drank a mélange of milk and honey with dried chamomile, and fell asleep for the night over her book, which was the last volume of *À la recherche du temps perdu,* a book she had been reading for eighty-three years and never quite finished. She kept at it, though, because her mother had met Monsieur Proust once at a party.

For himself and Paras, Étienne put together a pleasant degustation of shredded cabbage, withered apples (Paras smacked her lips, they were so tart and sweet at the same time), chopped beets, and more sweet potatoes. He offered her some pieces of cheese, his own favorite, but she wrinkled her upper lip and turned it down, as she also turned down the dark chocolate. Kurt, who was standing just inside the entrance to the rat palace, fluttered his whiskers at the odor of the dark chocolate. He would have liked a taste, but it was something Étienne never dropped and never left on the counter. After her meal, Paras took another long drink of water from the sink, and then went outside. Étienne huddled into his jacket and went outside with her. While they were gone, Kurt gathered up the remains of their meal, and also a single dried anchovy that he and Conrad must have missed from some earlier time. It was a mere fragment, but delicious all the same.

NINE

That night, Frida trotted back across the Pont d'Iéna exactly as if she knew what she was doing, and, in a way, she did. She hadn't been to the Place du Trocadéro since the leaves were fluttering off the trees; it existed in her memory as a place of comfort and richness — her little hiding place in the cemetery, her enjoyment of not only the provisions but also the well-dressed pass-ersby, the tiny dogs in their purses who would growl at her (for a long time, she'd thought that was what purses were for), the cigarette smokers lounging beside the walls (Jacques was a smoker when he could af-ford the cigarettes and occasionally he'd splurged on a bottle of champagne — he'd even given her some in her water bowl). Jacques had taken much pleasure in the lights and the busy social scene, had even thought himself, in a way, a part of it, since he had grown up on the Avenue de Messine, and liked walking past his old building when he could. One of Frida's favorite things had been to sit, erect and proud, on the top step of one of the two buildings at the Palais de Chaillot (she had heard humans talking about it — a museum about buildings in a large building). Jacques hadn't felt it worth his while to spend the money to go inside, though there were other museums he had entered, leaving Frida to guard his guitar on the street. She had also spent some time, while Jacques was asleep, exploring the cemetery that overlooked the square — he liked it because it was quiet there, enclosed, a good place for a long sleep.

As she trotted over the bridge, she was well aware of the enormous lit Tour over her shoulder, but she didn't turn to glance at it. She felt that she was somehow escaping its chilly aura. Once, she had asked Paras what she thought of the huge thing, and Paras had said, with bona-fide curiosity, "What difference does it make to me?," and Frida hadn't been able to answer that question. Raoul and other birds seemed to view it as a sort of tree/building hybrid, and he had told Frida that various flocks over the years had attempted to colonize it, not pausing to wonder, as he said, "why no

145

flocks had dared come before them — but every bird thinks of himself as an adventurer." Of course, he also remarked, the humans were not going to allow any flocks of Aves a free hand with that tower, not even *Corvus corax* in all of their many noble variations.

Once across the bridge, which was clear of snow but icy, Frida took a chance and did a thing she could not have done with Paras in tow, which was to go straight up the hill, beside the pool and then between the two buildings, as if someone were calling her and she had a right to be there.

And, indeed, the cafés around the square were ablaze with light, open for customers even if the night was chilly and slippery. Much of the snow had melted off during the day, or been swept to one side. The streets were shiny, and a few cars and taxis were making their cautious way here and there. Frida went over and sat beside the door of the Pâtisserie Carette, arranging herself so that she was facing outward toward the square, but also half looking in the window. She took a deep breath or two and waited.

With the wind blowing in her face, Frida suddenly felt cold for the first time — all day long, she had been on the move, up the

Avenue de Suffren, then back and forth across the Champ de Mars, then pacing in front of the house that her new horse friend had disappeared into. She had been distracted from the chill, first by the boy and then by events. At any rate, Frida was such a big, strong, muscular dog that she didn't feel the cold the way some dogs did. Her coat was short but dense, well suited for racing into rivers and lakes after ducks or into fields after pheasants, partridges, and other birds. No body of water that she had ever seen had intimidated her, including the Seine itself, which was plenty warm, even in the winter — at least, Frida thought so. But now, in the semidarkness, with the brilliant lights of the pâtisserie shining in her eyes, and the sight of the waiters relaxing, smoking, chatting among themselves as they wondered whether any customers would come in, she began to shiver. Was it fear or dread or cold? Frida herself didn't know. And the sky above was so dark that Frida could see nothing except the wavering lights of the giant tower across the river.

A voice said, "What in the world are you talking about?"

It was the voice of Raoul. Frida peered into the darkness. He was perched on the railing of the Métro entrance. Every so often, Frida had taken refuge in the Métro, but it was dangerous and loud, and the weather had to be very very rainy for her to choose the Métro. Frida sneezed, then said, "Hello, I was wondering where you had gotten to."

"I went to my nest, of course. A *Corvus* of my station has more things to attend to than one horse. But what in the world are you talking about?"

"What do you mean?" said Frida.

"Surely, you realize that you are always mumbling on about something?"

"No," said Frida. "I didn't realize that."

"My heavens," said Raoul, "I've been watching you since the summer. I've never seen such a talker. Mumble-mumble this, mumble-mumble that. I thought that that was the way *Canis familiaris* remembered things, by talking about them all the time."

Frida felt her shivering intensify. No one had ever said this to her, but she knew instantly that it was true. She hardly ever barked — Jacques had taught her that her bark was excessively loud and therefore dangerous if a dog (and a man) wanted to be left alone. And Jacques had not liked whining, and yet there were so many feelings and ideas that required expression of some sort. Even so, she said, "I don't really

148

know what you mean," and Raoul commenced to grumble and chat in a very doglike voice that Frida recognized perfectly as the voice of sometimes her only friend, herself. She sighed. Then she said, "That's a good imitation."

"Most Aves are adept at that," said Raoul. "You know about Psittaciformes, of course. They are an invasive order, but humans like them for their color, I suppose — humans are very shallow in some ways. *Corvus* are just as adept at different dialects as Psittaciformes, but we get far less credit —"

"What is a Psittaciform?" said Frida.

"A parrot, in common parlance, but of course there are many species. There have to be, because so many earthly beings are reincarnated as Aves. It's very educational for them. Or us, I might say. I feel that, in my former life, I was a government official; perhaps I was not as effective as I should have been. And look at Sid and Nancy. Terribly anxious, even for common mallards. My guess is that in a former life they were impulsive and careless. . . ."

Frida lay down, put her head on her crossed paws, and closed her eyes. There was a silence, and then Raoul said, "I do tend to go on, I know. It is a feature of age. I have learned so many things in my life that they just force their way out of my beak." Then he said, "I did peek in the windows at the Rue Marinoni today. The first time, it looked as though our friend was having a lovely nap, all stretched out on the floor, and the second time, she was eating from a very large bin. The boy seems to like her."

"No good can come of this," said Frida.

"Difficult to judge that," said Raoul. "The boy seems to do well on his own, for a boy. My view is that the danger is not to the *Equus,* it is to the boy. Over the years, I have observed that adult humans are very nervous if an immature human seems to be without a protector."

Frida's ears flicked at that word, "protector." With dogs, she knew, the question of who was the protected and who was the protector was always an open one. When you saw, on the streets of Paris, a human and a dog walking along, it could be either one, no matter how very small the dog was. She had seen dogs who might not even come up to her knees on the alert, not only looking this way and that, but barking, "Stay away, stay away! I will kill you if you hurt my human!" And it was true that, if there were three dogs together, it was the job of the smallest dog to keep an eye out and alert the larger dogs if danger was at hand. Had she been Jacques's protector? If so, perhaps she had not done a very good job.

Raoul said, "Pardon me, but there you go again. Talking to yourself. Is there something that you would like to communicate?"

Frida forced herself to remain silent for a very long moment, then said, "I suppose that communicating is rather dangerous."

Raoul said, "I hadn't thought of that. For Aves, not communicating is very dangerous. You never know when some hawk or owl might take silence the wrong way." And then he said, "Indeed. I will shut my trap now. Good practice." He flew upward, and the door beside Frida eased open.

The man who opened the door was not old, and he had a scowl on his face — Frida knew he intended to chase her away, perhaps to kick her — she had seen that in her day. But she felt too sad even to stand up. Let him kick me, she thought. She turned her head and stared at him. He stared back at her, and his face softened. After a moment, he squatted down and patted her on the top of her head. He said, "I have never seen such a sad face on such a beautiful dog." He stroked her several times, kindly and smoothly, as if he knew just how.

Inside, the man behind the counter said,

"Orlande! Close the door. What a wind! I don't know why we are even open this evening."

Orlande stood up, backed up, and then bowed, clearly inviting Frida into the pâtisserie. Frida was undecided — the interior of the restaurant was warm and light, and smelled good. There was no one there except the two men, but, still, it was *inside.* And at that very moment, Raoul flew up behind her and pecked her very smartly just above her tail. She jumped, Orlande laughed, and she stepped into the restaurant. She immediately sat down in her most dignified manner and offered Orlande her paw. He took it, shook it. From behind the counter, the other man tossed something. Orlande put his hand up and caught it, then showed it to Frida. It smelled good — it was a small warm roll. Frida took it politely, dropped it on the floor, ate it in as dignified a manner as she could. After she had done so, she dipped her head. Orlande patted her again.

"Beautiful dog," said the man behind the counter. "I've seen her around here before. I think she might belong to a family who has an apartment down the Avenue d'Eylau, but I thought they went to Cannes for the winter. I can't imagine that they would leave her here."

"Who would do such a thing?" said the first man. "André, she has a terrifically expressive face."

André set a bowl on the top of the counter. Frida could see steam rising off it. It was very fragrant. Beside it, he set a croissant, something she had shared with Jacques several times. He blew on the bowl. In the meantime, although there wasn't very much space, Frida did a few of her tricks — she put her paw over her eye, she lay down, curled up, and rolled over, she offered Orlande her other paw. After these, as if reading her mind, he took some bread that he had torn out of a loaf and set it on her nose. She paused a moment, then flipped her nose, tossed the bread, and caught it. Both men laughed, and the first man applauded. Then he brought the bowl to her — it was full of chicken broth — and the croissant. She ate carefully, trying not to make a mess. The croissant was delicious.

The view from inside the shop was most definitely different from the view outside — the windows were dark, and Frida herself was reflected in them; there was no surveying the landscape or seeing who might be coming. What with the talking of the two men, the banging of pots and pans, and the

153

scraping noise when her new friend moved a table or a chair, she couldn't hear much, either, and as for her most important and discerning sense, she felt rather as if she were being drowned in rich odors. Outside, there were plenty of smells — the damp in the air, the leaves, the trees, the birds and animals, the sharper scents of cars and trucks going by, the differing scents of humans (young boys — quite strong; women — almost nothing except occasionally the scent of a flower) — but they drifted past one or two at a time, always from a specific direction, easy to interpret, especially by a cautious dog such as herself. Being inside made her a little afraid to go back outside. It was, indeed, very very dark out there.

Orlande set a dish of water on the floor, and Frida drank it. She was quite full, and warm, too.

The door opened again, and four humans, two elegant young men and two young women in high heels, came in, laughing. André straightened up and began rearranging his offerings, and Orlande smiled, showed the four humans a table. They stepped around Frida without seeming to notice her. The next time the door opened, and another pair of humans entered, Frida slipped out as the door closed behind her.

From the railing of the Métro staircase, Raoul called out, "Good thing you don't have a long tail."

"I've often thought that," said Frida. She walked away from the Pâtisserie Carette toward the entrance to the museum, which was dark and no doubt chilly, but faced away from the wind. Raoul wanted to say, "The word among the Aves is that this unpleasant accumulation of frozen precipitation will be gone by the end of the day tomorrow. I gather from passing flocks of *Bombycilla garrulus* — some may call them waxwings — that warm weather is on its way." But, conscious of his recent moment of self-knowledge, all he said was "It'll warm up."

Frida estimated that she might be able to curl up in the corner of the entrance to the museum, entirely out of the way, and protected, maybe, from guards and the gendarmerie for most of the night. As she lay down on the hard surface, Raoul landed and walked back and forth, continuing to chat. "You know, by the way, that Nancy has laid six eggs." He wanted to say, "There could be more to come — mallards are a profligate bunch — but she seems to think she is finished. She seems content to be on her own, I must say. I might not have told you that I have a mate myself, and numerous offspring." He thought of Imelda, her "very large and important family down around Vincennes." Had Frida ever been to Vincennes? The question almost popped out. In Raoul's opinion, the *Corvus* of Vincennes were only exceeded in their sense of self-importance by the *Corvus* of Tours. But he was coming to understand that all importance is really merely self-importance. Though the thoughts unrolled in his head, he pressed his beak shut. He said nothing more, and so Frida drifted off to sleep — full, indeed, and surprisingly warm.

Not long after that, Paras was lying in the grand salon in the dark, enjoying the stillness as well as her own full belly (Étienne had spent the late afternoon soaking a bag of split peas for her evening meal, which he served with shredded cabbage). The house was so quiet that Paras could swivel her ears and hear all sorts of things — the sound of cars skidding along the Avenue de la Bourdonnais, the ruffling snores of Madame de Mornay behind the door of her room, even, perhaps, the sound of Étienne in his room, turning the pages of his book. Paras had long, slender, mobile ears. She had always

had good hearing — part of her skittish-
ness. She could hear the rumbles of her own
belly, which she knew was a good thing.
Étienne had decided, at least for the time
being, to rearrange the furniture of the
grand salon so that, if Paras was lying down
beside the back wall, a blind, deaf, ailing
old woman might not be able to sense her
there. Paras didn't mind — it was rather
like having a stall with a very high ceiling
and very low walls.

Paras was replaying in her mind her last
race, her second win, over the hurdles at
Auteuil. There had been not so many horses
in the race. Her previous win, also at Auteuil, had been rather like a stampede, a
rush over the hurdles that had made her so
nervous that she simply had to get out in
front of everyone and run away. The jumping part was the least of it. Hearing the
pounding of hooves and the snorting and
roaring of horses breathing behind her like
a great wind had driven her forward so
energetically that she had not really wanted
to stop even after the last jump and the finish line, with the jockey sitting up and turning her. She hadn't quite understood at that
point what a "win" was. But when they did
trot back to Delphine and Rania and Madeleine, and when the jockey gave her three

exuberant slaps on the shoulder, and when she saw that all the other horses (in particular the gray filly who had come as far as her hip and faded back) looked glum and exhausted, while she felt pleased and full of energy, she saw what winning was and knew that it was good. That had been in warm weather, the course fragrant and green. Her recent win at Auteuil was a more modest and autumnal affair, late in the day, not many spectators, but she had galloped with pleasure, jumped with ease, and stayed two lengths ahead of the chestnut behind her. She was again a front-runner, but out of curiosity rather than fear — it was strange and enjoyable, the way one hurdle seemed to lead to another, not frightening, but only a great big stride and then onward to the next one. She knew that when she was older Delphine would put her in jump races, where the obstacles would be bigger and more solid than "hurdles" (she had heard her say that to Rania). Paras had looked forward to that, so why had she walked (well, trotted) away from it all? Curiosity was the only answer. Or, as she thought now, sheer ignorance. Paras blew some air out of her nose and stretched out flat on her side. At once, she heard another scratching sound, this one inside the wall, and then there was a rat — dark gray, almost black, fat, but rather small, its whiskers twitching — right in front of her nose. She snorted at the odor, and the rat stepped aside but did not run away. He said, "Welcome."

Paras had a good view of the rat out of her left eye, so she didn't roll up onto her chest. She said, " 'Welcome'?"

"Yes, this is our territory. My father is Conrad and I am Kurt. Our castle is in the walls, but, as you can see, we have several courtyards, of which this is the largest."

"Do all —" She thought "little," but she said, "petite animals talk all the time about their property and importance?"

Kurt's whiskers twitched. He said, "In the first place, size is in the eye of the beholder, and in the second place, the only rats I know are myself and my father. All of the others who used to live around here, even the brown ones, have been killed or driven off by cats. There aren't many birds around, either, for that matter."

"What about your mother?" said Paras.

"I don't know," said Kurt. "We don't talk about that."

Paras, who had, as far as she was concerned, been separated from her own mother, Mapleton, far too soon (but no sooner than the other fillies — it was some-

159

thing the six of them who were turned out together had discussed endlessly), sighed in sympathy.

Kurt said, "My father says that you are a horse. Actually, we both thought horses were mythical animals, so we are a little surprised to see you, but what is, is. Rats are down-to-earth realists. Life is short, tunnels are long."

Paras didn't know what this meant, but horses also had their mottoes that were not all that understandable, like "Stay or go." She ruffled her nostrils. Kurt must have felt comfortable, because he coiled up, twitched his whiskers again, and sighed. He said, "I like you."

Paras said, "You don't know me."

Kurt said, "Your broadcast is calm."

"What does that mean?"

"Well, I see something with my eyes — that you are huge, reddish brown, furry, long-legged. I hear something with my ears — that your heart beats with a kind of roar. I smell something with my nostrils — that you have eaten split peas for your latest meal. I sense something with my paws — that, beneath where you lie, the floor sinks a little bit. And I receive something with my whiskers — that your global orientation is well adjusted."

160

"What is that?"

"If you don't know, I can't tell you," said Kurt.

But maybe Paras did know — maybe that was how you ran down a racecourse and jumped the hurdles and felt the ground moving this way and that and were not bothered by it, but found it enjoyable. She said, "You should talk to my friend Raoul. He's a raven."

Kurt shuddered. Silence descended, and Paras could hear rustling from Étienne's room. Then the door opened. Just like that, Kurt was gone, and since she had good night vision, Paras could now see the hole that he disappeared into, half hidden behind the leg of a piece of furniture. She rolled up onto her chest. Étienne's footsteps pattered around the couches, and he appeared. He immediately stroked her several times on the forehead and the neck. She knew it was time to go out.

She stood up and followed him down the hall and into the *cuisine*. Her own hooves sounded very loud on the parquet floor. He gave her a drink of water in the sink, and opened the back door. She went.

The snow was gone, the sky was clear, the moon was bright. Paras shook off the chill and walked around, enjoying the very act of moving. A gallop, she thought, would be nice, wouldn't it? It was true that she hadn't had a real gallop in a long time; thinking of her races had put her in the mood. Some racehorses saw galloping and racing as jobs they did, with food and shelter as the reward. Certain very good racehorses Paras had met seemed to be complainers, at least around the barn, always cocking a hoof or pinning their ears, dogging it to the practice course, needing a smack with the whip, then kicking out when they got one, but putting on the speed when they knew they had to, maybe so that they could lord it over everyone else and brag about their record. Others enjoyed it too much — everyone in the barn knew about horses who went out for a race and never came back, broken down. But there were those, and Paras considered herself one, for whom galloping was as natural as walking. Her problem had never been the gait — it had been her mix of curiosity and alertness. Delphine and Rania had been good with her, let her do it her way. And yet she had walked away from them. She lifted her nose and sniffed along the top of the fence — there was no looking over it — but she smelled nothing of Frida, nothing of Raoul. She was restless, and she kept walking. Étienne had closed the door

— she could see his face in the window, and then she couldn't, but the light stayed lit. She walked all along the fence, saw that there was a gate, but it was solid. When she kicked it or leaned against it, it didn't move. She walked and walked. Since she was protected from the wind, she wasn't cold, though her coat was fluffed up. She made several deposits and watered an old patch of asparagus.

TEN

The snow had presented Pierre, the head gardener, and his crew with plenty of extra work. They had to plow and shovel, though not cart away — Pierre knew that if he made paths the sun would do the rest. This was Paris! The sun in Paris was almost always cooperative. The fact that so few citizens came out early in the morning — using the snow as an excuse to stay home and relax — made his work all that much easier. Pierre didn't mind snow at all — he in fact rather missed it. His grandparents had lived in Arvieux, and he had visited them often as a child, enjoying many winter sports.

As he and his crew worked, he watched for Paras's tracks; he had seen them heading east, then fading out in a long patch of ice. He could let some nice hay drop off the back of a truck or a snowplow not far from the pond where Paras and (he thought) that dog lurked about, which he had still not mentioned to Animal Control. Pierre kept his eye on the newspaper and the Internet — but he'd seen none of the advertisements Delphine had placed. Pierre was beginning to think that he had done the wrong thing in turning a blind eye to the animal, in admiring the appropriateness of a beautiful horse in the Champ de Mars, where armies and cavalries once drilled, carriage-horses and riding horses once trotted along.

Could this be a horse who had escaped the slaughter truck? Pierre was not himself fond of horsemeat, but he knew old people who were. There were horsemeat purveyors here and there in Paris — one in Montmartre had neon-lit horse heads over the shop door. This horse was a beauty, though — lovely mover, prideful carriage, rich color, luxuriant mane and forelock, long, thick tail. If they were sending such horses to the abattoir these days, then times were even worse than he had thought.

It was a busy and exhausting day, and Pierre only wondered about the horse every so often. It had to be said that he missed the horse. He kept his eye out for any sign of a mishap — horse carcass rolled up out of the way, broken leg from the ice or snow, starvation, anything else. When he quit work late that night, he was tired and blue. He'd had a wife for a while, but perhaps she had not been able to stand the four cats in the end. She was now living in Montpellier with a man ten years younger than she was who taught at the university. She'd sent Pierre a picture of her apartment — no animals, no plants, no cushions or pillows, and only a futon for a bed. He wished her well.

As he headed for the École Militaire Métro station, he walked down the Rue Marinoni right when Paras was snuffling the top of the fence and pressing her shoulder against the gate. Paras had never seen Pierre except from a distance. She didn't know that the occasional apple that appeared beside the pond was left by Pierre. Now she smelled him (sweat, grease, gasoline), but didn't think anything of it. Pierre was so lost in thought that he didn't notice that the gate in that fence he'd passed so many times was bowing outward, nor did he hear the breaths Paras blew as she investigated her new world. Pierre decided to put off thinking about whether to call Animal Control and what to say (would they themselves be inclined to send the horse to slaughter?) until morning. Meanwhile, Paras decided to go to the door and tap it with her hoof. When she did, Étienne let her right in, and they walked to the grand salon, where she went to her corner and settled herself like a dog. In the evening, when he went to bed, Étienne prayed to Saints George the Dragon Slayer (Etienne didn't mind thinking about dragons — they were interesting to imagine and there didn't seem to be any of them in Paris) and Éloi, who were, he had read, the patron saints of horses, though whether they took under their care horses sleeping in grand salons in Paris, he had no way of knowing.

Raoul was sitting on one of the struts of the great Tour, useless, as far as Raoul could see, to humans, but a wonderful convenience for Aves. A few young *Corvi* were watching him. He performed several ownership rituals — I know everything about this neighborhood, come to me for advice, I won't kick you out if you are properly respectful, only respect, that is all I demand, no, request — best not to insert the "demand" gesture. The group of ravens watched him, looked away. Raoul walked around the leg of the Tour that was nearest to him, dropped down into the shadows, and flew away quietly. Freedom was what he cared about, like most worldly creatures of his degree of maturity, but youth cared about power, always had, always would. He crossed the Avenue de Suffren, then the river. He made a tour of the Place du Trocadéro, circled the chilled and motionless statue of the man on the horse two times, flew rather close to a couple of windows just to look, but he didn't see Frida inside or outside any shop. When he regained his territory above the head of Benjamin Franklin, he nestled there in a sort of resigned comfort — his morning sojourn had taken more out of him than he'd expected it to. He had seen himself in the window of the Pâtisserie Carette, a bit ragged, looking a bit blownout. There was grooming to be done, and he had only himself to do it.

When the sun was well up and she knew that it would be blazing through the great window that overlooked the grand salon on the southeast, Madame de Mornay hoisted herself to her feet and made her way to her lavatory, then to her door. She was too blind to really see the sun, except as a welcome brightness, but she could feel it on her arms and her head. She had lived in these rooms in this house for so long that she knew just how the warmth progressed about the place, and just where to go to receive some.

She walked slowly and a bit noisily, but Étienne, who was upstairs looking for a

168

book about horseback riding, did not happen to hear her. She opened the door of her chamber, moved across the hallway, paused, stepped, paused, stepped, paused, stepped again, until she could reach for the back of one of the wing chairs and move, chair by table by windowsill, to her favorite spot. When she got there, she groaned and sat down with a sigh. She was about three meters from Paras, who was standing by the fireplace, sniffing the very old logs piled on the grate.

Paras had eaten her breakfast and gone outside already — horses are early risers.

Over on the desk, Kurt was watching Paras and Madame. He could not help making a squeak or two, but he had no fear of Madame — one of his favorite tunnels opened into her chamber, and he was used to clearing away any crumbs that Madame might drop when she took tea and biscuits in bed.

"Ooh," said Madame, "good heavens! I am hungry!" She yawned, covering her mouth.

Very slowly, Paras eased toward her, her nose extended. She was as silent as she could be. She stood near Madame, and sniffed her all over, her nose maybe ten centimeters from Madame's face, her shoulder, her lap, her knees, her feet. Madame was very small: her feet hardly touched the floor when she sat up straight in her wing chair. Madame shifted, then raised her hands, smoothed her hair, tightened her bun. Her hand went past Paras's cheek but did not touch it. If she had, she would have been surprised, but, perhaps, not afraid — Madame was used to unusual events. Madame thought a soft-boiled egg would be quite lovely, with a bit of bread and some raspberry jam. She called out, "Étienne, where are you?" Perhaps Madame did get a little whiff of Paras, but perhaps not. She had smoked heavily for years — Gauloises. Or maybe she got a whiff and simply did not believe her nose.

Paras thought that Madame had quite an interesting and, you might say, well-preserved fragrance. There was a hint of floral and a hint of dust and a hint, but only a hint, of human. Madame picked up her knitting from the side table. Paras gently sniffed the knitting.

From the landing, Étienne stared down at them: his great-grandmama so tiny, poised in her chair, feeling her knitting with the tips of her fingers; the horse, so huge, her ears pricked, almost but not quite touching his great-grandmama. He coughed. Paras

170

turned her head, but only her head, her ears still pricked. She gently switched her tail. Étienne ran down the stairs and touched Madame de Mornay on the shoulder.

The old woman smiled and said, "Ah, little one! How are you?"

Étienne put his arm around his great-grandmama's shoulders, and received a light kiss on the cheek. In the meantime, Paras pivoted gracefully on her hind leg. Her hooves clip-clopped on the hardwood floor, but Madame felt them only as a little rumbling that reminded her of the Métro, and she didn't think anything of it. She was proud of the Métro — very forward-looking and typically Parisian for its day.

Étienne went to the door and opened it wide. Paras walked out into the sunshine. Étienne closed the door. He thought, sadly, that he might never see the horse — his horse — again, since the gate was open. But he went to Madame, took her hand to show that he was with her, and helped her into the *cuisine.* He had to make sure that she circumvented a pile beside the window, but it was a small pile, perfect for the raspberry patch.

Once they had left, Kurt zipped across the floor of the grand salon as fast as he could (which was very fast), clambered onto a chair and then onto the windowsill. He wished he had managed to get out the door with the horse — she was still out there — but he saw with despair that he had lost his chance. He was a buck, he needed a doe!

Outside, Paras enjoyed the sunlight and a warm breeze. She went over to the partially open gate and looked out. The street was darkly wet. The snow had melted and was flowing into the drains. The humans who were out were, as usual, looking downward, minding their own business, thoroughly convinced that they knew all about everything having to do with their world. Dogs noticed her — tiny little dogs in tiny little blankets trotting by on the slenderest of lead ropes — but none of them barked, and so their humans hurried on. One, a Jack Russell terrier about the same size as Assassin, looked at her steadily, then paused at Madame's shrubbery and lifted his leg. Paras snorted in derision at this property claim, but the dog ignored her, scratched a little in the wet dirt, and allowed himself to be pulled away by his mistress, who was reading the paper as she walked.

Paras had found her night indoors very restful — perhaps she had caught up on months and months of lost sleep. A grand salon was much better in its way than a stall

— more things to look at and explore, quieter, none of that constant sense of the other horses. In order to avoid having to make up her mind about going out through the gate, Paras explored the courtyard more carefully than she had the day before. The sunlight was now pouring in from above, and the snow had turned to slush. The riotous shrubbery covering the fences was brilliant dark green. Paras saw that there was a much larger entrance to the house, up many steps, very grand, like the entrance to a great stud barn. There was another gate, too, across from that entrance, also grand, with much curling brass-work. Paras saw that, just as the old lady had a room, and Étienne had a room, she could have a room — this nicely protected but airy spot, open to the sky, closed to the view of passersby, not quite as luxurious as the grand salon, but perhaps more suited to her needs, and, perhaps, a place that Frida would dare to enter. She walked about, looking here and there, sniffing this and that, listening through the growth to the humans and animals walking along the allée.

After leaving the front porch of the architectural museum, Frida moped up to the cemetery. Now that she knew it was there, she could see Raoul's nest in the tree above the statue of the sitting man, and she could even see the curve of the top of the raven's head, but he made no move, and she shuffled past him. The cemetery was a quiet place, with many hiding spots among the monuments, which Jacques had made use of. She wandered about for a bit, remembering Jacques, then went back to the street and turned away from the square and moped along the street for a while, her head down, her tail, such as it was, down. Perhaps she felt more alone than she ever had, even after Jacques disappeared. Her only choice, she thought, was to continue up this avenue to the Bois de Boulogne, where she had been a few times. In the Bois de Boulogne, she would try to hunt birds as a way of staying alive. She would dig herself a hole, and she would, perhaps, waste away, and why not? Jacques was gone, Paras was captured, Raoul was a mere bird (for all his talk about *Corvus corax*), the lady who had given her that sausage had walked away. Mumble-mumble — Raoul was right about that — she knew she was mumbling, could hear herself. Well, she was a mumbler, that was just who she was. She came to an intersection. She was depressed, even in despair, but she saw the gendarme look at her, look

174

around, heard him blow his whistle, knew that that whistle was about her — she could read humans with perfect clarity. She paused only for a split second; then instinct kicked in — she whipped to the left, and headed down that street, toward the river (she could smell it). And as she ran, having thought of a hole in the Bois, she remembered her real hole, the one with the purse in it. How was it that she had forgotten the money?

The gendarme chased her for a bit, then disappeared. He would reappear, she knew, in a vehicle, and so she ducked into an alley and waited until the screaming vehicle zipped by; then she came out of the alley, turned left, and trotted, head up, back the way she had come. There was a set of stairs where she and Jacques had sometimes passed the night — a very private spot that fronted on the river. She found the stairs, went down them, rested alertly for a while, until everything was quiet, and finally emerged into the street that ran along the river. Not long after that, she was at the pond.

"Good heavens!" said Nancy. "You're back!"

Frida said, "I am. How are you feeling?"

"What do you think? It's just one thing

175

after another! The water rose to right there" — she gestured with her beak — "and then receded. It was a nightmare. But I can explain these things to Sid until I am blue in the face, and he won't pay a bit of attention, you mark my words."

"I will," said Frida.

Nancy harrumphed and tucked her head back under her wing. Frida went to the spot where she had hidden the purse, and began to dig. The autumn, the rain, and the snow had not been kind to the purse, but because it was made of excellent leather, it now had a nice patina and a delicious semi-rotten odor. As soon as she dragged it out of the hole, she rolled on it, back and forth. Then she stood up and pawed it open. There were considerably fewer bills in the purse than there had been on the night when Paras carried it away from Auteuil. They were damp and a little grimy, but they were intact, their figures and pictures easily visible. In her weeks of shopping for vegetables at Jérôme's market, Frida had noticed how he received each bill. He preferred the brown and blue, so she had made it a point to take those. He had frowned at the white ones. Almost all of the bills left in the purse were now white. She did not find them interesting, but they were all she had. There were a lot of them.

She took the handle of the purse between her jaws. She normally went to the shop by way of the Avenue de la Bourdonnais, but the gendarmes were still on her mind, so she stayed in the Champ de Mars, simply trotting down the allée, under the trees, past the houses. She could not have said what her intention was, but she knew that if Jérôme saw the money in the purse he would be kind to her. Unlike Paras, and unlike Raoul, she did have faith in humans. Jacques had always treated her with generosity and affection. Jérôme might save her, somehow. Frida trotted along as quickly as she could; though she saw humans turning to stare at her, no one could have caught her even if they had tried. The two that she passed even stepped out of her way. She paused at the avenue where cars passed through the Champ de Mars, but they were few in number, though the sun was high and the snow was gone.

Paras, her ears flicking, heard her coming, or, rather, she heard a dog, and she recognized Frida's characteristic gait — smart and quick. Paras would not have said that she loved Frida, or even felt affection for her. She might have said that she felt affection for Rania, who brushed her so kindly

177

with that soft brush and fed her four times a day, but she had run off without a backward glance, and she had taken Rania's purse with her, hadn't she? It might contain something belonging to herself, Paras, but it had had Rania's characteristic smell all over it. Curiosity had trumped affection, and done so easily. Nevertheless, when she sensed Frida passing, Paras let out a piercing whinny.

Inside the house, Étienne, who was helping his great-grandmama make her bed, hurried to the window. There she was, in the front courtyard! She hadn't run away after all. Étienne finished his task, then ran up the stairs to fetch his book about horseback riding.

Kurt, who had emerged from the front tunnel on the *premier étage,* found his fur vibrating and his eyes rolling from the pitch and the power of the whinny. He had never heard anything like it. He passed out and rolled over, all four paws sticking straight upward.

Pierre, who was standing in the basin in the center of the Champ in his thigh-high rubber boots, cleaning mold and mineral deposits from the face and mouth of the fountainhead, heard the whinny rise on the cool breeze, and though he could not quite tell where it was coming from (he shaded his eyes and looked around), he was glad to hear it.

Raoul, perched on the Tour, also heard the whinny, but, then, he heard all kinds of things that simply told him that life in the Champ de Mars was much the same as usual, no matter what groundlings seemed to think.

Anaïs, who had finished her night's work and was walking down the Avenue de Suffren, heard it, too, just faintly, because the breeze was slipping around the buildings and carrying the vibrations of the whinny in her direction. The whinny aroused in Anaïs a hope that Paras would show up that night or the next night — with her own money, she had bought the horse some flaxseed to mix with her oats. And there were some delicious apples, Reinette de Cuzy, which had been aging in the cellar. She smiled to herself, and sped up.

The local gendarme, who was standing at the intersection of the Rue de Grenelle and the Rue Augereau, had almost convinced himself that his delusions of a horse going into that house on the corner were well and truly past. So, when Paras's whinny fluttered out of the Champ de Mars and fell upon his ear, he shuddered and went

179

straight into Le Royal for a nice glass of Burgundy. The gendarmes' union had recently certified his right to have a drink while on duty, and he felt like just a bit of a labor activist by exercising that right.

Frida slowed her trot, pricked her ears, but then continued. She liked Paras, but there was no protection to be found in a horse. Frida had passed where she sensed Paras, was almost to the corner. The whinny came again, even higher and more piercing. It made Frida's ears tickle. And then again. She stopped, turned, and crawled, though burdened by the purse, under the scratchy growth.

There Paras was, her tail up and her ears pricked, her neck arched. Through the ironwork, Frida said sharply, "Shut up!"

Paras said, "Oh, you found my purse." She came over and put her nostrils through the fence.

In her heart, Frida rejected the idea that this was Paras's, or solely Paras's, purse. Wasn't she the one who had carried those bags back and forth from Jérôme's market? Wasn't she the one who understood that currency was to be exchanged, and thereby benefit the larger economy of Paris? Wasn't she the one who had hidden and cared for the purse? Left to her own devices, Paras would have dropped the purse somewhere, having lost interest in it. That Paras should claim the purse was unjust, Frida thought. However, it was also true that Jacques had once found a very small purse, belonging to a man, lying open on the sidewalk. He and Frida had walked all the way to the Marais and returned the thing to the man, who had been very grateful, and given Jacques a sizable sum in return — enough for them to spend a lovely night in a pleasant room, where they both took showers and Jacques ordered a tray of food. It was not as though Frida didn't understand ownership — only that she felt that, in this case, ownership was unfair. She said, "Yes. I did. It's aged very nicely, I think. But you are making a spectacle of yourself. The gendarmes could be here any minute. I had a close call this morning, over in Passy."

"I don't see how we could find a nicer or more private spot than this. The boy is a decent sort, much smaller than a jockey, and he serves a lovely bowl of soaked split peas. Look over there — a little alcove where you could curl up, protected on three sides. I think it's a nice compromise between inside and out. I am sure he will let me out in the evenings, and with all of these bushes, you could climb over."

"Or dig under," said Frida.

Frida flexed her very powerful front feet. She hadn't had an enjoyable and challenging dig in a while.

When Étienne entered the upstairs library to retrieve his horseback-riding book, he immediately saw Kurt unconscious on the armoire. Owing to months of excellent provisions, Kurt was rather large, and Étienne was startled by his appearance. Of course, he knew that there were rats in the house — he could hear them late at night and early in the morning. But the only rats Étienne had ever seen were pictures in books. Those rats were thin and sinister-looking, with aggressive whiskers, narrow eyes, pointed noses, and bad intentions. This rat had a shiny, dusky coat. His whiskers did twitch, but more as a cry for help than as a threat. He looked, in fact, like a pet. Étienne went over to him and touched his fluffy white belly. It was silky. There was no odor. He stroked the belly. Kurt opened his eyes.

Kurt was intimately familiar with Étienne, in a way that Étienne was not with him. Once, against his father's, Conrad's, express orders, he had sat for quite a long time in the moonlight on the foot of Étienne's bed, watching him sleep. Étienne turned this way and that way, made human noises, once even sat up and lay down again without opening his eyes. Kurt had seen Étienne eating, bathing, helping Madame de Mornay, reading, staring out the window, washing up, going out, and coming back in. He had never seen Étienne doing a threatening thing, and so, when Kurt opened his eyes at Étienne's touch, he did not feel fear. He allowed the petting to go on, then sat up and yawned, which made Étienne laugh. The piercing noise was gone; Kurt's world resumed its usual sensory identity. Étienne, after pausing, now began to stroke Kurt's back, along the spine. After allowing this for what he considered the proper time, Kurt dipped his head in a little bow of thanks, and scurried across the armoire, over the back of one of the covered chairs, and into his tunnel. Étienne watched him for a moment, then found his book.

The digging was going very well — the ground was loamy and wet, and the roots weren't terribly intertwined. It took Frida only a few minutes to make a hole deep enough to push the purse through; Paras grabbed it with her teeth and dragged it under the fence. It did stink, she thought, wrinkling her nose. Dogs were so peculiar, in their preference for rotten over sweet.

Frida dug and dug, achieving a kind of whirling rhythm; finally, she saw that she could safely crawl under the fence, avoiding the pointed tips of the iron bars. Of course, there would be maintenance — there always was with a hole — but the freedom to escape was worth preserving. She stood up and shook herself. Dirt flew everywhere. Then she inspected the courtyard. She sniffed all along the base of the house, and the steps, and the base of the fence. She sniffed the air. The place smelled of age and cats, birds and their nests, dead leaves, and rotten grass. It smelled of isolation, but not filth, like the alley she had lived in after Jacques died. Perhaps because of the effort and pleasure of digging, she did not feel as glum as she had before. She investigated the alcove. She lay down in it, and she decided that it would do for now. In the meantime, Paras continued to walk around until, finally, she sought out a patch of sunshine, went over to it, and lay down. Paras took a nap. Frida took a nap.

Madame de Mornay, too, was taking a nap. Madame's window looked out onto the courtyard, but since she couldn't see it, she could only touch the glass with her finger-tips and imagine it — a graceful entryway, the brilliant brass gates wide open in the spring sunlight, the semicircular promenade curving past the steps, bordered with plots of flowers carefully tended by Clément, the gardener. An automobile was about to drive in — open top, black and silver. In it was her mother, wearing a gold velvet dress with beading all down the front, and a cloche hat with a waving feather. She would be taking Éveline for a little trip to Deauville — just a few days, to enjoy the ocean and the society of friends. Éveline had packed her own valise, and it was ready beside the door. They would eat fresh crabs in Trouville. In her sleep, she smiled.

ELEVEN

During the week before Christmas, Jacques had been in the habit of locating himself and Frida not in and around the Place du Trocadéro or the Left Bank, where he felt relaxed and comfortable, but near the Galeries Lafayette during the day and in the Boulevard des Capucines in the evening. He would put on his oldest clothes. He played Christmas tunes and instructed Frida to shiver and shake even when it wasn't very cold. She understood what Christmas was — bright lights and displays, pedestrians everywhere. People exclaimed about what an unfortunate dog she was, then came the clink-clink-clink of guilty coins in the bowl. Once in a while, someone had even taken them to a café and bought them supper — mostly soup, one time a lovely leg of lamb. Christmas was Jacques's busy season, and though he had grumbled about the hassle and the gendarmes, he was happy afterward. Frida quite liked Christmas. Because of the extra funds, she had eaten many a slice of turkey or goose, occasional bites of foie gras, and some delicious cheeses. Jacques had sometimes bought what he called a *bûche de Noël,* but Frida had never had a taste — no chocolate for dogs, said Jacques.

This year, Frida waited and waited at the house on the Rue Marinoni to see what Christmas would bring, but by Christmas Eve day, there was still no sign of anything. When Frida mentioned Christmas to Paras, Paras had no idea what she was talking about. Paras was going out every night now, and she, too, had noticed that there were more lights and more humans around (she assured Frida that she was being very careful — there was an hour or two in the deep deep dark when the streets were as deserted as usual). Was Christmas like the Arc, the race most of the trainers and the horses talked about? Was Christmas like the Grand Steeple-Chase de Paris? Races were what horses, jockeys, trainers, and owners got excited about — they talked about them for weeks and months. No, said Frida, but she couldn't explain any further. Raoul was not helpful — his explanation of Christmas was all about birds of various breeds mobbing and voicing, which was what humans seemed to be doing in the darkest time of the year, and in their most colorful plumage. He opined that it was a mass breeding ritual. However, and he thought Frida should note this, too, it was their most wasteful time of year, and for that he was thankful.

As a dog who paid attention to humans and was also prone to dejection, Frida could see through the window of the grand salon that Christmas was not making Étienne happy, that Étienne would sit beside Paras, his arm across her shoulder, as if he was dejected. Frida knew "dejected" very well. Once in a while, he would lay his cheek against Paras's coat, and if he was not sad, well, Frida didn't know sadness.

As a bird dog, Frida also understood the concept of offerings. Above and beyond food were sticks, balls, pinecones, abandoned shoes, inedible dead songbirds — all of which she'd carried to Jacques at one time or another. In return, he had bought her the occasional stuffed toy, knowing she liked to rip the toy open and pull out the fluff, and the occasional rock, because Frida had enjoyed carrying rocks in her mouth on walks. Offerings, she understood, pleased the recipient in some strange way that had nothing to do with food. Staring at Étienne, she felt that an offering might do him good. A rat was a possibility — she occasionally smelled a rat when she put her nose to the base of the door, but she was not going to go into the house just to kill a rat. She went to the purse (which was now stored in a basement window well) and took out one of the white bills. She chewed it a little so that it wadded up, then tucked it into her cheek. She crawled through the hole beneath the fence, careful about emerging — she waited until no humans were around, then shook herself and trotted with her customary flair to Jérôme's shop. She knew that Jérôme now thought she belonged to Madame de Mornay and Étienne. Perhaps she did.

But she did not want apples or onions or carrots or bread. That was food. She wanted an offering. How a dog might choose an offering was a mystery, but there were plenty of windows to look into, and perhaps there was some shopkeeper or another who would take her money.

The task was more difficult than she had expected. Most of the shops around Jérôme's were cafés, bread shops, or pastry shops. Beyond Jérôme's, she was out of her territory, so the best she could do was keep moving and looking. If she seemed idle, a gendarme was sure to notice. In some stretches, she found no shops at all, only buildings that humans entered and came out of. As she trotted lightly along, she tried to remember what Jacques had enjoyed — his guitar, of course, but that seemed impractical. Books, but according to Raoul and Paras both, Étienne had plenty of those. Items of apparel — Jacques had a very soft and sheepy-smelling scarf that he enjoyed wearing on cold days, and occasionally wrapped around Frida — that was a possibility. A bag to carry, a blanket to sit on. She had seen plenty of humans carrying electronic devices (small, glittering, hard things). Étienne didn't have one, but Frida felt, realistically, that that sort of thing was beyond her. Several dogs passed her, and not only small dogs — a wolfish male who was even larger than she was gave her the eyeball, but he was wearing a quite tasteless spotted coat, and when he saw Frida staring, he put his head down and slunk along in the shadow of his human. A very friendly, curly-coated medium-sized dog with a waving, happy tail also greeted her, but when the owner stopped and looked both ways, Frida trotted on without responding to the greeting. The friendliest owners of the friendliest dogs were the most likely to call in the gendarmes. Perhaps she should find a shop that sold these harnesses and leashes that the other dogs were wearing. Such a thing would be easy to carry to Étienne. But no. A leash could lead to other things, like going into the house and having Étienne lock the door.

It seemed to Frida that she trotted about for a long time, and it was surely true that if she hadn't had an excellent nose she would have gotten lost. These streets were complex, with many intersections. Finally, she gave up, and made her way back to Jérôme's shop, where she sat down beside the entrance, spat out her bill, and put her paw on it. The door opened, and a woman came out with two large sacks. Jérôme followed. He stood over Frida, his hands beneath his apron, and said, "Merry Christmas, my dear. How are you?"

Frida mumbled a few things, and Jérôme laughed. She moved her paw slightly, revealing the bill. Jérôme bent down and picked it up, then smoothed it on his knee. He said, "My God! You must be doing your Christmas shopping!"

Frida gave him her paw and he shook it. He held on to the bill, and invited her into the shop. It was empty of human customers.

The shop was tastefully decorated with a few flowers and ribbons. In addition to the usual squashes and potatoes and beans and oranges, Frida noticed boxes that she hadn't seen before, hard metal, with busy pictures on them. She touched one with her nose, and Jérôme set it on the counter. Of course there was food inside it, but the offering was the picture — humans liked pictures. Jérôme pointed to what smelled like bread, but was circular and covered with treats and decorations. Frida whined. Jérôme put it on the counter. There was another box, one she could see through, and in that one were elaborate cookies of many shapes. Since Jacques had had a sweet tooth, Frida had tasted a cookie or two, though she didn't like them. She nosed the box of cookies. Jérôme put it on the counter. One more thing, she thought. Jérôme touched a bag of nuts (she was familiar with nuts, because Jacques had sometimes eaten them). Attached to the bag was a tiny humanlike figure with big teeth, wearing a black hat. Frida put her paw over her eye and lowered her head. No sale. Jérôme laughed. After a moment, he placed the offerings in a heavy bag, also with pictures, and made Frida's change. He put the change in the bag, too. There was not much of it.

The bag of offerings was a good deal heavier than the purse, but Jérôme placed it carefully in her jaws, and then she squared her shoulders and headed back to the boy's house. Frida was reminded of a time when she and Jacques were working in the Jardins du Trocadéro. A stray terrier had kept pestering Jacques to throw a small stick. Jacques threw it a few times, then hid it. The terrier ran off, and reappeared minutes later with a rake — gripping it between her teeth, right in the middle of the handle, and balancing it as she carried it to Jacques. She dropped it in front of him, and barked, "Throw it! Throw it!" Jacques had laughed to himself for the rest of the day. Frida had had to admit that she was impressed. So now she thought of the terrier and carried her heavy bag down the street. At the very last minute, though, she saw another possibility. A shop door opened, and inside there was a bin full of balls. The door closed. She sat and waited, assembling her dignity, and when the door opened again, she looked into the face of the human who opened it as he was leaving the shop. He smiled and held the door for her. She went inside and over to the bin of balls, where she set down her bag.

The human who now slouched toward her

was the type of human she usually avoided — scowl on his face, sour fragrance, lank hair on his head — the type who might give a dog a kick if he thought no one was looking. Before he even got to her, he was saying, "Get out of here, you mutt! No dogs allowed!" Frida retained her dignity, gave him a level look, and placed her paw carefully on the bin, beside one of the balls. Then she nosed her bag. The human stopped with his legs apart, waved one arm, then put his hands on his hips. Frida knew right then that he was afraid of her. Well, some humans *were* afraid of dogs. She did what she had to do — lay down, rolled over, and then rolled back over the other way. The human took a deep breath. Frida rolled onto her stomach and crawled toward him. Then she waited. Finally, the human reached out his trembling hand, patted her lightly on the head. She waited. He patted her again, this time with more confidence. He smiled. Frida stood up slowly, turned, and went back to the bin, where she put her paw next to the same ball. He came over and took the ball out of the bin, then stepped back and tossed it to her. She jumped up and caught it. She carried it to the human's very large feet and dropped it. He picked it up, tossed it gently down the aisle, toward the back of the store. Frida ran after it and carried it to him, waiting until he opened his hand before she placed it on his palm (Jacques had been very particular about fetching). The human stared at her, tossing the ball back and forth between his hands, then walked away. Frida sighed, and went to her heavy bag. She took the handles of the bag between her teeth, picked up the bag, staggered slightly, then balanced herself.

But here came the human, with something in his hand. He removed the end of that something with a pop, and out of it rolled another ball. He bounced it, and it bounced very high. Frida dropped her bag, leapt into the air, and caught it. It was light and slightly furry, just the sort of ball she had been looking for. He laughed. She went to her bag and pawed at it, but although she could smell the money, she couldn't get at it. She dropped the ball into the bag and dragged the bag to the human. Then she did something that Jacques had warned her against. She barked. Only one bark. She put her paw on the bag. The human stepped back, but it seemed he understood — he came over, reached into the bag, and felt around. A moment later, he pulled out a bill. Now he really laughed, and he said,

"Well, I have to say, I've never seen a dog like you before." He bowed slightly, and said, "Would you please wait here, miss?" He slouched away. When he returned, he put the thing that the ball had come in into her bag, then helped her take the bag in her jaws. Finally, he squatted in front of her, patted her on the head, and said, "Merry Christmas, pretty one." He accompanied her to the door, opened it for her, and, after she went outside, locked it behind her.

The sky had clouded over, and dusk was beginning to gather. It wasn't far to the house now, but the bag was heavier than before. Sometimes she carried it, sometimes she dragged it, but slowly, gently. Though there were no humans about at all, there were lights everywhere, and the faint sound of music, too — the whole city was brilliant. Only Étienne and Madame de Mornay's house was dark and silent — just one small light in one window. The gate was open. Frida carried the bag up the step to Étienne's entrance and set it against the door. She was exhausted. She passed Paras without saying anything, and lay down in her alcove. She was asleep at once. Darkness fell.

An hour or so later, Kurt was watching

Madame de Mornay prepare herself for her expedition to the church for Christmas Mass — not Midnight Mass, no more of that, but afternoon Mass on the next day. The room was dark, but Kurt had good night vision, like Paras. The broadcast that he got from her through his whiskers was, he thought, the most interesting thing about her — she gave off almost no signal. According to his rat instincts, she was hardly alive — maybe *not* alive — and yet she was very active for a dead being. And she was especially expert and adept at grooming, something that rats paid considerable attention to. She laid out her clothes, brushed them off. She let her fingertips wander over the fabric, seeking rips and holes and suspicious little spots that might be stains.

Madame had been reflecting a good deal these last few days, and she was willing to admit that this might be her last visit to the church, at least under her own power. One thing that Étienne didn't know was that her birthday was January 6, the Feast of the Epiphany. When she was a child, she had celebrated every birthday with a Cake of the Three Kings, really a sweet brioche molded into a circle with some sugar sprinkled over it. There was a tiny little man hidden within, and that had been one of her birthday presents. She had been eight or nine before she realized that others celebrated the arrival of the Three Kings at the Manger as her family did. She would be ninety-seven! How could she be so amazed at that number? She had stopped celebrating birthdays when she turned sixty, but, alas, they had not stopped coming around.

Kurt was quite familiar with Madame's wardrobe. He recognized that the items Madame was investigating were for going outside. He was ever more eager to get there, and so, watching Madame, he contemplated his strategy for going with her. He had looked into her bag, which was in the center of the desk, but it was a cramped space. He had also eased himself underneath the hat she always wore, but that space would be filled with her head. He might sit on top of the hat and hope for the best, but he was too heavy for the hat, and he knew that Madame would notice if it was out of its customary shape. He might jump from one of the shelves beside the door onto her shoulder, but even if he made it, she would brush him off, probably violently, and then anything could happen. Conrad said that they were safe and well fed, and not every life was perfect, and that doe Kurt yearned for could show up at any time, there was always hope, but she never had, and Kurt had made up his mind to gamble on adventure rather than remain passive.

He'd thought that the boy might carry him outside, but as the days passed after the petting incident, Kurt lost his faith that the boy could be trusted. The boy broadcast a strong signal. Conrad, too, was suspicious of the boy, who was small but quick. Had he ever told Kurt the story of Hector, one of his ancestors? In this very house, many generations ago, there had been a human who left crumbs for Hector, who made agreeable little noises and seemed unusually friendly. After a whole season of this courtship, Hector had finally skittered onto the counter in the *cuisine,* going for some crispy fried pork fat, and what had happened? That human had banged the lid of a large heavy pot right down upon Hector, trapping him, breaking his tail, killing him. That was a human for you, according to Conrad, and Kurt had nothing to offer in contradiction. Conrad maintained that the territorial disputes between rats and humans had been going on forever and ever and ever and ever. Humans hated the very thought of rats claiming the taxes, in the form of food, that were their rattish right, of rats making perfectly good use of the otherwise useless spaces within walls. At some lost date in the past, rats and humans might have joined forces against cats, which were much more ruthless than any rat, but humans had been colonized by cats, and so that possibility was gone, and, Conrad advised, Kurt should look on the bright side, enjoy a comfortable life that even brown rats would appreciate.

Now Madame made her way to her bed and turned down the coverlet. She was humming. The room was dark, but that was all the same to Madame. She sat on the edge of the bed and kicked off her slippers, then arranged herself. It was Christmas, possibly her last Christmas. She closed her eyes and, looking within again, decided to remember a single thing from each of her ninety-six Christmases — that would be her celebration. Her first memory, she thought, and a vivid one, was of being carried into the grand salon in her mother's arms, and seeing the whole room lit with candles. She remembered hiding her eyes against her mother's silk collar, then turning to look again. She must have been almost two. Her second memory was of a doll, dressed in a red velvet gown, its tiny black shoes sticking out from under the hem of the dress. Perhaps her grandmother's couturière had made the dress? Somehow the doll and her grandmother rested together in her mind. The third Christmas would have taken place in 1915 — she had no memory of it, for it must have been a sad Christmas, the year her father died in the Battle of Loos. In 1916, she would have been four — her memory was of the *cuisine,* of standing on a stool beside the table, placing bits of candied orange peel on the tips of the meringues that Angélique, the *chef de cuisine,* was making. That was a happier memory. Madame de Mornay fell asleep.

Paras did not go into the house every night, nor did she visit Anaïs every night. Her days and nights had fallen into a pleasant rhythm, but it was only a rhythm, not a schedule. At any rate, on Christmas Eve, she had a nice long sleep in the courtyard, wondering only once where Frida had been and why she was sleeping and sleeping and sleeping. Paras of course noticed the bag beside the door, but it was not her purse, had no distinct odor. Raoul might have investigated it, but he was occupied in other parts of the city.

And so she shook her head, extended her foreleg to lever herself to her feet, saw that it was light though the sun wasn't up yet, the perfect time for a meal — she would climb the step, tap the door, perhaps. She rose. She stretched forward. She stretched backward. There was a breeze. She tossed her head. And now the door opened and Étienne came outside, stumbling over the bag as he did. He said, "Hey! What is this?" He lifted the bag and looked at it, then looked inside it, then went to the gate, which he saw was open, and looked down the street. Paras could see that he had no idea that the bag was from Frida. But it made him happy — that was evident. He turned, and said, "Grandmama! Grandmama! Father Christmas has made a visit!" He laughed and went back into the house, leaving the door open. Paras glanced over at Frida, who was now awake. She tossed her head toward the door, said, "Come in with me! Come on! It's warm in there! You'll enjoy it!"

But Frida trembled and curled up even more tightly. Jail!

Paras thought Frida might never enter the building. She snorted, went up the step and into the grand salon.

Étienne took Paras straight to the *cuisine,* where he had already filled her bowl with apples, carrots, and a pear. He petted her on the neck, rested his head against her shoulder. He seemed happier than Paras had ever seen him. Over and over, he said,

"Merry Christmas, Merry Christmas, my dear! What a Merry Christmas this one is!"

PART TWO

PART TWO

TWELVE

New Year's passed pleasantly — Étienne managed to make some crêpes for Madame, sprinkled with demerara sugar (and for Paras, and for Kurt, and even for Conrad, who was lurking in his tunnel near the stove). Madame's birthday came and went; she thought of it all day, but didn't say a word about it to Étienne. She knew he knew she was old, but she didn't want him to put a number to it. That was her main concern, vanity, until she lay down in her bed at the end of the day and her real concern hit her — yes, she wasn't going to live forever, and what in the world would happen to Étienne? If she lived to be a hundred, he would be twelve when she passed, and although he might see himself as independent, no one else would, nor should they. She knew she had funds that had been accumulating for all of her life, but, legally, he might have no access to those funds (how might she find out about this?). The funds themselves would lead the authorities to hand him over to a trustee or (God forbid, remembering her youth) an institution. What had she been thinking? She imagined this room, her room, in this sturdy building. Well, she had been thinking of how her home had protected her for her whole life, and as a result, she had failed, even when she could see, to look out the window at the large world. She tossed and turned all night, ruminating on these things, and in the morning, when he brought her cup of tea and croissant, she patted the bed, put her hand on his arm, got him to sit down. She couldn't see him, but she sensed his mood — lively, expectant, happy. She didn't want to wreck that, and so she made up her mind that she would come up with something soon, and said, for now, only, "Ah, my dear, you are very kind." He jumped up and hurried out of the room.

After giving his great-grandmama her tea and her croissant, wondering for a moment why she looked so worried, and then hurrying to the grand salon, Étienne went straight to Paras, who was lying on the carpet. As big as she was, she was careful in the grand salon, and graceful. She walked about, took naps, went to the *cuisine,* nudged the handle of the faucet for a drink of water if she was thirsty (and then nudged it until the water stopped running). Yes, having a horse was a lot of work. Even though the horse was pretty good about saving her deposits for outside (Étienne quickly learned that if she tapped the door he had to act at once), she ate far more than either he or his great-grandmama did — she was making her way through many stored root vegetables, dried legumes, fruits, and fresh vegetables. She would be expensive once the provisions in the cellar gave out. However, that would be sometime in the future, and Étienne knew that his future must include some very bad things — such as school, such as his great-grandmama's passing on. Indeed, his future was a yawning chasm of loss and mystery that he didn't dare look into.

This present — attending to the horse, petting her — was so enjoyable that he decided once again not to think about those things. Étienne often read while leaning his back against her as she rested. He liked to rub her with a cloth and brush her with an old hairbrush he'd found in one of the rooms upstairs. Lately, he had been sitting astride Paras as she curled upright on the carpet, her back hooves tucked neatly against her belly. She didn't mind — she yawned, then she looked at him. He could imagine riding — the horse's neck and ears in front of you, your hands entwined in her mane — but it was scary. Right now, his toes touched the carpet; everything was quiet; there was nothing scary about it. After a while, he "dismounted" (a word he had read in the riding manuals), and she stretched out on her side. He perched himself across her ribs then sat quietly on her hip. But even as he did so, he knew that he really wanted to ride.

When Étienne was asleep or in the library or taking care of the old lady, Kurt sat on Paras, too. In fact, he ran all over her, snaking under her mane, trotting across her shoulder, scrambling up her leg from her hoof to her elbow. She liked it — it gave her a good scratching, and meant that she didn't have to roll to take care of an itch. When Kurt asked her if she had ever had a rat as a friend before, Paras said, "Assassin wouldn't allow it."

"Who is Assassin?"

"A Jack Russell terrier."

Kurt thought she said, "Jack Russell terror." And, indeed, when she described the pleasure the dog always took in chasing rats, grabbing them, snapping their necks, he felt terror. Paras said, "He didn't eat them," as if that was a good thing. Why would he kill them, then?

"For sport. He enjoyed it."

He sounded to Kurt like a cat, but, then, you didn't get that feeling with a cat, that the cat was killing something because she enjoyed it — it was a duty for a cat, the essence of catness, to kill things.

Paras said, "Some of the horses were afraid of rats — not so much the sight of them as the sound of them. Horses don't like mysterious sounds. But rats were fine with the rest of us. However, it wasn't our business."

While they were having this conversation, Paras was in the *cuisine,* eating her chopped beets from a bowl Étienne had placed in the seat of a chair, and Kurt was sitting on the back of the chair. When Paras was finished, Kurt scurried down into the bowl and disposed of the scraps. Paras said, "You know where I need a little scratch?"

Kurt looked at her, his mouth full.

"Under my mane, just behind my ears." She stretched her head toward him and closed her eyes. He stepped lightly onto her maxilla and eased upward. When he got to her ears, he went a step farther, turned around, then entangled his back feet in the thick brush of her mane. She raised her head. It was disorienting, but Kurt held on. Paras said, "Ah, that feels good. I miss grooming. At the time, I thought there was too much of it, especially the everlasting baths, the water spraying in your face, but I liked the brushing."

She turned to look left and then right. Kurt felt as if he was being spun around, but he held on.

She said, "You're not that heavy. About the same as a bridle. But try to stay in the middle. It's easier to balance you."

She walked into the grand salon, went to look out the window. Kurt thought he might be sick, what with the beets and all. Down. Up again. A noise from the staircase — Paras's head swung to look.

Étienne's footsteps on the stairs. Paras knew that Kurt was afraid of Étienne, and since she generally took things as they came, she didn't try to dissuade him. But now she did a kind thing — she carried him over to the entrance to his tunnel and put her head down. He let go and dropped, sliding part of the way down her forelock. He went into the tunnel, which was dark and cool — relaxing, really. As he headed up the tunnel to his bedroom, he decided never to do that again, sit on her head. But he knew that he would, that sitting on her head was, perhaps, his best bet for getting out into the world and finding his doe, his desired mate.

Raoul had a winter project, too — making his most superior nest ever, the roomiest, the coziest, and the most aesthetically avant-garde (he had woven in several strands of silvery Christmas decorative materials so that they glinted in the moonlight in a pleasing pattern that reproduced the random effect of stars). He was now sixteen. Of course, that was in human years. An avian "year" had nothing to do with the sun or the earth, it was called a "segment," and had to do with vegetation and migration. He had lived for fifty segments, ten of them in Paris. Every male *Corvus,* upon reaching the age of fourteen segments, was required to challenge those around him in three ways — flights, speeches, and combat. Outside of Paris, these challenges were ritualized and traditional. For example, the topic of most speeches was either insect varieties or grains. Flights were sometimes for distance, sometimes for speed. Combat was ritualized, too — the old fellow who might lose the battle simply moved his family to a nest in a less prestigious tree — say, from a walnut to a beech. Relations in Paris were more chaotic and less friendly, and Raoul had been hard put to fend the youngsters off. Sometime soon, he would have to move his nest away from the statue of Benjamin Franklin, accept his banishment. And, yes, he was lonely. It didn't help that Paras and Frida seemed perfectly happy and not much in need of his advice over there at that creepy empty house with that poor child, that ancient humanlike creature, and that rat.

He might have done what he used to do — observe humans and Aves and develop his theories — but no one wanted to hear his theories. Tonight, his dissatisfactions were nagging at him, so he groomed himself until the roots of his feathers ached, and still could not settle in. The Place du Trocadéro was dead — all the cafés were closed; the two buildings of the architectural museum were like blocks of ice. Even the lights in the great Tour across the river looked rather forlorn. Raoul hopped to a higher branch, then spread his wings and flew, first upward, over the metal man on the metal horse; then he glided down the esplanade. The moon was a small pale crescent. He floated over the river, banked left. No one at all in the Champ de Mars except Mademoiselle Paras, trotting briskly across the damp wintry turf, her forelock bobbing, her tail up, and her nostrils flared. She was making plenty of noise, but the windows of every house were dark. Raoul circled her once, then landed on her rump. She snorted and said, "You can fly. You don't need to hitch a ride."

"I can't fly and talk to you at the same time."

"Other birds do."

"That is a misapprehension on your part. They are proclaiming, they aren't conversing. If we want to communicate, we park. I am parking on your hind end. You might halt."

"I'm hungry, and I don't want to be late." Nevertheless, she slowed to a walk.

"Where are you going?"

Paras explained about Anaïs, the baker: "She has access to grain. All different types of grain, in fact. You can't eat kale at every meal and expect to maintain your strength."

"I keep telling you Mammalia that insects are a wonderful source of energy and piquancy."

"How many flies would I have to eat per day? I weigh four hundred and fifty kilos."

Raoul admitted, though only to himself, that this might present a problem. He said,

"A bird eats seven times its weight each day."

"How much do you weigh?"

"Over a kilo. Maybe a kilo and a quarter."

"Ignoring the fact that I could not possibly process three thousand kilos of food every day, I also do not believe that you process seven or eight kilos of worms, flies, and *frites* every day."

Raoul didn't say anything. He flew off her rump, and she rose to a light trot. She had come to pavement, so her hooves made a crisp sound, but since she had lost her shoes a month ago, she no longer clanged. She turned left. Raoul followed her to the shop, where there was, indeed, a youngish human female working at a large table on the other side of the lighted window. Just as Raoul saw her, she glanced in their direction, smiled, and came to the door, which she opened. She exclaimed, "Good evening, dear girl!" Paras, who had dropped to a walk, and then halted, rested her chin gently on the woman's shoulder and snuffled a polite greeting in her hair. The woman patted her cheek and moved her forelock out of her eyes. Raoul found a perch on an empty vegetable display case in front of the shop next door. With mammals, it was an everlasting round of love, hate, sadness,

216

gladness, fear, and anger. All Aves knew that mammals said of themselves that they were "higher" than other animals. And all Aves dismissed this idea with a laugh.

Anaïs had become more comfortable with Paras. She had been sure that the horse would have been caught by now, but as far as she could tell, the horse was not even discovered. Certainly, where the horse lived was a mystery to Anaïs herself. On the day she heard that phantom whinny — before Christmas, it was — she had wandered around the Champ de Mars and seen no sign of a horse. Anaïs had then decided that Paras was a spiritual embodiment of some sort — one result of her very religious upbringing was that, although she rejected doctrine, she didn't mind visitations. And she knew from all the stories she had heard as a child that if a god or a spirit asked something of you, your job was to provide it in good faith and with a happy heart. And so she did. The horse came three or four times a week. Her provisions added maybe 1 percent to the wholesale expenditures of the bakery and the café, so Anaïs raised the prices of some of the luxury items that her customers should not be eating anyway, like chocolate croissants and lemon tarts, to cover it. And though Paras only trotted away when she was finished with her grain, and was not, at least for now, flying Pegasus-like into the empyrean, Anaïs had a remote hope that something amazing would happen someday — say, on the vernal equinox.

Anaïs loved her job, but since she was up all night, hers was a rather lonely life. She was isolated from her family because of the religious disagreements, and all of her friendships were based on business, not a sense of connection. She was now in her thirties, unmarried, hadn't had a boyfriend in four years, so it was a great pleasure to pet the horse, to feel the warmth of her coat underneath her mane, to sense her kindness and her enjoyment of the food Anaïs put together for her (tonight, a combination of wheat berries and flaxseed, with grated carrots mixed in). She rested her shoulder on the horse's neck, closed her eyes.

Then a raven flew up and landed on Paras's back. Anaïs was startled, but the horse only twitched, kept eating. The raven sidestepped forward along her spine, his eye on Anaïs — he kept turning his head, first one way and then the other. He was a little creepy — so utterly black in the dark. But every supernatural being had a companion, and at least he wasn't a bat. Anaïs held tight to the bowl, and thought that if the raven tried to peck her eyes out, she could put the bowl over her head.

But the raven simply started to caw — caw-caw-cawcaw-caw — not loudly, but, or so it seemed to her, conversationally, somehow. And then the horse tossed her head, and the raven flew back to what Anaïs now saw was his perch on Monsieur Curzon's potato bin. Anaïs set the bowl on the pavement; the raven sailed down to it and pecked up a few tiny bits. Anaïs laughed. Meanwhile, Paras quietly inspected the pockets of her benefactress's apron. Anaïs cupped a lump of brown sugar — the one most preferred by customers — in the palm of her hand, and Paras took it, let it sit in her mouth, melting for a bit, then crunched it down. The raven looked up at Anaïs. Anaïs squatted down and offered him a lump of sugar. He took it in his beak, dropped it, pecked it, then picked it up and flew off with it. For a woman who had never had a pet because of her mother's allergies, this experience of living in a world of horses, birds, and other animals was a pleasure to be cherished, even if they should turn out not to be embodied celestial beings.

A few days later, when the weather was fresh and almost warm, Frida was lying in her spot with her bag nearby (a nice cloth bag that retained the fragrances of any vegetables or bones that had been carried in it). She waited, as a bird dog knew to do, and, sure enough, Madame de Mornay and Étienne shuffled out of the house, then opened the gate. Frida followed them. Etienne knew she was there, as he knew she stayed with Paras in the garden, but she was so shy that he hesitated to acknowledge her, and was waiting to see if she would acknowledge him. Madame used her cane with one hand and laid the other on Étienne's shoulder. Étienne pulled the little two-wheeled shopping trolley along and kept his eyes forward. Frida assumed her place two paces behind them.

The surface of the shopping trolley, which was made of fabric, fluttered, catching Frida's attention. The three of them crossed slowly at the traffic light. Autos did not honk, though Frida sensed their bursting impatience. Madame was steady, impervious. They passed the sporting-goods store, and Frida glanced through its glass door, but the fellow who had sold her the ball was not visible. The surface of the trolley fluttered again. Frida sped up, and she could smell the bad smell now, over and above the vegetable fragrance of her own bag. It was a grimy, sour odor. The odor of rat. Frida's nose twitched.

But there were other things to attend to. There was that man running behind her, almost on top of her. Frida shifted her weight to the rear and the side. The man, who said, *"Mon Dieu!,"* was deflected off the curb, and Madame remained safe. The man slowed to a walk — much more appropriate, Frida thought.

Étienne and Madame stopped, unusually for them, in front of the chocolate shop. Étienne said something, then Madame said something, then they stepped inside, leaving the trolley on the threshold. The fabric of the trolley fluttered again. Frida stepped up to it, dropped her own bag, put her paw on it, nosed open the flap. Yes. He was inside the trolley — a small, dark, glossy rat. He had been scratching around, but now he went quiet and stared up at her, his eyes large and frightened. Frida bared her teeth.

Kurt said, "I'm sorry. We haven't met, but I've seen you through the window. You are friends with Perestroika." He added, "My friend."

Frida understood that she had overreacted. She cleared her throat and said, "Yes, I've heard about you. I understand you are not game." Even so, her whiskers twitched.

Kurt said, "Where are we?"

"Rue de Grenelle, outside the chocolate shop."

"What is a chocolate shop?"

Frida, who saw Étienne and Madame approaching with a box, said, "Curl up in the corner and find out. But keep your paws to yourself." She stepped back. Étienne, still attending to Madame, put the little box into the trolley without looking. He closed the flap, and they walked on. Madame was saying, "Nothing wrong with an occasional treat. I bought a box of candied orange peel dipped in dark chocolate. Some other nice things in the box, too. Take good care of it, my darling."

Étienne patted his great-grandmama on the back of her hand.

They walked on.

Frida took a few deep breaths, and at the fruit-and-vegetable market, where Jérôme was absent for some reason, replaced by a young woman, she waited until Étienne and Madame began inspecting vegetables (always a long process), then nosed open the flap. The little box was untouched. She said, "Why did you come along?"

"I didn't mean to. I was sleeping in here, and suddenly we were out the door. I always wanted to get out the door, but now I'm not so sure. Do you see any rats around — females, perhaps?"

"Not a one," said Frida.

"Oh dear." Kurt sighed.

"It's too busy for rats. There are humans and automobiles everywhere. I can't say that I smell a rat in the neighborhood right now, but I've gotten a whiff from time to time."

"My father tells me that cats did away with everyone. We are the last living rats."

"He's exaggerating," said Frida.

Kurt curled into a ball, his paws over his face. Frida let the flap drop and sat down in her attentive and statuesque position beside the trolley. She was a predator, but even so, she did not want the rat to be squashed by groceries. It was a conundrum — if Étienne merely dropped the bag of vegetables into the trolley, that might endanger the rat (but also the chocolates); if he reached in to take out the box of chocolates, he would see the rat, and then there might be chaos. There was a reason why Paris was home to so many fat cats — the rat's father was wrong about numbers, but not about culture. Étienne and Madame went deeper into the shop. Frida bumped the trolley, knocking it over so that it fell on the fabric side, then put her nose down as if sniffing it, and said,

"Ease yourself out under the flap. I'll lie down close to the wall of the building, and you can hide between me and the building." She arranged herself. Kurt slipped out. He looked rather striking to Frida, but the Parisians had their chins in the air, and if they saw him, they did not react. He pushed in behind her. He whispered, "The boy petted me once," but after that said nothing. She barked one gentle bark, and Étienne appeared a few seconds later. He stood the trolley back up, said, *"Bon chien!,"* and pulled the trolley into the shop. Frida had no idea what to do next. She lay quietly, ears forward. Humans saw her and smiled, but did not, apparently, look closely — there were no screams or gasps. The feel of the rat's fur against her leg was warm and soft. The stink was not overpowering, not unlike the stink of every mammal, including Madame de Mornay. Every so often, the rat gave out a little squeak, but it was so soft and high-pitched that humans could not have heard it.

Étienne and Madame came out of the vegetable shop, went into the meat market. Frida remained still, arranging herself to look as proud and supercilious as she had ever done before, even in her days of solitude in the Place du Trocadéro. As a result, the woman in the meat market didn't chase her away.

Now Étienne and Madame came shuffling out, dragging the trolley. Humans stepped aside to give them space. Étienne was pulling the trolley, and it was full. The flap, partially open, revealed the box of chocolates nestled into the moist greenery of a bunch of carrots. Frida rose to her feet. She said nothing, but Kurt did what she would have advised him to do: he walked along underneath her, exactly within her midday shadow. He made no sounds. Fortunately, Madame was tired, and she and Étienne proceeded deliberately, rather close to the wall of shops, out of the way of passersby. Frida was a little nervous, but what would anyone do even if they did see them? The rat was inside Frida's territory. Even a human would deduce from that that the rat belonged to her.

But of all the humans, only the gendarme saw the rat scurrying down the street, within the stride of the German shorthair. It looked like an optical illusion, especially when the dog paused with the boy and the old woman for the streetlight, and the rat paused, too, and then skittered off the curb and across the intersection in the dog's shadow, perfectly in time with the dog's step. Did the dog know the rat was there? The gendarme couldn't tell. After the four of them disappeared around a corner, he stood scratching his head and wondering what he had really seen. He checked his watch. Lunchtime. He went into the nearest bar and ordered a shot of brandy; then he wondered if perhaps he might be transferred to Montmartre, where strange things happened all the time and weren't so disconcerting.

That evening, Kurt could not sleep at all: he was still too amazed at his first foray into the great world. He thought that it was no use telling Conrad about it — Conrad would not believe that their kingdom here, so huge to them, was relatively so small and dark, or that the number of humans in the world so defied all of Kurt's powers of perception that his sensory mechanism had broken down completely. He might believe that the sunlight was so bright that a rat could not open his eyes for more than a second, and that the noise of humans and their doings was overpowering, but he would not believe that a dog had saved Kurt's life, that cats were relatively few and far between, or that Kurt could not wait to go out there and look again for his doe.

THIRTEEN

Pierre thought that perhaps they were due for an early spring — the Champ de Mars had gotten plenty of rain since the December blizzard, but was now drying out quickly. It was Pierre's job to make a meadow in the midst of a city, to give it beautiful flower beds and swaths of color. And no one in Paris was willing to step in a puddle. It did not matter if a man or a woman purchased his or her shoes at Hermès or at Monoprix, those shoes were not to know muddy water. Pierre had been to the U.K. and seen "wellies," but never on a bona-fide Parisian. And so he had to take care of the allées and the grass (which was wet and tender this time of year, reaching for the sunshine) and the fences, which got rusted and bent over the winter, by whom and how Pierre was not quite certain. It was a hectic time, which was fine with Pierre, since he had no one at home but his four cats, and because there were four of them, they viewed him even more superciliously than the citizens of Paris did — the mere fact that they outnumbered him rendered him incidental in their eyes. He knew from that piercing whinny before Christmas that the horse was somewhere nearby, but he hadn't seen her or any of her products recently. It gave him a pleasantly eerie feeling when he happened to think of it, but he hardly ever happened to think of it, he was so busy.

When Pierre was growing up on a farm west of Saint-Céré, five hundred kilometers due south of the very spot where he was standing, and infinite worlds away, he had cared nothing about the apple orchard, the plum trees, the sunflower fields, the cows, or the sheep. He'd wanted only to get to Paris. When he got here, he tried various forms of employment, and at the first one, a travel agency, he'd met his wife. And they had traveled a bit — to Greece, Italy, Morocco, Scotland, England. But the tightness of the office made him restless, so he tried driving a taxi. The streets of Paris were both confusing and frustrating — once he had been stopped for an hour in a traffic jam over by Montreuil in which the cars were so crammed together that even a police vehicle blowing its siren had been unable to get through. Then he'd found this job, and his restlessness faded away, or, rather, dissolved into the very sort of work he had left behind down south. Here he was, active, orderly, as solitary as his father had been. Almost fifty. His father had died at fifty, pulmonary embolism.

Then, as he was sorting rakes in the gardening shed and inspecting the upper hinge on the shed door (screws coming loose — the door needed replacing), he saw a stray dog trot past. The dog was a German shorthair, sleek and elegant, with a confident air. A striking dog, which was why Pierre recognized her — she was the dog that belonged to that busker. Pierre had seen the two of them several times in various places around the arrondissement, particularly across the Pont d'Iéna, over by the carousel and the architectural museum. Everyone knew the fellow was quite a musician, had a guitar worth as much as an automobile, made a lot of money, could have found a place to live if he had wanted to, but you could tell by his look that he was a bit of a renegade, the kind of old fellow, maybe sixty, who had always been a renegade. Pierre had given him a euro or two. What was that song he'd played —

"Malagueña"? Something classy. Pierre stepped out of the shed enclosure and watched the dog trot away, then looked around. The busker was nowhere to be seen. The dog was trotting north, carrying a shopping bag. Pierre laughed, pleased with the distraction. He thought, well, once you have decided that a stray horse is none of your business, then a dog with a shopping bag is truly none of your business.

After eating her meal, slowly, as she always did, as she always had — even oatmeal had interesting flavors if you ate it slowly enough — Madame de Mornay made her way into the grand salon, feeling the warmth of the sun as she went. She paused at the second window and touched the glass. It was almost hot. She turned the crank that opened a lower pane and felt the breeze. Her ninety-eighth spring! Had every single one been so full and rich? She did not regret any one of them. She took a deep breath and then made her way to her chair, where she sat quietly for a while, sensing the flow of the air around her. Then she put her hand out, found her knitting, and commenced. Her project was a useless one, a coverlet to be pieced from the squares she knitted, using up a lifetime of leftovers, most of them merino wool, her favorite. She had made many a sweater and sock in her day; no doubt her bin of remnants was a riot of colors that did not match. But she knew her stitches by heart, by feel. She didn't have to see what she was doing to know whether to knit or purl or pass the slip stitch over. She could do a simple lace if she kept proper count. It was rather like saying her rosary or playing the piano, orderly and reassuring.

Perhaps the onset of spring was why those feelings of dread for Étienne that she had had around her birthday had receded in favor of hope, or even confidence. She still understood the stakes, but the boy was taller all of a sudden — she had to lift her hand fairly high to put it on his shoulder — and somehow this calmed her. Yes, she had been selfish to keep him here; however, she herself had never gone to school, had had a governess who was quite well educated, who had taught her to read, write, and do mathematical equations, had introduced her to Stendhal, Balzac, Flaubert, Rousseau, Poincaré, Colette, and George Sand. A music tutor had taught her to play the piano. She was allowed free run of a library that included many eyebrow-raising texts, and she had read them and discussed them with her tutor and her mother numerous times. Étienne might have started school at five, but Madame had decided that the school nearby was a sterile, unpleasant place, not right for her darling.

But once she felt better, then she felt worse — truly, she had been selfish. She had wanted Étienne all to herself, and had also wanted to prevent anyone, everyone, from access to the life they led here on the Rue Marinoni. Her experience of Paris was that if you went about your business with dignity and cleanliness, no one dared to investigate. Yes, she had plenty of money in the bank — her bills were paid — but she didn't remember the name of the bank — the old one had been taken over more than once, and no doubt the bills were no longer even paid by a human, but by a computer program. As she remembered, she had crept to the bank some years ago — four? five? — and the man she met there, very well dressed, had reassured her that the bank had only her best interests at heart. Did she believe him? How might she decide? If someone were to investigate, she and Étienne would be separated, and both of them would be put in separate places to be "taken care of." Her extreme age was against her, her failing sight was against her, her deafness was against her. It would be easy for "an authority" to assume that she could no longer live independently, would it not? Easy and profitable for a hospital, a facility, a "guardian." She remembered the orphanages and institutions of her youth, cages for children where beatings abounded, food was scarce, and the adults embezzled the funds. Whether these things were true about real orphanages, or whether she'd read them in books, she could not now remember, but the images were as clear to her at ninety-seven as they had been at six, when, walking down the Avenue de la Bourdonnais, she asked her nurse why children were alone on the street, why they were so dirty and thin, why they came up to her and grabbed her elbow. Her nurse, a kind woman, had handed out what change she had, shaking her head, saying, "The war! The war! Our Father who art in heaven, have pity!" Madame could reassure herself that Étienne was better off than those children, at least. Every day, she ran her hands over the boy's clothing to discover if he was dressed properly, and, every day, he was, and she detected no bony protuberances or emaciated upper arms — he was no wild child, like that boy she had seen in some film, when was that? A friend had taken her, then introduced her to the director, a handsome man whose name always made her think of truffles. Étienne was clean, fed, responsible, an avid reader. She shook her head, came back to the present, thought of the future: "What next?"

The horse was about to stand up; Étienne wrapped his legs around her sides and twined his fingers into her mane. Underneath him, she tilted back, then heaved forward, and then he was up toward the ceiling (not too near the ceiling, since the ceiling in the grand salon was five meters high). She stood quite still. He could see through the window from a different angle, too, and what he saw was the top of the fence outside, the buds on the shrubbery that enveloped it, the house across the street, and a bit of brightening bluish sky — it was just past dawn, and his great-grandmama would awaken soon. He had stood on the back of the sofas once or twice, and looked out the windows of the library upstairs, and he ran up and down the staircase every day (he had been known to slide down the banister, until that became rather boring), but this was different. He felt Paras's warmth. Perhaps he even felt her heart beating and the blood coursing in her veins. He felt her skin tremble and her

234

tail switch easily to the left and easily to the right. She was still, but she was alive. It was frightening and it was exhilarating. She took a step forward. He felt her right hip shift slightly; then her right shoulder moved, then her left hip, then her left shoulder. Her head lifted and dropped. She paused, and then she took another step, and another. Her mane was thick enough so that his hands were full — it was rough and warm, and underneath it, her coat was silky. Her ears flicked toward the window; then she paused, alert, as if she was listening to something. Her ears, though deep reddish brown, were edged in black. He hadn't noticed that before. He bent down, put his arms around her neck, took in her smell. There were so many wonderful things about being on her back that the riding books never mentioned.

He had set up the furniture in the living room so that, though his great-grandmama's favorite chair and table were just where they'd always been, everything else was bunched together in the middle, to give Paras a place to sleep and some room to get around. From on top of her, this looked a bit like a racecourse, and so it was — she now walked the circuit in a leisurely fashion, and as he went around on her back, past the fireplace, the window, another window, short wall, long wall, doorway, short wall, window, window, fireplace, her steps were muffled by the carpet but his feelings kept rolling out. The first circuit was a vertiginous thrill, but he didn't fall off, and then he felt himself get used to the movement and the rhythm, which was much more pleasurable. He sat quietly, let his back sway in time to her steps. By the third circuit, he was feeling a gentle rapture. None of the riding-school books in the library had ever talked about this, either. Time passed, step by step, and then the door opened to his great-grandmama's chamber, and there she was, neatly clothed in her usual black outfit, her hand on her cane. She called out, "Étienne! Where are you, my boy?"

Paras halted. Her ears flicked. Luckily, she was right beside one of the sofas, and so, still gripping the horse's mane, Étienne slid down until his foot touched the upward curve of its back; then he dismounted as best he could. Though he knew she couldn't hear him, he said, "Right here, Grandmama!" Paras stood stock still. Étienne skipped over to the old lady and guided her into the *cuisine.* On the way past the front door, he opened it wide. The air was fragrant. That it seemed like spring surprised Étienne. With the horse in the house, time passed more quickly than it ever had before, perhaps because there was so much to do, so many books to peruse, and even memorize, about the nature of horses.

When he came back after giving his great-grandmama her breakfast, the horse had gone outside. In his exhilaration over his ride, Étienne had forgotten to feed her, and now he didn't know quite what to do — Grandmama would certainly sense something if he were to let Paras back in and give her her usual basin of steel-cut oats and legumes. He ran upstairs and looked out the window. She was snuffling among the shrubbery along the fence. The dog was lying in the sun nearby, and the raven was perched on the head of the sitting lion that still adorned the left column. There was grass, at least some. She seemed fine enough for now. And then he gazed around the courtyard, imagining himself sitting on her back, striding here and there. He could not wait.

Out in the courtyard, Paras was not terribly hungry. Anaïs had given her an especially rich mixture of wheat berries, bran, flaxseed, and grated beets the night before, and, anyway, the grass in the Champ de Mars was coming back — rich and full of flavor. Grass in the courtyard was sparse, but what humans called "weeds" were plentiful, young and delicious. She ambled here and there, nosing for this bit of clover, that bit of dock. All the horses at the stables in Maisons-Laffitte had enjoyed the bits of herbs that got into the early hay, giving it more flavor and variety. Really, she thought, she might be a little thin, but, between Étienne and Anaïs, she now had a more varied and interesting diet than she had ever had in her life.

When Raoul presented himself at Nancy's nest, the edge of the water wasn't far from where Nancy was sitting dutifully upon the eggs, muttering to herself. Raoul thought but did not say that he had advised Sid to situate the nest on higher ground. Sid had insisted that higher ground was too exposed — was Raoul really and truly unaware of the hawks and the owls that flew about, focusing their gaze from above every moment on nests of duck eggs? Duck eggs were far and away the most delicious eggs, far surpassing geese and, what was it they were called — "Chickens?" offered Raoul — that humans ate by the hundreds. Sid was far more hysterical than most Aves, even mallards, that Raoul had ever encountered. How he flew into the empyrean with his mallard friends Raoul could not imagine, but, on the other hand, he had seen flocks of mallards squawking constantly, as if shouting to humans, "Shoot me! I can't stand myself any longer!"

Nancy said, "What will happen will happen. I say that every year, and I truly believe it, but I would like a rest every so often. At least the dog is gone."

"She isn't far gone," said Raoul.

"Oh dear," said Nancy. "You never know with a dog."

"I've never seen a dog as nice as Frida," said Raoul.

"Yes, but with any dog, something snaps, and there you are, she's wringing your neck for you, tossing you aside without even eating you."

"Has this ever happened to you?" said Raoul.

"It happened to a third cousin, out in Chatou. It was the talk of the family for years. The dog appeared to live with the flock in comity and peace, sniffed the ducklings, herded them a bit, and then, who knows, my cousin said the wrong thing, the wind blew from the wrong direction, the dog got up in a mood. Jumped on Pearl and did her in, in seconds. Left seven ducklings. Some humans baked Pearl for supper that night. Served her with oranges from their greenhouse. No, it doesn't matter what a dog *says*. A mallard has to keep her wits about her. Better for the dog to be gone."

"Life," said Raoul, "is always a chancy business."

"You are telling a mallard this? A mallard, for whom a moment's peace is a rare and precious thing?" She tucked her head under her wing and went back to muttering.

Now that she was living with Frida, Paras was a little surprised by her canine habits (it was Raoul who'd taught her that they were "canine"): She slept off and on all day; you could tell her something, but she didn't believe it unless she checked it out with her nose (not her ears — equines relied upon their hearing); she could not control her tail — everything she thought was expressed before she knew it by the movements of her tail. She had a strange attachment to objects, which she stashed here and there and kept watch over (one time she had lost the "ball," and then, when she found it, she rolled it with her paw, took it between her jaws, and tossed it in the air, trembling with pleasure). But the strangest thing was that, even though she still would not go into the house, she treated the boy as her very own

240

human — she wagged that tail when he came out and when he looked out the window. He seemed to notice her — he smiled, and sometimes he even petted her when they went to the market.

Raoul, who was perched in the crook of a tree limb that arched over the top of the fence, said, "My dear girl, I have never seen a *Canis familiaris* who was truly independent. Those who don't have humans run around in packs with one another. When I first saw our friend Frida after her human was carted away, she didn't leave the neighborhood over there. Ah well. And, you may not know, not all Canidae are familiaris." He lifted his wings. Frida continued to sleep. "You ask me, the best type of Canids are *Vulpes*. They have a poor reputation among the other canids, but they think for themselves."

"I've seen foxes," said Paras. "I've seen them in the Champ de Mars."

"Of course you have," said Raoul. "They were certainly more surprised to see you than you were to see them."

Paras said, "I need to make a wider circuit. I would enjoy a good gallop."

Raoul fluffed up his feathers, sidestepped, plucked an insect from the base of a leaf. He said, "Mmm. Not bad."

241

Frida stretched out, groaned, and then woofed, very softly, in her sleep.

The fact was that Raoul was thinking of abandoning Benjamin Franklin entirely. Those youngsters over there! The whole lot of them were from Dijon, pushy and populous in the Dijonnais tradition. He skipped upward from branch to branch in the tree. Certain forks or crooks in its branches had been utilized by earlier generations of Aves, but there was nothing at the moment, though in the adjacent tree there was a stick nest belonging to a pair of *Columba palumbus*. They were talkative and rather messy Aves, but they minded their own business. He hopped upward again. The branches of the tree got smaller and bouncier, the air got fresher. It wasn't a bad tree, a plane tree, a common tree. But he didn't have to think of it that way if he didn't want to. When you got old, your priorities changed, did they not? He cawed a few times to Paras (though she didn't look up at him) and stretched his wings.

Delphine hadn't spoken to Madeleine since Christmas. What was there to say? Delphine had exhausted herself looking for Paras, and had gotten to the point where she could only imagine bad outcomes — stolen by

Louis Paul, with him gloating. He might have even sent her to the slaughterhouse, because her skills were a threat to his own chances for a win. . . . She smacked herself on the side of her head to rid herself of this thought. Madeleine had not sued her for negligence — she was too kind to do that. Nor had Paras been insured. But the whole experience had driven Madeleine out of the horse-racing business. She had retired her silks, put her other two horses out to pasture, and contributed fifty thousand euros to a horse-rescue organization. Delphine's barn was full — she had had to borrow three stalls from her neighbor, and what she would do if he wanted them back she did not know. Sometimes, when she was out training, she would see a horse go by that reminded her of Paras — same refined head, mobile ears — but it was never Paras, never had that parallelogram-shaped star right over the cowlick between her eyes, never had that avid, curious gaze.

As for racing, Delphine was doing well enough — already this season, she had won two flat races, at Cagnessur-Mer and Hyères, had a series of four seconds in a row in Lyon. She liked her horses, and she was looking forward to the season, both on the flat and over fences, but she could not keep herself from gazing at races that Paras might have done well in, imagining driving Paras to the course, imagining telling the jockey to let the filly do it her way, reliving the pleasure she had felt when the filly came home first, and then first again.

When her mobile rang and it was Madeleine's voice on the other end of the line, her heart fluttered, as if, as if Madeleine had some news. And she did, but it wasn't about Paras. She had a new project, devoting herself to rebuilding a small abandoned convent in her village as a museum. Delphine thought it was a good idea — that village was at a crossroads where Gauls, Romans, Franks, and countless other peoples had paused, looked around, and decided to settle. The earth there was a swamp of artifacts. Madeleine sounded as if she was trying to be enthusiastic, as if she had made herself call Delphine in order to be friendly. She went on about potsherds and coins — there was one with a figure of a horse on it — Gaulish. Looking at it had made Madeleine rather sad. At the end of the call, just as they were hanging up and Delphine was watching Rania head out toward the gallops with the American horse Jesse James (fast, but still not comfortable, Delphine thought), Madeleine said, "I did look at a horse."

Delphine said, "A racehorse? What's his name?"

"Alphabezique."

Delphine remembered seeing the horse run; he was very good on the flat, big, and big-boned, a nice mover. She remarked that he had been a good horse — run fifth in the Arc, made a fair amount of money — but then said, "I thought he was retired."

Madeleine started to cry, and said that, yes, the horse was retired, she wanted to buy him as a breeding stallion; she loved him. And even as Delphine was counseling against this, saying that the horse wasn't good enough for that, that only a fool went into breeding, best leave that to those with endless money, she started crying, too, so much so that she could not see Rania and Jesse James for the tears. Delphine could not say that Madeleine was persuasive. She did not end the conversation any more in favor of this crazy idea than when she began, but she did agree, the next time she headed south, to stop and look at Alphabezique. It seemed the least she could do.

After the morning training was over, and the horses were quietly eating from their hay nets and Rania was listening to a tune on her iPhone, and Delphine should have been heading to her office to make out bills, she got into her car and drove into Paris. It was not that she thought Paras was in Paris. But she did think that getting away from Maisons-Laffitte might somehow give her a new idea about what to do — either how to find her or how to give up on finding her.

It took about an hour, and there she was on the Périphérique, on the west side, and she could not help herself, she got off at Neuilly. She often got off at Neuilly, but she always turned south and headed down the Avenue de Malakoff. Now she went east, toward the Arc and the Champs-Élysées, something she hadn't done in years. She disappeared, as she felt, into the maelstrom. Part of the problem was motorcycles zooming everywhere, the machines and the riders the same color, carrying the same brilliant shine, curving around her inside a cloud of noise. As she circled the Arc, the other cars seemed to swarm like bees attacking. She felt lucky that there were no bumps, that she was spit out at the turn into the Champs-Élysées without mishap in some mysterious way. Delphine had ridden in horse races, some of them with fifteen or twenty entries who bunched and spread out at fifty to sixty kilometers per hour. But, maybe for that very reason, she didn't trust cars. Cars had no sense of a herd, no perception along their bodies of where the other cars were. Cars relied on their drivers much more than horses relied on their jockeys. She was panting as she passed Cartier, Swarovski, the Hôtel George V. These expensive places were routine for Madeleine, so why should the woman not do whatever she wanted with her money? Beautifully pruned horse chestnuts rose above the traffic like cliffs above a canyon, and all the pedestrians seemed to be staring at her, watching her drown. There was of course nowhere to pull over, so she kept her hands on the wheel and her foot on the gas, but she did not know why she had made this trip, or what it meant. All she knew was that her horse had disappeared, just a horse, not a great horse, not a horse even as good as Alphabezique, a pretty horse, an interesting horse, but horses came and went all the time. Why could she not get over this one? But, of course, it was the mystery of the whole thing, the possibility that Paras had died in some cruel way.

Then there was some greenery, then there was the Place de la Concorde, then there was some more greenery — oh, yes, Les Tuileries. Sometime late in the afternoon —

nowhere near dark, but the shadows were lengthening — she came to. She was on the Avenue de Suffren. It was hard to say where she had been — the Parc Monceau came to mind, but so did Montparnasse. How could she have ranged so widely without realizing it? There was a parking place down the street from the soccer field. She whipped into it, turned off the car, and sat there for a long moment. Up since 4:30 a.m., she was worn out. She emerged from the car and walked around it. No new dents, no new scrapes. She must have stayed out of trouble. The thing to do was to call Rania and have her take the train into town and pick her up. She would think of something to say between now and then.

But when she checked her phone, she saw that it was dead. So, if she wanted to come to her senses, it would have to be coffee, then. She walked into a café and bakery.

After her second cup, she was back to normal. What it was like, she had to admit, was the day she rode her first race as an amateur jockey. She didn't ride races anymore, but at that time, ten years ago now, she'd had a wonderful old gelding, a horse with dozens of races under his belt at eight years old, still sound, still ready to run. She had forced herself to do it — to ride, to get in shape, to work the old fellow every day — and then she had entered him in a race right there in Maisons-Laffitte. But from the moment she woke up on the morning of the race, she might as well have been on Mars — she couldn't breathe the air, she didn't feel as though she was sticking to the Earth when she walked, and all through the race everything seemed to move slowly and at light-speed at the same time. They had come in fifth, she had won a thousand euros, the sense of being lost in the universe had lasted for the rest of the afternoon, and then, all of a sudden, she was awake, she knew that they had both survived, and for some reason that escaped all logic, she was committed to racing again, to having a few more horses, to embarking on this career. But for years after that, when people asked her about her first race, she'd said, "I don't remember a thing." She took a bite of her roll. It was an odd version, maybe something from down south, buttery but not a croissant, sprinkled with fennel seed. She took another bite. She might have liked a second one, but she had to keep her weight down if she was going to do her share of the training and stay in the horse business.

Anaïs saw her. Anaïs came in once a week to help in the afternoon and to sort out the books before they went to the accountant. A woman, not old but all dried and brown, sat quietly at a table by the window, in tight pants, dirty boots, horseback-riding clothes. No one had dared wear such apparel in this bakery for years, if ever, and the other servers and the patrons looked offended, but Anaïs was fascinated. The woman seemed to be enjoying Anaïs's own modest fennel-seed creation, so she picked up a little tray and walked over to her. Yes, the woman gave off a countryside fragrance, you might say, but it wasn't unpleasant to someone who had laid her forehead against the neck of a horse about twelve hours before. She said, "Good day, madame. May I offer you something else? Another small roll, perhaps?"

The woman looked up at her. She looked exhausted. She said, "No, but thank you very much. This one is quite delicious."

"Thank you, madame. It's my own creation. I like to make new things to amuse myself. Our customers do seem to particularly appreciate this one." Now was the time, Anaïs thought, to ask about horses, to ask if a real horse could possibly wander the streets of Paris at night, accompanied by a raven, who sometimes perched between the horse's ears in order to receive a grape, a horse who disappeared at the break of dawn, whose gaze seemed uncanny, almost flickering with light, who, she sometimes thought, had just the ghost of a halo hovering above her. She said, "Excuse me, madame —"

And the woman said, "No thanks!," sounding as if she meant "No, thank you, do not address me, I need nothing from you," and so Anaïs decided once again that it was better to keep her nighttime escapades to herself.

FOURTEEN

Although Étienne was somewhat uneasy about how much his great-grandmama was sleeping lately, she was still eating her usual amount, still making her trips to the shops, and seemed to be happy, so he made use of the fact that she took a nap after her breakfast to go outside and ride Paras around the courtyard. It was easy now. There were ten steps from the courtyard to the portico. He climbed to the sixth step, and she sidled up to him. It was easy to grasp her thick, tangly mane and slide his leg over her back. She always waited quietly until he felt evenly balanced, and then, before he said, "Go!," she ambled away, here and there over the grass. He was high enough to look in the windows, but not over the tops of the shrubbery, so he could hear people walking, talking, or running (he could tell by the quickness of their stride), humming, and he could hear a dog bark every so often, but he couldn't see anyone, and, he was confident, no one could see him. Sometimes the two of them walked here and there for hours, and as they did, he let his mind wander. Because he had lived such an isolated life, there was no place for his mind to wander except around the worlds of the books he had read, but that was enough for now. He could imagine twenty thousand leagues under the sea, cold and black; he could imagine Emperor Hadrian; he could imagine the plague; he could imagine Gargantua and Pantagruel, though possibly no one in the world would recognize what he was imagining. Étienne was willing to read anything, even if he only understood one word out of ten. He could even imagine London, since one of the books he liked to read was a French translation of *David Copperfield,* an edition that had been lovingly perused by someone — there were all sorts of spidery notes in the margins. He had looked for another Dickens, but not found one.

All the time he was imagining, Paras's legs were moving, her ribs were shifting from side to side, her ears were flicking this way and that, she was pausing to gaze at something, pausing to eat a bite, pausing to scratch an itch. She breathed in, she blew out the air, she snorted, she tossed her head, she yawned, she nosed the sweet dog as if to investigate where she had been.

Frida was in and out under the shrubbery. The entrance she'd dug for herself was quite a tunnel now, smooth and rather large. Frida and Étienne, Étienne felt, were friends, even though he couldn't lure her into the house. Frida came to him, her head down, her stump of a tail wagging fast, and he stroked her silky ears or tickled her chest. She brought him her ball, but as yet she had not given it to him, and he had not taken it — they both knew it was hers. She had, indeed, shown him where the purse was, and he had seen the money and counted it. He had no way of knowing how much had originally been in there, but now there were a thousand euros. He had looked, in good conscience, for some sort of identification, but there was only a tag that said, in English, "Lucky Brand," which might be a name, but he guessed it wasn't. Since the bag had a magnetic flap, not a zipper, like his great-grandmama's bag, all sorts of things might have fallen out. And it was a terrible muddy mess. Money, he saw, was quite durable even when wet. But it was Frida's money. He left it in the bag.

How comfortable he was, astride his

horse! At first, she had seemed slippery and wiggly, always moving out from under him. It had made him tense, and he had nearly fallen off three times, but then, one day, when he was tired from a long night listening to that rat in the walls (and it did sound as if there was more than one), he got on her anyway, and that was the first time he stopped paying attention and sort of thought about other things (the rat, for one), and as he did so, his body seemed to relax and settle like a bag of flour, and he came to the realization that if he didn't tense up, but just moved with her as a jelly might jiggle on a table, she would not leave him behind. When he tensed, he got taller, more like a stick. When he relaxed, he felt her all up his spine, deciding where she was going to go before she even turned her head.

Of course, they had not trotted, much less tried a little gallop — the courtyard was not big enough for that. Knowing this drew his imagination into the Champ de Mars. He still opened the gate before he went to bed. He still knew, partly from looking out his window in the night, that she left and came back, but he didn't think about it much, except at those times when he pictured himself going along for the ride. He planned, this very night, to follow her, for at least a little way, just to see what she did. As he thought this, she stopped, pricked her ears, snorted, then shook her head, as if, perhaps, to say, "No, this is my business, stay home." But then she walked on. All the books (well, both of the books — one called *Cours d'équitation,* which was much older than his great-grandmama, and another called *Le Cheval,* by a man whose name started with an "X") prescribed saddles and bridles and martingales and all sorts of things that Étienne did not have, and so he skipped those pages. Actually, he skipped most of the pages and looked at whatever drawings there were, and sometimes let a sentence about how a horse should be obedient and limber sink in. As far as he could tell, Paras was both obedient and limber. After a while, Paras went to the steps and eased her shoulder and hip toward them, and waited. Étienne knew how to take a hint — he slid off onto the sixth step. She walked away. Through the window, Étienne could see that his great-grandmama was out of her bed — out of her room, perhaps, though he couldn't see much through the leaded panes. It was such a warm day, he thought. Time to start leaving some windows open.

■ ■ ■ ■

Kurt was in the old lady's room, lying on his back in a spot of sunlight, waiting for something to happen. He had been waiting for something to happen for a very long time, but nothing had happened — or, rather, since he had gone out into the world, everything that had happened subsequently seemed like nothing at all, because that thing that he wanted to happen, meeting his doe, hadn't happened. Two times he had waited near the door for Paras to go out, so that he might follow her, but he wasn't fast enough on his own to get his whole body plus tail through the closing door, especially since he didn't want the boy to see him. When he had proposed to Paras that she take him with her, she had refused — she had a ways to travel, she wanted to gallop, it wasn't safe, what would she say to Conrad?

"You don't know Conrad."

"I've seen Conrad."

"You've never spoken to him."

"I don't want my first words to him to be about how I carried you outside and you were taken off by an owl."

"What is an owl?"

"For your purposes, a flying cat."

"Get Frida to take me."

"When Frida talks about the last time, she trembles all over."

"I can ride you. The boy rides you." She'd had no answer for this, so he still hoped that she might eventually be persuaded. "Just let me sit on your head again." She'd let him sit on her head again. Then she lay out full on the carpet, and he ran along her side and up and down her belly. She liked that a great deal.

Now Madame de Mornay was making her way through the grand salon. Kurt rolled over, yawned, and followed her. She called out for Étienne twice, but not very loudly. He must be upstairs in the library, forwarding his schooling. There was sunshine everywhere — she could feel it. Every time Madame paused to enjoy the warmth, Kurt paused to enjoy the warmth. Every time she pushed open a window, he took a whiff. He wasn't terribly hungry — provisions around here didn't allow for that. He knew he would be better off if his and Conrad's estate were a little leaner and more populated — but that part he wanted to fix, he really did. In the *cuisine,* he sat quietly under the table while Madame groped her way about, making a pot of tea. He was just grooming his whiskers when the back door opened unexpectedly and there was the boy, who looked first at the old lady and then at Kurt. Then again at Kurt. Kurt's whiskers twitched involuntarily. Although the boy had scratched his belly that time, it had been in the bedroom. They both had been able to pretend that Kurt's full figure was not due to a lifetime's expropriation of Mornay family wealth. Now, right here, they found themselves at the scene of the crime. Conrad said, over and over, that the last place a human wanted to find a rat was in the *cuisine*.

The boy went to the old lady and took her hand. She smiled, said, "Hello, my dear." He kissed her on the cheek, and moved the tea kettle to the burner that was actually flaming, then opened three different cans of tea and held them under her nose one by one. She chose the second one. As a rat, Kurt could count to six. Conrad maintained that cats could only count to five.

Madame pulled out a chair, felt her way around the table, sat down. Kurt moved toward her. Really, there was no smell at all now, so she was closer than ever to nonexistence — he and Conrad sometimes marveled at her ability to hold on. He was not touching her, but he was near enough so that any attempt by the boy to swat him would result in her being swatted, too. He eyed the entrance to the network of tunnels, but the boy was standing in front of it, and, anyway, he sensed no rage from the boy, not even any dominance. He remained still, semi-crouched on his hind legs, one forepaw on the floor and one lifted, ready to run. The old lady said a few things, and the boy said a few things, something was put on the table above him, and then something else. He waited. He didn't mind. He enjoyed feeling brave. There was, he saw, a dead cockroach in the shadow of the pantry. How had he missed it? It was dry and flat, no odor. He and Conrad were failing at their job.

Madame shifted her feet, and her toe touched him, but lightly. He moved over one step. More chitchat from above. Madame always spoke softly; Kurt found it soothing. Now another chair moved, and, moments later, the boy sat down. Kurt was surrounded by feet. The boy had taken off his boots at the door — Kurt could see them and smell them from where he was; they were the most exciting things in the room, fragrant with dirt and flowers and horse dung and a dozen other things that Kurt should be able to recognize but could not, because of his housebound lifestyle. The socks were fragrant, too, and a little grimy. Kurt crept over and peeked into the cuff of the boy's trousers. There was the bud of a flower there, tiny. Kurt extracted it with a flick of his paw and tasted it. Bitter. He spat it out. Above him, more chitchat. He got bolder. He went back to Madame. There was fluff on the toe of her slipper — nothing to eat, but he flicked it away, then scratched at her slipper to see if it might give off an odor. It did not. He was getting very bold! Now the chairs pushed back, the humans stood up, and Kurt could see by the arrangement of their feet that the boy was helping the old lady out of the *cuisine.* He waited, then skittered to the doorway. She was going to her chair in the grand salon. She sat down, still talking, and picked up her knitting. It was the only thing Kurt ever saw her do in the house besides eat and sleep.

She kept talking, but the boy turned and came back toward the *cuisine.* Step by step down the corridor. Kurt didn't move. The boy got closer. His gaze was on Kurt, right on him, and Kurt did not look away, but he did start to tremble, he did start to feel the tunnel entrance drawing him, he did start to wonder where Conrad was, and to long

261

for that safe darkness. He squeaked, and then squeaked again. The boy squatted down in front of him and stretched out his hands, palms upward. Even a rat knew what palms upward meant — it meant "give me something."

All was quiet, except for the comforting mumble of Madame counting her stitches. Kurt swallowed.

The boy smiled.

Rats do not smile, but they do open their eyes wide and make a little "o" with their mouths when they mean to be friendly.

The hands were still extended. Kurt crept forward. It was possible, Kurt thought, that the boy was the one who was essential to all of his hopes and dreams. He was right at the hands now. He touched one of them with his nose, and then flicked his whiskers across it. He put his paw on the hand. And then he went up into the hands, which were slightly cupped but did not curve around him, did not grasp him. After a moment, he coiled himself, and then the boy stood.

That time before, when the boy had tickled his belly and then his back, Kurt hadn't been brave enough to look the boy in the eye. He had looked at the ceiling of the bedroom, where the light coming through the window seemed to be a part of that piercing noise that he now knew was a whinny that came and went and came and went and then was gone. The boy had been polite, Kurt had been polite, but then he had left, and that, it seemed, had been that. Now he uncurled himself, and sat up, looked at the boy, eye to eye, a difficult thing for a rat. His whiskers fluttered. He stopped them. He tried to be dignified but friendly-looking. The boy said, "I forgot how silky your fur is. Indeed, you are handsome."

Kurt smoothed his whiskers with his paw. No one had ever called him handsome before. Perhaps that boded well for his reproductive aspirations.

Kurt didn't know what he wanted from Étienne. Certainly not food. Perhaps this was enough — acceptance. When your own father went on and on about the injustice of rats being outcasts all over the world, about how every rat had a story of escaping the trap, or the broom, or the dropping shoe, a story of being greeted by screaming, by barking, by hissing, by a fog of ill-smelling and sickening gas, then acceptance was the oddest thing of all. He no longer had to look at the horse and ask himself, "Why do humans like horses, but not rats?" When he told Conrad about the dog saving him,

Conrad had snorted in disbelief, said, "Must not have been hungry, then." Here was something he would not do — tell Conrad about sitting in the boy's hands. The boy bent down and set Kurt on the floor, then tickled his back for a few moments. Kurt walked in a leisurely manner, but, he felt, with a certain grace, to the entrance of his tunnel. It was broad day now, time for a nap. But he would return.

Jérôme considered himself taciturn. He loved vegetables, he loved his neighborhood, he kept his eyes open, he knew it was not his job to gossip about his customers. Now that the dog always accompanied the boy and the old old lady to the shop, he felt that his original instinct, that the dog had been ferrying provisions to that household all along, was proved correct (as were most of his instincts). In this neighborhood, he had seen plenty over the years, and a man walking down the street on Monday with his arm around the waist of a pretty blonde and then walking down the street on Tuesday, laughing convivially with an elegant brunette, was the least of it. A shopkeeper in the Seventh Arrondissement was wise to keep his opinions to himself, and Jérôme always did so. But, nevertheless, there he had been, on a

Saturday morning, talking about the boy and the dog and the old lady to Hélène, from the meat market next door, his hands under his apron, Hélène having a smoke, out on the street as if they lived in some village in the country, and, yes, Jérôme had been aware of someone in the shop behind him, but he'd thought she was squeezing oranges or selecting potatoes.

On Monday, late in the afternoon, this woman came to him with someone else, a man. It turned out that they were from the elementary school up the street. They came into the shop and more or less pinned Jérôme to the wall behind the cash register. It was true that Jérôme himself had not had a happy school experience — he had been a little wild, had hated studying, and excelled only in cultivating the school vegetable garden, which had been fine with his father, who had owned this shop before Jérôme did. They were polite enough, but that air of strictness that all teachers had would come out. Who was this boy? Jérôme had called him "Étienne" and had said that he appeared to be eight or nine. There was no boy at the school named "Étienne" other than a boy in the first grade. Jérôme had been talking about a boy he saw in the neighborhood with some frequency. Did he live in the neighborhood? How long had he been coming to the shop? What was this about a very old lady, maybe a hundred years old?

Jérôme said he knew nothing about the boy or where he lived or went to school. Strictly speaking, this was true, he knew nothing if you did not count the boy's gustatorial preferences. Jérôme put the officials off. Let them look for the boy, let them spy on his shop and follow the boy home — that was their business, not Jérôme's. But he did wonder how to warn that boy that something was in the wind.

Which was the reason that, the next time Étienne came home from Jérôme's shop, he found, folded up among the dried figs he had bought as a treat (for himself and for Kurt and Paras), a note letting him know that some people from the school were nosing around for information about him. Jérôme's handwriting was neat; even so, Étienne read the note three times before he comprehended what it meant. It meant that he had to come up with a plan before those people found him, before they found his great-grandmama. Before they found the horse. He made himself put the vegetables away, but he saw that his hands were trembling as he did so.

The school may have not noticed Étienne until now, but Étienne had noticed the school, and it looked to him, as it looked to his great-grandmama, like a noisy trap. The riot of the children (he thought of them as "the children" rather than "the other children") was bad enough, but the noise of the adults was worse — stiff, raised voices, clapping hands, commands. Étienne had never in his life received a command. Even when his great-grandmama told him to do something, she phrased it affectionately, as something that would be done to please her if he cared to do it. And, therefore, he always did it. Nor had he ever issued a command. Whom would he command? The horse? The dog? They seemed to read his mind — or not. He could go to the sixth step in the courtyard and stand there. He could know that Paras knew he wanted a ride, but that she wasn't ready at the moment to give him one. If he commanded her to do so, was she likely to agree? Not at all. She was likely to move away. As for the dog, the dog watched his every move and was ready at every minute to follow him, to go ahead of him, to present herself to his great-grandmama for support, to carry something, to wait for him. She would not give him that silly ball; a command would

267

not cause her to do so. It was her ball.

There were plenty of books about school in the library. No one in any of those books had ever liked school; every author remembered school with horror. Beatings and deprivations were the least of it. According to every single author, the attempt to have a thought of one's own was the gravest sin. Étienne's whole life was made up of having thoughts of his own, exploring them, enjoying them, comparing them to the thoughts he found in books or overheard on the street.

And then there was the question of, if he went to school — which looked like an all-day affair, except for Wednesday, when the school was quiet — who would watch over his great-grandmama? And even if there was someone, would that person try to command the old lady? Try to order her and organize her? This did not seem to Étienne like a project that could turn out well. As for the dog and the horse and now the rat and maybe the raven, well, he didn't want to think about that. He stared at the note, then wadded it up and tossed it into the bin. Perhaps, he thought, he could write notes himself, to Jérôme, detailing what he and his great-grandmama needed to buy. The dog could do the delivery. Just the day before, he'd taught her to put her head through the handle of the trolley and push it. She'd only pushed it a meter, if that, but maybe it was possible that she could push it to Jérôme's shop. Étienne finished putting away their purchases, peeked at Madame, who was now knitting a purple square; the evening before, the square had been green. Then he went upstairs and looked out each window for a rather long time. He made note of every human he could see that seemed to pause or look up at the house, especially the gendarme. He had seen the gendarme plenty of times — you couldn't do anything about a gendarme — a gendarme walked the streets and made your business his business — but he had never felt that he or his great-grandmama had attracted the attention of the gendarme in any special way. Now, as he watched, he did not sense that the gendarme was curious about them, at least for now. But if the school authorities happened to consult the gendarme, perhaps the gendarme would have a thought or two. After watching for a while, he went downstairs and found the old lady dozing, her knitting in her lap. He touched it with his fingertip. It was a lace pattern. It reminded him of pictures of snowflakes.

Paras finally felt comfortable visiting Nancy and the ducklings when the ground was dry and the turf was thickening up. There was no moon, and the Champ de Mars was especially dark — always good for a ramble. It was so late that none of the buildings had even a lighted window. Of course the great Tour was lit, and beyond that, the bridge across the river. The river itself shimmered and gave off a warm vapor. It could not be true that Paras smelled or sensed the two racecourses so far out in that direction. It could not be true that Paras felt a little pull in that direction. This life was a well-fed pleasure — what more could she want? She came to the fence around the pond, trotted a little bit back and forth to test the footing, then popped over it at an easy canter. That was also a pleasure, and one that she had forgotten. Jumping. She had been particular about hurdles, in training and on the course, never touched a one. She wasn't a careless type who came back to the barn complaining about this knock and that blow — she pulled her knees right up to her cheeks and kicked out behind. If you had been a nimble filly, the sort who could curl up in a ball to sleep, it was as easy as could be, and more fun than galloping — perhaps a bit like flying.

Nancy started quacking as soon as she saw Paras — the ducklings were in grave danger every single day, and should they survive, it would be a miracle solely attributable to Nancy's alertness. Paras, having seen hawks and owls and a fox and two large cats as she trotted around the Champ, didn't doubt her. The ducklings, so far, were Male No. 1, Female No. 1, etc., down to Male No. 3 and Female No. 3. They all looked like Nancy, and even though they were quite young, they were already swimming vigorously, according to Nancy; at the moment, their sleeping heads were arranged around her in the nest. That they all looked like Nancy was a triumph in itself, because Nancy had been sure that one of those shoveler ducks you see all over the place had introduced an egg into her nest, and it was all very well for certain ravens to say what's the difference, but the difference was evident — that hideous beak. Nancy stopped quacking, sighed, rearranged herself among the ducklings. All was quiet. Everything was quite lush here, in the shadow of the parapet. Paras nosed out a few herbs and chomped some grass. She said, "Where's Sid?"

271

"He'll get back anytime now," said Nancy. "Depends on air traffic, which can be a little vicious. He isn't the kind who goes scouting about for stray hens. He's faithful and knows his job."

"What's his job?" asked Paras.

"Look around," said Nancy. "Six ducklings is a lot of work. Do horses produce offspring?"

"Yes," said Paras, "but usually only one at a time."

Nancy started quacking softly to herself. Paras didn't say anything more, pulled a few weeds out of the water, just to taste them, and looked out there again, toward the big bridge and up the hillside to the grand buildings on the crest. They drew her; she jumped the fence beside the pond without even testing the footing (but of course it was fine — without shoes, all footings were manageable). She made her way along the edge of the lighted area, always cautious, and stood among the buildings not far from the bridge. A few cars passed, but there were long moments of darkness and silence. She saw that if she was going to get there it would be at this time of night. But what would she do when she got there? She was overfed now because of the rich grass, and no longer fit because of the intermittent exercise. The other horses would pass her with ease, kicking dust in her face, and then pretending concern when the race was over. She was a four-year-old, a mare, no longer a filly. And she looked like a mare, she was sure, one of those graceless beings that you respected but didn't care much about, who did, indeed, as she had told Nancy, produce one offspring at a time. She lifted her head and flared her nostrils, recalled that long trot she had taken into the city the first evening. She had been in the forest, and she had followed her nose, and then she had crossed something that brought her to a small fenced area of grass, and she had jumped in there, and then she had jumped out, and then she had trotted down the street, her shoes clanging on the pavement, and then she had found that other patch of grass, and Frida. It was hazy, had always been hazy. But it wasn't so hazy that she couldn't find her way back, she thought. She flicked her ears. Was now the time?

And then she was startled into rearing up by a huge rumbling van that flew by, a van that would have hit her and killed her had she made the move she'd been thinking of. She stood quietly, her head down, her breathing fast, sweat breaking out on her flanks. Sometime later, when she had calmed down a bit, she turned, went past the fence and the pond and the bridge, and over to the allée, and cantered home. The gate was open, Frida was sleeping. The windows were dark. The courtyard was peaceful. Paras stood quietly by the shrubbery until the sun came up and Étienne called her in for breakfast.

Pierre, unable to sleep, had come to work at dawn. If he got there early enough, he could watch the baby squirrels, doves, owls, ducks, coots. Of course, there were the pigeons and the rats. Part of his job was to control them, because tourists hated them, but he was of two minds about that: every city was an ecosystem, and Paris was more complex than most. The horse manure, fresh, still greenish, two piles of smallish clumps, surprised him — he hadn't seen it in weeks. One pile was west of the Tour, a few meters from the Quai Branly. That one he pulped with his shovel and mixed with some of the soil he had in his cart. He piled the mixture around the trunks of a few trees. The other, smaller pile was where the Allée Adrienne Lecouvreur crossed the boulevard. He was looking at it when a voice behind him said, "What is that?"

He turned around in surprise. Maybe he had never met anyone in the park this time of the morning. He thought he recognized her — she was wearing a light jacket and a red cap — but he couldn't place her. He said, "I'm guessing it's horse dung." He tried to make himself sound impersonal, indifferent, but, really, he was happy — well, thrilled — that the horse was still alive. He hadn't realized how convinced he had become that the horse had gone to the slaughter. The girl — well, she was so slight, she seemed girlish, but her face was the face of someone who knew what she was about — said, "How can there be horse dung in the Champ de Mars?"

Pierre said, "Historical precedent, perhaps," and the woman smiled, not what Pierre had expected. He said, "Horse dung isn't unhealthy, and, at any rate, we clean it up."

Now the woman smiled, and said, "It doesn't bother me. In fact, I'm happy to discover proof that there is really a horse. I thought it was something much spookier."

Pierre said, "What are you talking about?"

And Anaïs, who had decided to cross the Champ de Mars in the pleasant weather and take the RER train home from work, avoiding the two transfers she normally had to make, told him about her horse, her myste-rious nighttime visitor.

Pierre knew Anaïs's pastries perfectly well — he'd bought *galettes* and coffee there several times. He said, "You work in that café? Or the bakery? I've never seen you there."

"I'm a baker."

Pierre couldn't quite contain his relief that the horse was still alive. He knew he was grinning. He said, "When was the last time you saw the horse?"

"The day before yesterday, during the night, and she ate a bowl of oatmeal with flaxseed, corn flour, and grated carrots."

And then they looked at each other, not saying anything, both smiling. Anaïs was thinking that something around here was crazy, but at least she knew now that it wasn't her, and, by the way, this gardener had a nice demeanor, comfortable and kind. Pierre was thinking that Anaïs must be a good-hearted woman, and those *galettes,* and the rolls, too, that he had gotten from that pâtisserie were chewy and delicious. The sun lifted itself into the heavens, just a little bit, and shone brightly on the pile of manure.

FIFTEEN

As a result of spying through the windows of houses and apartments around Paris for many segments and watching the humans lined up at the foot of the Tour, Raoul had noticed that it took humans forever to do the least thing. There they stood, looking around, waiting waiting waiting, shuffling forward, hardly speaking to one another. Ten flocks of Aves might rise into the heavens, sort themselves out, and billow off into the west or the east in the time that it took one human to creep onto the elevator, look out over the landscape, return to the earth, and toddle away. Or you could watch humans eat in their cafés, a spectacle affording no drama whatsoever. The food was dead before they even saw it, and yet they sat there, poking the dead things with their tools, their mouths working and working. And so, though Delphine planned to renew her search for Paras, though Pierre planned to keep his eyes open, though Anaïs planned to follow Chouchou the next time she came for a feed, though the authorities at the school planned to ask around the neighborhood and at police headquarters about a stray boy, the days went by, the same as always, pleasant and fragrant, occasionally rainy, occasionally cool. The herd of runners in the Champ de Mars swelled, but they noticed nothing, partly because, though Pierre didn't look for the horse, he did clean up after her, trusting that she would appear. Anaïs always found herself up to the elbows in dough, in no position to take a long walk — merely feeding the horse used up plenty of time. And she knew that if she found the horse, if the authorities (including that kindly fellow — Pierre, his name was) got involved, the visits and her pleasure would be over: the horse would be claimed by a real owner. Only Jérôme actually planned to do nothing, say nothing, simply to supply the vegetables and the bread and the bones, to pat Frida on the head when she came to the shop with the boy.

In the meantime, Madame de Mornay knitted, made her bed, napped, ate a bit of this and a bit of that. She chatted with Étienne, she held her hat in her hand and stroked the feather, she thought of her husband, that dapper heartthrob, her mother and her brother, her son, and her grandson and his wife, Étienne's parents, and she hoped some idea would come to her. No one had ever suggested that death was voluntary, unless you counted heading off to war a voluntary act, which it sometimes is and sometimes is not. Her father had died a commandant, which meant that, if he had not embraced that war, he had embraced his duty therein. Her husband had sent Madame and their son to Domme during the second war, then fought with the Resistance, died in a bombing raid upon Lyon, killed, ironically, by his own allies. And then her son had gone to Oran as a representative of de Gaulle. He had intended to stay eight days and had been killed by a ricocheting bullet on the second day; her grandson was a year old at the time. Her grandson had used his portion of the family money to live in Alaska, Hawaii, Hong Kong, Australia, Kuala Lumpur — anywhere that was not like Paris. Perhaps he had married, perhaps not. He returned home with a lovely girl from Dublin, twenty-five years old to his forty-four. The three of them had lived well enough in the house — Madame kept to herself on the ground floor; André and Irene ranged through the upper stories. André made big plans to renovate the whole place, to return it to its former undusty glory. His friends showed up, of all types, speaking all sorts of languages, but Madame was already fairly deaf by that time, and could make out very little. Irene's French was good. Though her accent puzzled Madame, she'd liked the girl, the girl who was driving the night they were killed, the girl who got confused and entered the Périphérique going the wrong direction. Étienne was two and a half. Madame did not know if he remembered his parents — and if she were to ask now, she would not be able to hear his reply. She did not remember her own father. It was their fate as a family, perhaps, or merely luck, merely a part of being French in the twentieth century, when wars came and went like terrifying, unstoppable tempests. She had been spry enough when Étienne was two and a half, when he was five, to care for him, and then their roles had switched. Truly, she had done ill by the boy. And then she stopped thinking about it and returned to her knitting basket. The wool was running low — she could feel only three small balls in there. She had stitched each section to the others, and the afghan spread out over her bed and draped to the floor on every side. It was almost complete.

Étienne and Kurt thought only about riding. When Étienne was not caring for his great-grandmama or hastily dusting here and wiping there, he was staring at Paras or sitting on her or stroking her with a soft rag. At least he ate. Kurt no longer knew himself. All he wanted to do, inside the house and outside, was entangle his four little feet in that thick mane and go about from place to place. His former greatest pleasure, eating, now looked to him like a waste of time, and as a result, nothing was left on his bones except muscle and fur. Frida lay in her corner in the courtyard and muttered and grumbled about rats knowing their place, and their place, if they were smart, was indoors. Even Conrad occasionally looked out the window on the second floor in dismay, but Kurt could not be stopped. He was delirious with pleasure and desire.

As for Paras, after her near-death experience, she was willing to do anything. Otherwise, she might have discouraged Kurt from running over her and sitting on her constantly, but his feet, light and tickly, reminded her that she was alive. Any reluctance she'd had about presenting herself at the sixth step to Étienne was completely gone — he fed her and gave her a place to live, he cleaned up after her (and the shrubbery and the raspberry patch had never looked more richly green), he talked to her about horses in the books he read. She owed him, if not her life, then her living. Paras thought she might like to chat with Raoul about her conflicting feelings — he would certainly have something to say, and even if it wasn't relevant or helpful, the sound of his cawing would be soothing. But it was spring; he wasn't making much progress on his new nest in the nearby plane tree — he was off doing ravenish things, whatever they were. Paras was happy, but her happiness felt like a scarf of morning mist floating above her, ready to blow away any minute.

Raoul had been seized by a desire for one last circuit. He had enjoyed visiting with his cousin Liam Corax Corvus, who lived in the Jardin des Plantes, so he flew there again, but though Liam was welcoming, the garden was as tame as could be. He longed for something more, one last adventure. Out to Vincennes was the obvious alternative, but just when he was almost there, just when he recognized his youthful haunts, he veered around and headed west. He flew and flew and flew — a long way for an old bird whose idea of a voyage was from the Place du Trocadéro to Montmartre, but he rather gloried in his power, the way he once had, at least until the very end, when he came to a screeching, plummeting, aching halt, and landed, pretty wobbly, in the middle of the training track at Maisons-Laffitte, gasping for air and stumbling across the sand, even as a large black horse galloped toward him. He closed his eyes, didn't move — and the horse galloped on. He heard the rider exclaim, *"Mon Dieu!,"* and, with the last of his strength, he hopped up to the limb of a slender little tree and sat there, his wings trembling, wishing only for a drink, maybe his ultimate drink, of water. Some ravens, ones he didn't recognize, gathered across the horse track, on a wire between two poles, but he could hardly lift his head, and so they chose to ignore him.

When Delphine got back to the barn, she told Rania what had happened — a raven had fallen out of the sky right in front of them, had not moved. Whiskey Shot, the English-bred three-year-old she was riding, galloped right over the bird without even flicking his ears, didn't touch him, maybe didn't notice him. Then they chatted about how you might think that birds would be falling out of the sky on a regular basis, but no one ever saw such a thing — it was peculiar. Whiskey was a bold horse, their great hope — entered in the Poule d'Essai des Poulains at Longchamp, the first horse Delphine had ever entered in a Group One race. And he was young, had turned three in April. He had plenty of growing to do.

Raoul sat for a long time in that small tree — long enough for the other ravens to finish one squabble and begin another. He found a puddle underneath a spigot on the edge of the course. He drank some (sandy) and paddled his feet around in it, refreshing himself a little bit. He was not quite sure where he was, but the ravens would tell him (while commenting on his ignorance) once he was revived enough to approach them. That was for later. For now, he flew back into the small tree, settled himself in the fork of one of the branches, and took the opportunity to survey the landscape. There were plenty of trees, and so there were many more Aves and of greater variety than he was familiar with in Paris. And they were all fat, especially the sparrows, the bee-eaters, the finches, the swallows swooping here and there. Wood pigeons, magpies, lapwings, even a furtive pheasant or two — never saw those in the Champ de Mars. He could see the outline of the head of a baby owl in a nearby tree, and then another one appeared beside it, peeping out. The mother would be nearby. Otherwise, there were horses everywhere. Several shot past him, but others came along more slowly, their riders curled on their necks. The horses progressed along several routes, not only the dirt track where he had landed. Some stood quietly with their riders, here and there, watching. He saw plenty of dogs, too, though attached to humans, not running free like Frida. And there were cats in the shadows. The world was full of cats — every Avis knew that. He could see a pair of them from this tree, gray and white, sliding around in the ragged grass. He adjusted his wings. He was beginning to feel stronger, and also rather proud of himself for making the trip.

He must have dozed off. When he woke up, he was thirsty again, so he flew down to the spigot, took another drink, investigated for and found an ant colony. And there was the carcass of a rabbit, a fair amount of dried meat on the bones, plus the tang of maggots and a most delicious carrion beetle. He was just pecking around for a few bits when shadows gathered above him, and a flock of something big landed in a pond on the other side of a small hill. Oh, mallards.

He flew to the crest of the hill and looked down. It was a small group of drakes, well colored, fit, and sleek, homeward-bound, Raoul suspected. It was that time of year.

Just as Raoul was eavesdropping on their conversation about how far they had flown altogether — it was farther than last year, and, yes, that landscape off to the northwest there was an interesting one, an exceptional gathering place if you wanted to meet Aves from all over the world, but was it really worth going there, over so much ocean, and with the storms — if you went northeast, though, there were plenty of Aves from odd places — one of them said, "A little closer to home is better for me. I don't like to stay away longer than I have to," and all of the others squawked in mild skepticism, and then the mallard turned his head and stared at Raoul. Moments later, he stepped out of the water and strode up the hill, meep-meeping quietly: How are you, good heavens, what are you doing here, that can't be you. Raoul was hard put to maintain his superior demeanor — embarrassingly, it was Sid who had recognized him, not the other way around. But this drake was not the Sid Raoul thought he knew, the screaming, panicked fellow who preened until half of his feathers were plucked. This Sid was easygoing and good-humored, a comfortable member of his cohort.

Sid seemed to be happy to see him. How are they? How many are there? I didn't want to stop here, I just wanted to get home, is she okay, have any been taken, I hope not.

Raoul arranged himself as best he could, and said, "Sid, your offspring are too numerous to count, perfectly healthy as far as I can see, and awaiting your return." Sid glanced back at the other mallards and sighed, then settled down beside Raoul. He said, "I think it will be a wonderful summer. I've gotten a lot of counseling this trip. I feel more in control and better prepared for the chaos. I am up to the challenge."

"I'm sure Nancy will be overjoyed to see you."

"Every summer is a new beginning, that's what I've learned. I don't have to carry the past with me. My approach to the dangers of reproduction is my choice. I am in charge of who I am and how I view things. I own my fears."

"That's a wise —"

"I've had my eyes opened. We had many group discussions as we were migrating, and I was given to realize that certain experiences I had as a duckling have had a strong impact on my worldview, especially the death of Male No. 3, who was just above me in the nest, taken by a hawk right out of the middle of the group, and then the hawk, instead of flying away, swooped around us the whole time my mother was hurrying us to shelter. I mean, this is not an unusual experience for mallards, but I think that I must be especially sensitive, which is nothing to be ashamed of. This autumn alone, humans shot two of our flock right out of the sky as we were flying over Marmande. Did we stop? Did we panic? No, we bade them adieu and flew onward. But I've come to understand the effect of duckling experiences much more thoroughly now, and also to understand fate. Fate is simply fate — you are here or you are not. You have to yield to the nature of the cosmos."

"Very true," said Raoul.

"I'm glad we've had this talk," said Sid.

"Yes," said Raoul.

"By the way," said Sid, "you should explore this area. If I thought I could get Nancy away from that pond by the tower, I would bring her here. It's very lively."

"I hardly know how I got here," said Raoul. "I usually go east."

"As the raven flies," said Sid, "it's forty-five degrees southeast, about an hour's flight if you aren't in a rush."

"I'm not in a rush," said Raoul, stretching his wings.

"You can go with me. We are taking off in a bit. I leave the group at Nanterre. They are all from around Le Chesnay. They live in the country. Very sane compared with us Parisians."

Raoul wondered what those ravens he had seen would think of a *Corvus* of his stature flying off with a pack of lowly mallards, but then he said, "Yes, I think I will go along with you."

Sid said, "Happy to have you, believe me. I'll explain who you are. Everyone's eager to get home. You might want to keep your opinions to yourself, however. Just a suggestion."

Raoul cawed softly, then said, "I understand."

All of the mallards were young, healthy, and well traveled. They were, of course, *Anas platyrhynchos,* so their conversation (to which Raoul did not contribute) was about feats of strength or endurance — what regions they had visited, where they planned to visit in the future. They all had mates, but everyone except Sid chatted easily about other females they had gotten to know, offspring they suspected they had in various far-flung districts. Raoul felt that it was not his task to judge. Every Avis knew that mallards had their place in the avian world, and in many ways, their place was as game. Sure enough, Sid knew exactly where Nanterre was. He was flying with the group, and then, without even looking around, or down, he lifted his right wing and tilted away from the others. Raoul followed him. When they were floating smoothly above the Paris suburbs, he said, "How do you do that?"

"Just pay attention to the signs, is all."

"The signs?"

"You know, the magnetic grid. There's a little interference around here, but not much. My first time coming home, a few years ago, I ended up in Orléans for the night, but haven't made a mistake since. You get more sensitive with practice. You ravens . . . ?" After a moment, Raoul said, "*Corvus* are more locally oriented, I guess you would say."

Sid made his little meep-meep noise, and they flew on. They were at the Tour by late afternoon. Raoul landed on one of its rungs and watched Sid hit the water, swim in a circle, and then head toward the nest. One by one, the ducklings popped up; then they formed a group, and Nancy, her wings lifted and her neck arched, herded them toward

their sire. She was quacking like mad —
Here he is, don't be shy, close up on the
right there, go on, move on, quack-quack-
quack. Sid did not come out of the water,
but swam quietly in circles, and one by one,
the little brown birdlets came to the edge
and launched themselves toward him. Pretty
soon, the whole family was swimming
around that end of the pond, and the
humans below Raoul were exclaiming and
cooing at the sight. If Raoul had ever seen a
human who didn't turn to mush at the sight
of a baby animal, he couldn't remember
when that was. Nancy's loud quacking
subsided, and everyone swam in peace.

How long had Raoul been away? Since
sunrise, maybe. Not much of a circuit. (He
had to admit that, in spite of himself, he
was impressed by the grandness of the
mallards' journey — to a place where bar-
ren mountains stretched from sea to sea,
and steam rose right out of the ground,
where daylight gave way to almost no darkness, and they met Aves that had traveled
from places ravens did not know existed.)
Yes, the mallards had met the legendary
Sterna paradisaea, white Aves with black
heads, who cared for nowhere on Earth
except the farthest north and the farthest
south. Most *Corvus* pooh-poohed their exis-

291

tence. Could it be possible, thought Raoul, that *Corvi* did not know what they were talking about? Raoul sighed, lifted off the tower, and headed toward the Rue Marinoni.

Madame de Mornay had missed May Day. Her mother had loved May Day, every year had made for Madame (in those days, Mademoiselle Éveline, of course), with her own hands, a little sachet of flowers. At any rate, when she was a child, she and her mother and brother had celebrated by eating only what they most enjoyed, whatever it was — it could be foie gras and meringues or it could be champagne and morels sautéed in butter, it could be lime sorbet and a wedge of goat cheese. Whatever appealed to them on that very day was what they ate their fill of. And so, one morning, though she could not say what day it was, when she opened her window, even she could smell that her lilacs were in bloom, that the scent was like a mist, entering and filling up the room. Invigorating. And so she found the trolley, and when she came upon Étienne, who was sweeping the corridor between the grand salon and the *cuisine,* she put her arm around him and suggested they go to the market. Since his great-grandmama had not seemed well or happy in weeks, Étienne at once put away his broom, took hold of the trolley, and guided Madame out the door, leaving it open so that Paras could go outside when she had finished her breakfast. He hoped very much that the raven, who was sitting on the horse's haunches in the *cuisine,* and Kurt, who was sitting on a shelf above the basin, would exit with her. He liked them, but they were becoming unmanageable.

Usually, Étienne walked slowly, sometimes very slowly, and Madame de Mornay tottered along behind him, Frida on the alert. Étienne didn't know whether Madame was curious about Frida — she never alluded to her or asked about her, but when her hand went out, flailing a bit, and Frida stepped up and pressed against her leg to steady her, Madame understood what was happening, and accepted the assistance. Today, though, Étienne had to exert himself to stay ahead of his great-grandmama, she was walking so fast. When they got to the vegetable market, the first thing she did was take Jérôme's hand and give it a good squeeze. But she was difficult to please — Jérôme showed her the best new peas, the best baby artichokes, the best bouquets of basil, new potatoes, watercress. She touched it, she smelled it, she shook her head. Perhaps a little frustrated, she went to the flowers, and chose two pots of sweet William, already in bloom. Étienne recognized them — they'd been in the garden, but not for a couple of years. She came back to the vegetables. She stood in the middle of the shop, her hands lifted and her eyes closed. Jérôme and two other customers gazed at her in a kindly manner, but Étienne was a little worried — he had never seen her do this before. Finally, she stepped forward and let her hands drop, and there was the asparagus, a mound of slender stalks. She smiled, took two handfuls. She gave Jérôme the money and refused the change. Jérôme laughed and slipped it to Étienne. Now the meat market. Suzanne, the meat seller, was not as good-natured as Jérôme, but today she was patient, only staring at Frida for a moment, and stepping back as Madame entered the shop. Madame, of course, couldn't touch anything, but she walked along the length of the counter, whispering to Étienne — chicken, filet mignon, sausage, veal, pork chops, lamb. She could not decide. Alise waited, tapping her pack of cigarettes with her fingertips. Étienne hoped that his great-grandmama would not choose something so exotic that he couldn't manage to prepare it. Finally, she said, "Some confit! Ah, that would be very good."

Alise handed her one of her own concoctions — a cassoulet in a jar. She even opened the jar for Madame and let her smell it. Madame said, "Ah, yes! Perfect!" She closed the jar with her trembling hand, placed it carefully in the trolley, and handed Suzanne the money. On the way home, they bought a strawberry tart. Étienne could tell she was excited. At home, she still seemed restless — no afternoon nap, insistence upon being taken for a walk around the front courtyard (where Étienne planted the sweet William and Paras stayed out of the way). While Étienne prepared the asparagus, Madame sat in her chair with her giant afghan on her lap, fingering the patterns she had created and the seams between the sections. She insisted that they eat in the dining room rather than the *cuisine.* She sat quietly in her old chair while Étienne set the table, carried in the asparagus, warmed up the cassoulet. When they were full and could eat no more, he brought in the tart and set it before her. She took a spoon and ate the strawberries one by one off the surface of the tart, then a few bites of the custard. All of this as if it were the greatest indulgence she had ever known. She said, "Ah, you are a good good good boy." Then she drank her nightly cup of mint tea (the mint in the garden was doing as well this year as everything else — sharp-flavored and richly green). She said, "May Day is a day of marvelous pleasure." And then she sighed, because she still had not solved the puzzle of what to do about Étienne. She went into her room and fell asleep before the sun dipped below the courtyard fence.

SIXTEEN

Of course Paras does not "talk" to Étienne — none of the animals talks to Étienne — but Paras does make her wishes known, and one morning a few days after Madame's feast, Étienne wakes up very early, when the world is still absolutely dark, and he cannot go back to sleep. When he looks out his window at the horse, she is standing, staring upward at him. He puts on his clothes and goes to her silently. When he gets there, he sees that Frida is asleep, and the raven, too, is quiet in his nest. There is a bright, silent moon — that is all. Paras sidles up to the sixth step. Étienne slides his leg over her back, wraps his hands in her thick mane, and settles himself. He is as wide awake as he has ever been. Paras walks out the gate.

Toward the Avenue de la Bourdonnais, there are a few wan lights, but no cars, no activity. Toward the Champ de Mars, there is nothing. The trees, which seem short and

297

orderly during the day, now seem to muffle everything — light, sound, activity. Étienne can feel Paras's walk speed up — longer strides, quicker rhythm. His hips shift back and forth. She turns right, down the dark allée between the row of trees and the row of fences that hide the houses. Her walk speeds up again, and then they are doing it, the very thing that he has read about so many times: they are cantering. He tightens his grip on her mane, tightens his legs around her sides, but her movement is light and smooth, rocking gently forward, gently backward. The sharpest thing about it is the cool air in his face, his hair blowing upward. Paras makes a noise with each smooth leap, a ruffling sound out of her nostrils, one-one-one-one. It is comforting and dreamy, as if she is counting. They come to the end of the allée and loop around the Tour and the ponds and the fences, passing the dark, still vans belonging to the vendors, passing the lights of the Tour beaming onto the empty dirt, rounding the trees. They then proceed (it now feels almost like a ritual movement, this graceful rocking) up the allée that parallels the Avenue de Suffren, a street Étienne has never explored — too far for his great-grandmama to walk. Halfway up that allée, Paras slows, first to a jerky gait that dislodges him, then to her regular walk. Étienne takes a deep breath, shakes his head. He unclenches his fists, strokes her on the neck underneath her mane. Paras, too, takes a deep breath, and tosses her head, obviously pleased with herself. They walk along. Behind the great building at the far end of the Champ, just the thinnest string of brightness appears. Étienne does not want to get caught, but he leaves everything to Paras. She wends her way back to the house. As she enters the gate, Étienne sees the headlights of a car on the Avenue de la Bourdonnais. Once he dismounts, he is careful to close the gate, so that they are back inside their leafy sanctuary, quiet. Étienne discovers that he is so tired from his exciting adventure that he falls asleep in the grand salon, stretched out under one of his great-grandmama's ancient coverlets. He doesn't even wake up when Kurt runs across his body two times. Kurt gives up, goes into the *cuisine*, helps himself to grated carrots and a few croutons that have fallen on the floor. Kurt is wide awake, but, indeed, he seems to be the only one. The windows brighten.

It was Conrad who discovered that the old lady had vanished. Oh, yes, her husk was still present in the bedroom, neatly covered so that only her nose was visible. Conrad hadn't intended to discover this — he had never skittered over the old lady, or any human, before. But the bed was so flat, and the room so empty of energy, that he thought she was in the grand salon, and so he planned to check her night table, where there was often a crust of something. When he saw the nose, Conrad squeaked in surprise, but the nose emphatically did not twitch. He crept up to it. It gave off no vapors. He touched the tip of it with his own nose. It was cold and hard. Conrad sat back on his haunches and curled his little fists against his belly. He stared at her and was silent, which seemed appropriate.

Nevertheless, Kurt had to be told, and so Conrad finished his foraging, then entered the tunnel. Although the tunnel was his home, it seemed a little darker than the old lady's room, darker than he was used to its being, darker, colder, a bit narrow. He could feel the top of the tunnel, and the sides pressed against him as he ran, almost squeezing him. He did not know how old the old lady was, or how old a human could get to be. Every rat in his family had known the old lady more or less intimately. She predated every story he'd ever been told.

Some rats said that humans were immortal, but other rats said that this was impossible — all you had to do was receive their broadcast and sense how they varied in order to understand that immortality was unlikely. Conrad stopped, flicked his whiskers. He heard Kurt's characteristic squeak, ran again, and popped out in that room where the books were. Kurt was sitting on the windowsill, looking out at the horse. Conrad joined him without saying anything. The horse and the dog were still sleeping, even though it was full day. The raven was perched on the greenery that flowed all around the courtyard, picking at something with his beak. Finally, Conrad said, "Remember that talk we had about broadcasts?"

"Which one?" said Kurt. "You talk about that all the time."

"Do I?" said Conrad. "I don't mean to repeat myself."

"If we got out a little more, I think we might have more to talk about," said Kurt.

After a long moment, Conrad said, "Son, you are right. You are exactly right. And the fact is, everything is different now." Kurt's head spun toward him, and he nodded. Then he said, "Every rat has a different theory about human power and mortality, but we all agree on one thing, and that is that when a human vanishes a rat's world turns upside down."

In the meantime, Étienne slept on, and the house grew so quiet that when the gendarme passed it on his morning round, he looked at it twice, so still and cold did it seem, right here, today, in the brilliant warmth of the green spring.

It was Frida who woke Étienne up, barking like mad in the courtyard. Paras lifted her head and said, "Why are you making that awful noise?"

Frida paused and said, "I don't know," and resumed barking.

Paras hoisted herself to her feet, walked over to Frida, and stood over her. She pinned her ears, narrowed her eyes, and switched her tail in a threatening manner, but it was evident that Frida didn't know horse body language, because she just kept barking. At last, and with some misgivings, Paras bumped Frida with her knees and knocked her over. There was silence.

Paras said, "What is going on?"

"Everyone needs to know."

"To know what?"

"I don't know. Something. Something important. Whatever it is, it is making my skin tingle and my hair curl."

"Your hair isn't curling."

"That's what it feels like." She rolled energetically in the grass, twisting her body this way and that; then she rolled onto her stomach and put her paws over her ears. At last, she said, "I felt this before, but I didn't know what it was. Now maybe I do. It was when my human vanished."

Paras looked up at the window. There was Étienne, staring at her. She said, "The boy is fine."

Frida blew out a long breath.

Thanks to the barking, Étienne was wide awake, but a little disoriented. Why was he sleeping in the grand salon? What time was it? Where was his great-grandmama? What was for breakfast? He staggered a little as he went toward the *cuisine*, thinking that the answers might be there, and the staggering reminded him of his nighttime adventure, cantering around the Champ de Mars in a dream. This had the effect of making him feel more rather than less disoriented. It wasn't until he had scarfed down a piece of bread, some cheese, and a large glass of water that he felt like himself. At that point, he yawned and cleaned up the *cuisine* as best he could — just the day before, his great-grandmama had run her hand along the top of the table and made a sad face.

Not a scowl — she was not angry — but it was clear that, distracted as he was by the horse, he was doing a poor job of maintaining the house. Kurt could have told him that his own distraction had resulted in his complementary failure in waste management, but Étienne had never known how great a contribution to his efforts Kurt had made.

Only after wiping the table, rinsing the sink, sweeping the floor, and closing all of the drawers and cabinet doors did Étienne bring his attention fully to the old lady. He thought that she had to be somewhere — perhaps, given her energy when they went to the shops again just the day before, she had gotten dressed and left the house! And so he hurried out of the *cuisine,* through the grand salon, across the hallway. He knocked, even though she would not be able to hear him, and then put his hand on the door to her chamber, eased it open. The room was quiet. Like Conrad, he at first didn't see her — she *had* gone out! But no — her hat with the feather was in its customary spot. Then he did see her. Her covers, including the great coverlet she'd been knitting, were drawn up over her chin, with her pillow hiding her forehead. He stared at her for a long time, and then he crept toward the bed. After a moment, he slipped his own hand under the covers and found hers. He squeezed it. It was small and cool and stiff. The day had come, Étienne thought, the day when he no longer knew what to do, down to the least little thing.

Jérôme, at the market, also felt uneasy for some reason. He found himself stepping out into the street without meaning to, looking left, looking right, making himself go back into the shop, only to step out into the street moments later.

Anaïs, in her apartment, was brewing herself a cup of tea. She poured the boiling water right onto her hand, cried out, put her hand under the cold tap, and started to weep. Anaïs hadn't wept in years, she thought; as for burning herself, she did that all the time, but this time was different, somehow.

Pierre, who still had his earplugs in from his morning operating the leaf blower, stepped out of the equipment shed and saw dark clouds to the north — unexpected, because the forecast had been for days of sunshine. He went back into the shed, felt a chilling breeze, found a jacket. When he'd finished hanging up his tools and making the signs he had to redo every year to remind his crew where to put things, he went back outside. Brilliant sunshine. Unaccountable, really.

The gendarme made up his mind to consult his superior officer about that house. There was something funny about the place, and the gendarmerie needed to look into it. He knocked on the office door, then knocked again. Another officer went by, told him that the boss was in Nanterre for the afternoon. Whatever it was would have to wait until tomorrow, but tomorrow was his day off. Okay, he could wait two days.

Frida was not barking anymore. She was lying quietly in her dip, silent, not even mumbling, almost invisible under the vegetation.

Paras continued to sample the grass and weeds. She knew that Frida thought she was insensitive or indifferent. She wasn't. She was preparing herself.

Raoul knew exactly what was going on. He stood on the sill of the old lady's window, tapping. He could see that she had passed, and he knew that it was the animals who had to save the boy.

Delphine felt nothing special, apart from the anxiety she always experienced before a big race. Since she trained horses for both jump races and flat races, her worries were different for each. When she put a horse in a race over the hurdles or the jumps, she imagined the horse falling more than anything else. Now she stood, leaning on Whiskey Shot's stall door, watching him gobble down his hay. He was a flat racer, less likely to fall, especially since the ground was dry and firm. But was he too fat? Was he too tall for his age? Would the jockey be able to control him? He liked to come from behind, always a hazardous strategy. If they bunched in front of him, would he try to barrel through the pack, putting himself and everyone else at risk? Delphine wiped the sweat off her forehead with the sleeve of her shirt.

Because Étienne didn't know what to do, he did what he knew he should have done before this, which was to clean, clean, clean, first the *cuisine,* then the grand salon, then the library. He put away, he threw away, he wiped down, he swept, he straightened. In his great-grandmama's chamber, it soothed him to walk around her, picking up this and that, placing her cherished possessions exactly as she would wish them to be if she were, indeed, a ghost (she had never said anything about ghosts, but there were ghosts in books, just as there were horses in books

307

— a horse had shown up, so perhaps a ghost would also show up). Several times, he went to her and kissed her on the forehead. He made very little noise, because he did not have a vacuum cleaner, and so the gendarme, who altered his route in order to peek through the fence with all of its vegetation and to listen for telltale noises, could make out nothing. Yes, a raven was tapping on a windowpane, up on the first floor — that was unusual, but it was not against the law, or even a matter for Animal Control. He had other things to do until his shift ended, but he thought he might come back, even though tomorrow was his day off. He could explore a little more aggressively — not in his uniform, but as an interested private citizen.

As Étienne made order in his great-grandmama's chamber, he got more comfortable with what most books would have called the *cadavre* or the *restes humains*. He did not know what he should call it, but both of these terms seemed too final. He glanced out the window. Paras, Frida, and the raven were standing together, as if they were conversing.

Étienne couldn't hear them, but Frida said, "Where can we possibly take him? We'll be captured!"

308

Raoul said, "My relative Liam Corvus Cor—" But then he tossed his head and shut up.

Paras said, "I have an idea."

Perhaps, Étienne thought, he should go to the church and find the curé, but Étienne knew that as soon as he let the curé, and whoever else, into the house, they would take him and his great-grandmama out of it. He needed one last night with her, one last night in his own room, in his own library, in his own *cuisine*. Having made up his mind, he went down into the cellar and began sorting through the vegetables and other things stored there. At suppertime, he came back up with a bowl of some very nice beets and carrots, some oats, and the last of the apples, now wrinkled, but fragrant and firm. For himself, he put some cheese and dried fruits on the table, and in honor of his great-grandmama, he set a bowl of walnuts and a peeled orange in front of her chair. His great-grandmama had always been very fond of walnuts. He ate properly, as if she were with him, thinking of how good she had been, but also how interesting she had been. Then he went to the front door and opened it. The animals were still standing together.

The sun had gone down, and the only lamp Étienne turned on was a single wan bulb in the grand salon. Because of his great-grandmama's poor eyesight, he was in the habit of turning on only the lights he needed for reading or thinking or helping her go about the place (not that, after so many years, she needed much help). But now, sitting beside the table, holding his book on his lap, and looking around, he began to cry for the first time. That was when he knew that she was dead, that, underneath all of the silence, there was no longer the even "sshh" of her breaths. From where he was sitting, he could see the shadowy emptiness of her yarn basket, like a hole in the ground, a drain to nowhere. Now fear began to infuse his sadness. He wondered whether elsewhere in Paris there were eight-year-olds sitting quietly by themselves, with no one anywhere nearby. Yes, her corpus was in her room — and what would he do with that? — but, truly, she was gone, alive only in his memory of her care and her good humor. He could hear himself sniffling, feel the tears running. He put his face in his hands.

First to appear, but not from outside, was Kurt, his nose twitching in the rush of evening air. He emerged from his hole

(Étienne could hear him better than he could see him), zipped across the carpet, and crouched beside Étienne's right foot. Étienne took his hands away from his face and looked down. He leaned forward, cupped his hands. Kurt stepped into them. Étienne straightened up, placed the rat on his knee. The next to appear was the raven, who came in the usual door, cawing. His cawing sounded very specific, but only Kurt knew that he was saying, "Well, at last! In circumstances like these, and believe me, Aves understand the ins and outs and ups and downs of death perhaps better than any other class of Chordata . . ." He fell silent. And here came Paras, not through her usual door, but through the big door, the door that required her to mount ten steps to the great portico. She whinnied a few things to Raoul, and then came to where Étienne was sitting, snuffled his hair, and put her chin gently on his shoulder. Her warmth spread out around him. He put his hand in the silky spot under her mane.

And now, at last, after so many months, here came Frida in through the small door, her tail down, her ears down, half slinking, a sad but determined look on her face. She looked exactly the way Étienne felt. She came all the way to him, and stood, trem-

311

bling slightly, as Étienne petted her on her silky head. She mumbled a few things, the raven cawed, the rat squeaked, and Paras nickered gently. Étienne knew that they were talking to him, though not in his language, and he felt comforted. One by one, they settled in — the raven in his great-grandmama's empty yarn basket, Kurt in the corner of the sofa, Paras in her usual spot in front of the windows, and Frida right there, right at his feet, her lovely head resting on her paws. Very soon, there was quite a bit of snoring, which Étienne found so soothing that he, too, put his head back and fell asleep.

Sometime later, Paras woke up, levered herself to her feet, and went into the *cuisine*, where she turned on the spigot and had a drink of water, then finished the last of the supper. It was that time of night, the deepest deepest dark, when she customarily went out into the Champ de Mars. The doors were open, and she could come and go as she pleased, but when she came back into the grand salon, she went over to the boy and poked him with her nose. He woke up at once. Frida woke up. Raoul flew up and perched on Paras's croup, and Kurt scrambled to the back of the sofa. Étienne understood that they had a plan.

Étienne now remembered his outing of the night before, the pleasure of it. If the horse wanted to do that one last time, Étienne was all for it, and, indeed, he suddenly felt that he had to get out of this house. Paras placed herself next to the sofa and put her head down. The rat pulled himself up her mane and settled just behind her ears. Étienne followed them out the smaller door. Frida was at his heels. Paras waited while he opened the gate, and then they walked around to the staircase, and he climbed to the sixth step. She positioned herself. He put his leg over her back and hopped on, entwining his hands in her mane. The rat hadn't gone with them the previous night, but he looked eager. Frida was mumbling. The raven continued to sit on Paras's haunches until they were out of the gate, and then he rose gently on the breeze and stayed a few meters in front of them, only lifting and lowering his wings a little bit, swaying from side to side.

The horse walked down the allée, loosening up, relaxing, and then she eased into that canter again, and there they were, swaying and leaping, almost airborne, the trees passing them on the left, ping-ping-ping. At the pond, Paras slowed to a walk. The farther they went, the more Étienne wanted to keep going, the more it felt like escape rather than pleasure. Now they were in front of the Tour, just outside its circle of light. Paras's walk was energetic. Frida trotted beside her. The rat made little squeaking noises, but he was sitting up straight, his tiny ears pricked, as if he was as interested in where they were going as Étienne was.

Paras paused. The raven landed on the fence. They waited. A large truck went by, and then it was so quiet that Étienne could hear the river bubbling and lapping against the embankment, and after that they were walking across the Pont d'Iéna. They passed the carousel, turned left, and headed up the dark path beside the great building, and every single step was into somewhere that Étienne, native Parisian, had never been before.

Paras was not normally of a philosophical turn of mind, but she was surprised at how natural this was, how easy, really. This was nothing compared to a workout around the dirt track at Maisons-Laffitte. So far, this was a sprint, hardly enough to cause a stayer like Paras to breathe hard. Why had she waited so long? That was the price of indecision, wasn't it? And yet it was also the price of freedom. Although she now felt herself responsible for Étienne, as well as drawn back to Delphine and that former life of fitness and purpose, she understood that her days of doing what she pleased when she was pleased to do it were behind her. As she climbed the path, she drew in many deep breaths, not because she was winded, but because she loved the air, the smell of spring, of grass, of plants and flowers and dirt, so different from the smell of oncoming winter and dead leaves from the last time she was here. She could feel the boy swaying as she walked, his legs relaxed, his body never moving out of plumb. He was, as Delphine would have said, a natural. And he was her responsibility now. Well, she didn't mind that. She was four years old, a mare — mares took responsibility for almost everything groups of horses might do.

Ahead of her, Raoul flew from tree to tree. He seemed to have nothing to say. Just for a moment, Paras regretted not having paused to say goodbye to Sid and Nancy. They would have been sleeping, but saying some last word was the friendly thing to do. She continued to climb, the dark bulk of the huge building warm and protective. And now there was the gate, the gate Frida had opened all those months ago. She halted. Frida stepped forward, got up on her hind legs, and opened the gate again. They went through. It was still darkest dark, and the Place du Trocadéro was empty. All the shops were lightless, the huge buildings were solid black, and that strange horse still stood up there in the sky, unmoving. Paras looked around. She could smell the forest, but how to get there was a bit confusing.

Raoul did not mean to be preoccupied with his own petty concerns — he had re-entered his former territory, and there was cawing, some of it on the order of "Oh, heavens, I thought you were dead!," some of it on the order of "You need to watch your step!" He did not think there would be a mobbing, but you never knew. At least, it was less likely in the dark like this, in the spring, with nestlings everywhere. Even so, he perched not far from the horse, not far from Frida.

For her part, Frida also felt the gravity of returning to the Place du Trocadéro. She hadn't seen the Pâtisserie Carette since her last sad meal. She could feel a train rumbling beneath her feet, which reminded her of those terrifying times in the Métro and where her hiding spot had been, behind the café, small and gritty. And up the avenue there, the one that ran not far from the river, was where Jacques had sat down one

316

morning, played his instrument for a while, and then lain back, never to get up again.

Only Kurt was living in the present moment, and in the present moment Kurt saw cats, crouching here, sitting there, hiding everywhere. He squeaked and squeaked again. A cat crossed the street; a cat went behind a bush in the green area. Kurt dug all of his claws in even deeper, and just then, Paras ruffled her nostrils and Raoul and Frida shook off their blues and headed north of the cemetery, down a lovely avenue lined with dead cars, fluttering trees, and many buildings enclosing many sleeping humans, just the sort of outing Paras enjoyed. Her hooves clopped neatly on the pavement, tock-tock-tock-tock, big walking strides. Here and there birds flew up around them and a fox peeked out at them, but Paras moved along, Étienne's fingers in her mane, his heels tapping her rhythmically. With every step, she could smell the turf and the leaves, hectares of greenery.

Étienne had not intended to get so far from his great-grandmama. He felt his thoughts about her getting no less sad, but thinning out among his other thoughts, his pleasure in this adventure, his curiosity about where they were headed, his sense of being surrounded by these friends. He, too, smelled a difference in the air, sensed a difference in himself, in his attachment to the horse. He knew every move she was about to make as she made it — his own back and legs connected with her back and legs. It was hypnotic. He was watching the scenery go by, noting lights in windows here and there, but all of that seemed unimportant compared with this tock-tock-tock-tock.

All Kurt cared about, since he was so strong now, was that they seemed to have left the cats behind.

And now they were into the woods. The turf beneath Paras's hooves was springy and green. Frida took off at a run, disappeared, must have looped around, returned with Raoul not far behind. Her ears were up. Raoul was talking about some nearby statue, of his very own ancestor Raoul Corvus Corax, the thirteenth of that name, cawing, cawing, and then he shouted to Frida, "I can't believe you never saw a rabbit before!" Frida barked, "It's a hare!," then put her nose to the earth and trailed the scent into the trees, as if in ecstasy. Paras followed after her, newly relaxed. They went deeper into the greenery.

318

SEVENTEEN

The gendarme had a nice breakfast, as he always did on his day off — a mushroom omelette, two pieces of nine-grain toast, a dish of strawberries, two cups of coffee, then a medicinal slug of aged Cognac. After that he performed a few other Saturday rituals — filing his nails, scraping his tongue, trimming his nose hairs. At last, he went to his closet and chose his outfit for the day, something uniform-like, but not a uniform. He spent five minutes choosing his shoes: he had a new pair that were very elegant, but a little stiff. He went back and forth, eventually opted for comfort over vanity.

Delphine, too, was getting dressed. All of the important decisions were over — the jockey, the training regimen, whether to enter Whiskey Shot in a race with so many other well-bred horses, whether to scratch him just out of sheer anxiety — all done. All she had to do now was choose a sweater

319

— she had two worthy ones, a green Hermès and a blue Alexander McQueen. The question was not which one looked more flattering, but which one was luckier. She stared at them as the sunlight brightened through the window.

It was a beautiful morning in the Champ de Mars — perhaps, in terms of the plantings and the fixtures, the peak day of the year. Pierre and his workmen had all of the grass trimmed, all of the flowers weeded, all of the allées raked, all of the fountains spraying sparkling streams in the air. They might as well have polished the Tour itself, because it rose brilliantly into the sky, as gleaming as the day when construction was completed and it stood as the gate to the 1889 World's Fair. Even the ducks and ducklings in the ponds looked as though they had been personally groomed by duck-grooming specialists. The tourists and runners and strollers and dog walkers parading along were well turned out, too. Pierre still had some work to do — sorting autumn bulbs — but he chose to stroll around and enjoy the fruits of his labors. When he first noticed the emergency vehicle on the Rue Marinoni, he didn't think much of it, but after he turned around and headed back toward his shed area, he got more curious;

the emergency vehicle was still there, more people had arrived, and a police car as well. He went around that corner where the shrubbery was so thick, and saw that the gate was ajar, and so he peeked in.

A door opened, and two men, supervised by a third, emerged, carrying a stretcher. They didn't seem to be in a rush, and so Pierre deduced that the person in the stretcher was dead. He stepped backward, deeper into the courtyard, and of course he recognized the smell, the rich, sweet aroma of horse manure. He looked around. There was plenty of it, deposited in three spots, though a good deal had been distributed, as Pierre would have done, beneath the flourishing raspberry patch (Pierre plucked a few berries for himself — they were juicy and flavorful), along the roots of the shrubbery, and at the base of a row of ash trees, which were also vibrating with health. So this was where she lived, the whinnier. He walked around the larger courtyard, noticing the evidence — not only a mound of fresh manure, but well-cropped grass and weeds, a shallow depression where she must have been in the habit of rolling. As he was looking at this, he saw the tunnel underneath the fence, big enough for a large dog — the dog had lived here, too. He put his hands in his pockets, then went up the staircase to the grand entrance. The doors were wide open. He called out, "Hello?"

From deep within came an answering "Yes? Who are you?" And he recognized the fellow who popped out, not in uniform but, indeed, the gendarme who patrolled the local area. He said, "Good day, I am Pierre Duman. I am the caretaker in the Champ de Mars. What is going on here?"

"Ah well, the old lady seems to have died a while ago — one day at least. Most certainly died of old age, no sign of anything suspicious. How long she's lived here? Difficult to say." Then, "You may enter, but please don't touch anything. We have to treat it as a crime scene for the moment. You know these people, perhaps?"

Pierre said, "No, I don't know them," but he did step inside, and he did walk around, keeping his hands in his pockets. The place was like one of those museums in a small town, where the prominent families and the bureaucrats simply hoarded everything that could possibly be of interest, from an old coin found in a garden to the stuffed head of a gazelle that someone carried home from Africa a hundred years ago. There were paintings on the walls, but they were fogged with dust — impossible to say whether anything was of value. Books were piled on every table; the furniture that was uncovered was upholstered in frayed but ornate brocade. The place did not have the air of death or abandonment. When he looked down at the inlaid flooring, he saw the faintest print of a hoof. He bent down and touched it with his finger. It was still damp. He looked around, and saw another one, which he had missed, right beside the big door. Well, he thought, Paris beat all for strange goings-on, and who was he to deny that?

When he was walking back to his shed at last, turning these thoughts over in his mind, he nearly bumped into that young woman, that not-so-young woman, who did the baking at the café. What was her name? He looked into her blue eyes, and thought, "Anaïs," and smiled. She said, "Ah, hello, how are you this morning?" She seemed so pleasant and friendly that he turned and walked along with her, and told her about the house on the Rue Marinoni, the old lady and the antiquated interior, yes, but primarily the manure in the courtyard, the evidence of the horse, and Anaïs said, "I always wondered where she lived," and they started to compare recollections, all the way back to the late fall, when Pierre first noticed the horse's presence, and then about the feedings, and the raven, and the mysterious whinnies now and then, and Anaïs reminded him that she had hoped that perhaps the filly was the incarnation of some magical being, especially after seeing the raven walk along her spine, and Pierre said, "Too much manure," and Anaïs said, "She did have an appetite! She is an eating machine." And so they laughed, and each recognized that the other was both appealing and often in the neighborhood. But Pierre had to get back to work. He said, "You'd think she'd be easy to find, but she isn't."

They both shook their heads.

Rania put Whiskey Shot into his stall. He was behaving himself, but Rania knew that Whiskey knew that it was a big day. His ears were pricked, and he looked fervently at every passing horse, passing jockey, passing groom. This was his fourth race, first at Longchamp. He had two wins and a place. "He wouldn't know bad luck if he saw it," thought Rania, "and may Allah provide that things stay that way." Here came Delphine with the owners, a pleasant couple who bred a foal or two every year, but had bought Whiskey Shot at a sale in England upon Delphine's advice. They were very happy so far, as well they should be. The odds on him were 5–1, just where Rania was hoping they would stay. Rania was a smart bettor and had a nice wad of euros in her bag, which she was going to put right down on Whiskey's nose at the last minute. It was about an hour until post time.

In the woodland, Paras was the first to wake up. Étienne was leaning against her, as he had so often in the grand salon, and Frida was stretched out under a nearby tree, snoring. Kurt was under Paras's long, thick mane — she could feel the weight there. As soon as she woke up, he woke up. They had walked around for most of the early morning, exploring the woods. There were roads and plenty of buildings, but you could stay in the grassy parts, among the trees, away from the dead cars on one side and the speeding, lit-up vehicles on the other. At one point, they had followed a low fence, then entered a gate to get away from the road. After a while, they had been overtaken by the fatigue of their long night, and found a secluded spot among some weeds and trees. Now Paras snuffled her nose in the grass and ate a bite. It was rich and moist. She felt the boy come to life. He sat up, then stood up. He yawned. Frida continued to sleep.

Paras's ears were long, delicate, and sensitive. As she lay there, they flicked to the front, to the back, to the left, to the right. She could hear both high sounds and low sounds. The woodland was full of small scuttling animals, blowing leaves, creaking branches, calling birds; the city was nearby, and so she could also hear cars and trucks and the shouts of people. An airplane howled overhead. Humans walked past without noticing the wildlife, chatting with one another, rustling paper. They came and went, came and went. Underneath these sounds were some very low sounds that surged rather suddenly as a kind of pounding, half aural, half visceral. Paras knew what they were — they were the sounds of a field of horses racing around a track, many sounds melded into one sound, approaching, then receding. She felt her whiskers move, the hair on the edges of her ears prickle, her heavy mane and her tail lift slightly. She could not help herself. But she lay there and she waited for Étienne, and pretty soon he put his leg across her back. She stood up. At once, Frida was on her feet, her ears pricked, her nose in the air. Paras said, "Did you hear it?"

"Hear what?"

"The race. Galloping horses."

Frida looked at her and cocked her head.

No, she hadn't heard it.

Now Kurt emerged from under her mane and went to his usual spot between her ears. He squeaked a little.

She walked along. The race had nothing to do with her. All she thought was that she had not realized the track was so close. In her mind, her trek from Auteuil had taken forever, all night, sunset to sunrise, had covered miles and miles. She had felt as though she were pressing herself through a dense fog that pressed back, slowing her progress, draining her strength. She had stopped in the one green area, eaten some grass, gone on to the other green area, where Frida had found her. She had seemed to herself to have left one world and entered another. Since her journey always remained in her mind in this way, she was now a little disoriented by the nearness of that thumping sound. Still, the boy's heels tapped against her side, and his hands gripped her mane with trust and pleasure. Frida said, "Where are we going?," and then, "I wonder where Raoul is?" She lifted her nose. Paras would not answer the first question, and she could not answer the second one. She walked along.

Okay, she was curious. She was still a curious filly, although she was now a mare. It was perfectly understandable that a curious mare would be curious about her old friends, would enjoy seeing a horse that was not cold and inert at the top of a tower, would enjoy hearing some of the gossip — who was winning, who was in from the countryside, what they thought of her disappearance. Surely, they would enjoy hearing her adventures, too — horses liked to gossip.

They walked in the direction of the noise, and then came the sound of the crowd, rising and falling, the sound of a human voice pouring out into the air, naming names. There was a tall barrier — she could see through it, but it was above her head — and then they found a break in the barrier. Paras stepped through, and the others followed her. Now Raoul appeared, landed on her haunches. He said, "Ah! A contest!" The course ran away from them, vast and green, mowed, trimmed, leveled, springy, but no jumps. It did not look like the course where Paras had won her purse, the course she had cantered away from so blithely.

She heard the runners before she could see them, dark and chaotic in the distance, thundering toward her. She told herself they were flat runners, not her business. But still she kept shivering and soon she was stamping her feet. They came on, strung out, not bunched. It was early in the race — no one was trying hard, but they were stretching, nostrils flared. Paras snorted, lifted her head. Her tail went up. She remembered that the boy was there just as Frida said, "What is wrong with you?" She calmed herself, but they got closer, eating up the turf. No, she didn't recognize anyone, not really, but she recognized herself in them — not only in the bays, but also in the chestnuts, the two grays.

She snorted again, and Frida stood on her hind legs and pulled the boy off. He fell in a heap, and Paras leapt the railing — it was as low as could be — and as the field passed her, she joined it. Yes, the jockeys stared at her, but the horses just said, "Welcome!," and on she galloped, pacing herself by keeping up with one of the chestnuts — rangy, four white feet, decent stride. They were neck and neck. He was friendly. His jockey said, "Oh my God!," and then Paras pulled ahead. She had never run in the pack before, since she was a front-runner. After a moment, she was almost in the clear — only two horses ahead of her, and only the one pulling away. She ran neck and neck with the other one, a nice-looking brown, no markings. They sped up, lengthened their stride. The horse eyeballed her, trying to intimidate her, but she wasn't tired, since she wasn't carrying any weight at all. The other horse, a bay, pulled ahead by another length, and they were deep among the screaming humans, and then they crossed the finish line, and everyone except Paras slowed down right away. Paras kept going until she heard Kurt squeaking like mad. She had forgotten he was still in place. His paws were digging into her, and through her own panting she could hear his. Then he said, "I am going to die."

Paras said, "No, you aren't," and she turned around and trotted back to where everyone else was standing. She did so willingly; she didn't realize until she got there that the human saying, "God in heaven, God in heaven! It's her!," was Delphine. She was holding the bridle of the winner, and that horse's jockey was jumping to the ground, and then Delphine collapsed and Rania appeared and, what do you know, she came over and put her arms around Paras's neck and leaned against her and started crying. The giant human voice in the air said, "Something very strange seems to have happened as the horses were running! Ariane, can you provide us with any sort of an explanation?" And then there were humans everywhere, and some man was approaching Paras with a halter, and so she backed away, and trotted, then galloped to where Frida, Raoul, and the boy were still standing.

They could have gotten out, they should have gotten out, but no one, least of all Paras, remembered where the break in the tall barrier fence was, and so they were trapped, and so they were caught, and so, Paras thought, her fate was decided.

Jérôme was wrapping a half-dozen prunes in a sheet of newspaper, making small talk with his customer, and keeping his eye on the street for a particular old man who had walked past, who sometimes helped himself to the fruit. A few days before, he'd taken a handful of excellent strawberries — Jérôme had seen him eating them one by one as he ambled down the street. If the man were to simply ask, Jérôme would give him things — Paris was full of homeless people, and everyone knew someone who'd had a bad season or two, and there you were. But this fellow . . .

Jérôme's eye caught the face of the boy, looking up at him. He flipped the package of prunes over, and there was the face of a horse, too. The picture in the newspaper was of the boy and a horse, cheek to cheek. Jérôme unwrapped the fruit, wrapped them in a sheet of ads for Monoprix, took the money, made the change. When the shop was momentarily empty, he read the article. There was the dog, too, offering her paw to the horse trainer who had found them, or whom they had found. The horse had jumped over the outer railing, into a race, run with the other horses, then fled back to where the boy and the dog were standing, way at the far end of Longchamp, where no one but the mowers ever went. It had been a great sensation when it happened — not only had the horse joined the race, she had nearly won it; not only had the horse appeared, but she was the very horse that the winning trainer had lost in the late fall, when the horse slipped out of her stall and disappeared. Into the Bois de Boulogne? Could she possibly have survived in the Bois all winter? The boy seemed terrified by the whole experience. However, the boy and the horse and the dog all seemed well fed and healthy. Yes, said Jérôme to himself, as well they might be, since he had fed them, and he stocked only the best. A customer came in, bought a substantial bunch of commodities, paid, and left. Jérôme went and knocked on the window of the meat market.

Alise raised her hand, came out a minute later. Jérôme showed her the article. They both began laughing. For the rest of the afternoon, Jérôme looked at the picture every so often. Nothing about the old lady — well, that wasn't surprising. What was surprising was that the old lady had lived to make her way to the market as long as she had.

Toward late afternoon, here, at last, came the gendarme. Jean, his name was. Jérôme had never even spoken to him, but they had touched their caps to one another, smiled, nodded, acknowledged each other's business in the neighborhood. Jérôme waved him over, and he came, with dignified steps. Had he seen the paper? Jérôme pointed to the pictures of the dog, the horse, and the boy, and the gendarme pushed his cap back and gave a satisfied sigh. Then he said, "So that's where they went. The old lady died, you know. In her bed. Just the sort of death I wouldn't mind."

"I'm not surprised," said Jérôme. In a way, the horse wasn't a surprise, either, when he reflected upon how many carrots, apples, and beets the boy had purchased over the last few months. He said, "Where did they live?"

"On Marinoni, just beside the Champ de Mars."

After closing the shop, Jérôme walked down the Rue Marinoni and looked at the place. It was all closed up now. He tried peeking through the fence, but the vegetation was too thick — that should have been a giveaway right there. He stood with his hands in his pockets in the deepening dusk and wondered why he had never thought to do this — follow the boy and the old lady and the dog home, just to see. Would it have been better if he had?

He was standing there quietly when Pierre approached him. Jérôme knew why. All he had to say was "Have you seen the newspaper?"

Pierre shook his head.

Jérôme took the folded article out of his pocket — the boy, the horse, the dog. Right before their eyes the whole time. When Pierre got to Anaïs's café, she was there. She had the paper, too. She'd found it on one of the tables when she came in to begin the evening's baking.

It was an odd thing, to meet this person and that, to compare notes, to solve a mystery that you didn't even know existed, to answer questions that you had not thought to ask: Who was this boy? (The last in a long line of unlucky ones.) Who was this dog? (Don't you remember that busker? Unkempt, but a musical genius, a fellow who had walked away from a promising career. Jacques Seul, he had called himself — no one knew his given name, but that had been his stage name — he had cut two records in the 1970s.) Who was this horse? Perestroika, by Moscow Ballet out of Mapleton, by Big Spruce, four-year-old, two starts, two wins, bay mare, white star, no other markings — what else did you need to know?

EPILOGUE

Delphine saw at once, the evening of the race, that no one would know what to do with them. Paras was the smallest problem: Could she go back to racing? Would she? The dog needed a home. And the boy — even though some people had suspected he existed, and the authorities were hard at work figuring out his antecedents, no one had a plan. So Delphine let him stay that night in Maisons-Laffitte, with the dog, in a room right above the stall where she put Paras. She saw in the way he looked at Paras and stroked her that he was very attached, so she showed him how to ease out the door and go down the stairs if he wanted to be with her. Early in the morning, she found him in the stall, leaning against Paras, one arm over her back. The dog was lying beside the door of the stall, her head on her paws. And a raven was picking his way sideways along the top of the stall door, cawing, you might say, informatively. Rania brought in the morning bran mash, and Paras got to her feet. The boy stood, yawning. Delphine took him by the hand, said that she had a few rolls and a — And just then she saw the rat, who was sitting in the nearest corner, watching Paras eat from the bucket. Assassin, standing in the doorway of the stall, stared at him, not a single bark. Both Delphine and the boy laughed.

Delphine was happy happy happy. She had called Madeleine, who had fallen out of her chair, she was so thrilled at the news, and would be there later in the day. She hugged Rania, who had made a thousand euros on Whiskey's win. After the morning feed, she walked that wonderful fellow herself, around and around the courtyard. His legs were cold and perfect, he seemed sound and full of beans. Every so often he turned his head and glanced at Paras eating her hay. Yes, Delphine thought, she is a beauty, and well you should admire her.

It was a lovely morning and a lovely afternoon that would be followed by those events that had to play themselves out, but, Delphine thought, enjoyable all the same.

Madeleine chose to keep Paras in training, at least for now.

After Madeleine left the training center to

return to her place near the Parc Monceau, Delphine took Paras out of her stall to walk her around the yard. She saw the boy looking out the window above the stall, and then he came skipping down the stairs and through the doorway. Paras dragged Delphine over to the mounting block, and the boy slid onto her. After a skeptical pause, Delphine handed the boy the lead rope, and he started riding her around the yard. His balance was good. His sense of where Paras might go was good. There was an obvious feeling of attachment between them. Delphine saw that he was doomed to be a horse trainer, shook her head, and suspected that her own mother had once had the same feeling about her.

The authorities came the next day. After nosing about for an hour, they decided to allow the boy to stay with the horse, at least for now: Delphine had space, it was too late in the school year to find a spot for him, and there was no school for the summer. When Delphine took the boy, Étienne Denotre, to pick up his clothing and other possessions, Frida jumped into the car and went along without being asked. As soon as they went through the gate of the property, she ran into the raspberry bushes and dug up the purse. It was deeply brown, damp, fulsome. Inside were two hundred-euro notes. Delphine returned the money to Rania, who told her that two hundred euros was just what she had bet that day on Paras's race. Rania allowed Frida to keep the purse.

The old lady had a small but lovely funeral, and was buried between her son and her grandson. Étienne stood between Delphine and Rania during the burial, and both of them touched him, held him, comforted him as he cried.

The bank oversaw the cleaning of the house and the disposal of the furnishings, the books, and the extremely healthy crop of mushrooms growing in the cellar. The bank saw no reason to sell the place, at least until the housing market rebounded; when it did rebound, Étienne might inherit a goodly sum. And there was plenty in the old lady's account. The art collection was sent to an appraiser, who felt that there might be some nice objects among the rest of the junk.

Pierre and Jérôme enjoyed the raspberry crop a great deal, and Pierre carted away the horse manure and dug it into his compost heap.

Delphine bought Frida her own bed, cozy, not too large, which she put inside the tack room, within sight of the door. She always left the door ajar so that Frida could go in and out.

Raoul made himself an excellent nest in the fork of a chestnut tree not far from the training track.

And Kurt was quite taken with Noelle, an agile black rat, a month or so older than he was, whom Assassin had never been able to catch. Their first litter had three pups, two females and a male.

Anaïs and Pierre decided that they were made for each other, and started going to races from time to time as Delphine's guests.

Paras enjoyed her summer of training. She was only four, after all. Jumpers could go on for years. The American horse Jesse James, whose stall was beside hers, chatted incessantly about his pedigree (his accent was better now). There was one horse — "Independence" was his name — who raced until he was ten, seventy-four starts, two track records. Of course, those days were gone. The American horse snorted, went back to eating his hay. Independence, Paras thought. A wonderful name, a name to remember.

Étienne enjoyed his summer, too. The authorities were patient — they let him get used to the idea of going to school, and they tested him a few times, so surprised were they at what he knew and did not know. Rania said that she would keep him at her house; there was a school around the corner, and she had an empty room. The authorities said that they'd consider her proposal, but they said so in that particular way that indicated they'd already thought it was as good a proposal as any — and, after all, why make things more complicated than they really had to be?

ABOUT THE AUTHOR

Jane Smiley is the author of numerous novels, including *A Thousand Acres,* which was awarded the Pulitzer Prize, and, most recently, The Last Hundred Years Trilogy: *Some Luck, Early Warning,* and *Golden Age.* She is also the author of several works of nonfiction and books for young adults. A member of the American Academy of Arts and Letters, she has also received the PEN Center USA Lifetime Achievement Award for Literature. She lives in Northern California.

The employees of Thorndike Press hope you have enjoyed this Large Print book. All our Thorndike, Wheeler, and Kennebec Large Print titles are designed for easy reading, and all our books are made to last. Other Thorndike Press Large Print books are available at your library, through selected bookstores, or directly from us.

For information about titles, please call:
  (800) 223-1244

or visit our website at:
  gale.com/thorndike

To share your comments, please write:
  Publisher
  Thorndike Press
  10 Water St., Suite 310
  Waterville, ME 04901